THIS PERFECT WORLD

Suzanne Bugler lives in south west London with her husband and two sons. She has also written two novels for young adults: *Staring Up at the Sun* and *Meet Me at the Boathouse*.

By the same author

THE CHILD INSIDE

THE SAFEST PLACE

THIS
PERFECT
WORLD

SUZANNE BUGLER

PAN BOOKS

First published 2010 by Macmillan

This edition published 2011 by Pan Books
an imprint of Pan Macmillan, a division of Macmillan Publishers Limited
Pan Macmillan, 20 New Wharf Road, London N1 9RR
Basingstoke and Oxford
Associated companies throughout the world
www.panmacmillan.com

ISBN 978-0-330-51069-1

A CIP catalogue record for this book is available from
the British Library.

Typeset by Ellipsis Books Limited, Glasgow
Printed and bound by CPI Group (UK) Ltd, Croydon, CR0 4YY

Visit www.panmacmillan.com to read more about all our books
and to buy them. You will also find features, author interviews and
news of any author events, and you can sign up for e-newsletters
so that you're always first to hear about our new releases.

Acknowledgements

With thanks to Sara Menguc, Jenny Geras and the staff at Macmillan, my husband Nick, and my family and friends for their support and enthusiasm.

ONE

Heddy Partridge was never my friend. I have to start with that.

Heddy Partridge was never my friend because I was pretty, popular, clever and blonde and my friends were pretty, popular, clever and generally blonde, too.

Heddy Partridge was none of these things.

Heddy was dark and lumpen, with heavy eyebrows and an unfortunately large mole on her left cheek, right below her eye. Heddy wasn't popular. In fact I couldn't tell you who her friends were at school, but I certainly wasn't one of them, even though she was always there in my life like a misplaced shadow, a stain, a sort of negative of myself, until we were streamed in the third year of senior school and I was put in the top stream and Heddy in the bottom, confirming her as thick and finally shunting her out of my life, to be more or less forgotten, until now.

When the phone rings I am distracted, caught off-guard.

It's a hot afternoon in May. Arianne is in the garden with her little friend Molly and Molly's mother, Belinda, and I'm on my way indoors to fetch cold drinks. Soon it will be time to collect Thomas from school. I snatch up the phone when it

1

starts ringing and this rusty voice crackles down the line saying, 'Laura Cresswell? Can I speak to Laura Cresswell, please?'

'It's Laura Hamley,' I say automatically, stuffing the phone between my chin and my ear, and holding it there with my shoulder while I carry on into the kitchen, 'speaking.'

'Yes, dear,' this tired voice comes back at me while I take glasses down from one cupboard and plastic cups from another, 'of course it is, dear.' There's a pause then, and I get the strangest sense of *relief* coming down the phone; *that* gets my attention far more than the use of my maiden name. In the garden the girls are singing 'Le Chat à la Promenade' at full volume, with Belinda leading the way. I move away from the window, away from the noise, and that thin voice says in my ear, 'It's Mrs Partridge here, dear. Helen Partridge's mother. You remember me, don't you, dear? You remember Helen.'

Oh, I remember Helen all right. I remember Heddy.

Memory comes rushing back – dormant, never gone. I stand in my kitchen with my phone against my ear, waiting to be accused.

'I got your number from your mother,' Mrs Partridge says, 'before she moved. She said you were living in Ashton, now. It's nice to keep in touch, I said to her. Your family were always very kind to us. It'd be nice for Heddy, you know, to hear from you. You were such good friends, once.'

She's lying, saying that. Oh, my family was nice to her family all right, but Heddy and I were never friends. She breaks off again, and the heat is burning in my face. There's want in her voice, though she isn't getting to the point. I can hear that want in every word. Though what it could possibly be that Mrs Partridge wants from me, now, after all this time, I cannot imagine.

They've stopped singing outside. It's nearly a quarter to three and Belinda is calling through the kitchen window, 'Do you need a hand in there, Laura?' I can see her face through the glass, distorted by the sunlight, looming.

'It's lovely to hear from you, Mrs Partridge,' I lie into the phone, 'but I'm really sorry, I can't talk now. I was just on my way out.'

'Can I call you back then?' she asks quickly. 'Later?'

'Yes, yes, of course,' I say as I take water from the fridge, and orange juice, and start pouring.

'This evening?' she persists. 'Would that be convenient? Say half-past seven?'

When I walk back through the conservatory and out into the garden, carrying my tray of drinks, Belinda is singing another song, French again. 'Frère Jacques' this time. She knows all the words, and the actions to go with them too. And she's teaching them to the girls, moving her mouth and arms in this ridiculously exaggerated way. She's kicked her shoes off and she's crouching down at their level, bare toes spreading into the grass. She squats the way they show you to squat at antenatal classes, legs open, like she's about to give birth. In between gestures she plants her hands on her thighs, for added balance, and bobs up and down slightly, like a toad. Her trousers have scooped down at the back, revealing an expanse of white skin and the top of her blue-grey pants. I can't help noticing the label sticking out over the elastic: M&S size 16.

In my head I join in with the other version, the school-dinner chant of:

Mashed potato, mashed potato,
Soggy peas, soggy peas,
Sloppy semolina, sloppy semolina,
No more, please.

I think maybe I'll tell Arianne my version later; she'll like that. I especially think she'll like that when I see her poor little face peering at me over Belinda's shoulder. Molly is doing *so* well, earning big nods of approval from her mother, but Arianne looks totally bemused; one hand is up by her face, two fingers up her nose and one in her mouth. With the other hand she half-heartedly tries to join in with the actions, and gets it wrong.

'Drinks, girls,' I say, putting Arianne out of her misery, and Belinda turns to look up at me, pushing her bobbed hair back behind her ears.

'You should send her to French classes,' Belinda says, sitting back on the grass and stretching out her legs. She has very short toes, attached to very short feet; I try not to notice as she wiggles them shamelessly. She is badly in need of a pedicure. 'Molly goes every Tuesday, after Tumbletots,' she says all enthusiastically. 'It's amazing how quickly they learn, at this age. Josie Hall's sending Katie; they're bringing her up bilingual. They're teaching her the French word for everything, as well as the English. Isn't that such a good idea? She'll have such a head-start when she goes to school.' She takes the glass that I hand her and gulps down her drink. 'Of course they're a bit worried because she's still not talking yet, but they're getting her seen by a speech therapist. And Josie says Katie loves it when they talk French to her.'

*

Later, when she is still warm and damp from the bath, I wrap Arianne up in her fluffy white towel and curl her up on my lap like a baby. The ends of her hair are wet from the bubbles. Gently I rub at them with the edge of the towel and watch the curls spring back. Holding her like this is such a joy. I can never do this with Thomas, he'd wriggle and squirm and escape, always off somewhere, always busy.

'Mummy,' Arianne says suddenly, snuggling deeper into my arms, 'why does Molly's mummy sing strange songs?'

'They're French songs.' I press my face against her hair and breathe her in; she smells of heaven.

'What's French songs?'

'Songs people sing in France,' I say.

She turns in my arms and looks at me, a little frown creasing her forehead. 'Are we in France?'

I laugh. 'No, darling, we're not.'

That little frown gets deeper. 'Is Molly in France?'

'No, darling, she isn't. Nor is her mother.'

'Then why do they sing French songs?'

'I don't know, darling,' I say and pop a kiss onto her serious little face. 'I don't know.'

No wonder poor Katie Hall has got delayed speech. The poor child is probably totally confused. Bilingual, indeed! Non-lingual is more like it.

I slide Arianne off my knee and start putting her into her pyjamas. 'Listen,' I say. 'I know some funny words to that song.'

Soon she's running round her room singing, 'Mashed potato, mashed potato, soggy peas,' and Thomas comes bounding in wearing nothing but his Bob the Builder pyjama top, and joins in.

'Soppy Semolina, Soppy Semolina ... Who's Semolina?' Arianne asks.

'It's *sloppy* semolina,' I say. 'School dinners.'

'Argh!' Thomas clutches at his throat and falls to the floor, dead. 'School dinners – argh!'

I think Mrs Partridge won't call back, but she does, at bang on seven-thirty. This time she's concise, to the point. I have the feeling that she's been there all afternoon, by the phone, waiting until the allotted hour.

'It's about poor Heddy,' she says. 'You know she hasn't been well. Your mother would have told you ... I often used to see your mother down the High Street, before she and your father moved away. She always asked after poor Heddy, she was always so kind. So kind to take an interest.' I can't remember what my mother may or may not have told me about Heddy Partridge over the years; whatever she said would have gone in one ear and out the other, not interesting me. Not relevant any more. 'She's not been well at all, dear, Heddy hasn't. She's in the hospital now, in St Anne's, out past Hounslow. You know it, don't you, dear? St Anne's? They have a unit there. That's where Heddy is, in the unit. They're keeping her there. I have the boy, Nathan, staying with me now. I had them both staying with me till all this ... And glad to have them with me too, I am. I do my best for poor Heddy, but ... It isn't right that they're keeping her there. It isn't doing her any good. She isn't getting any better ... '

Her voice starts to crackle and she breaks off on a cough. I have to say something, but all I can manage is platitudes. 'That's terrible, Mrs Partridge,' I say, 'I am sorry.' It's kind of disturbing the way she assumes I'd already know all this.

When she speaks again her voice is clearer, bolder. 'I need to get her out, dear,' she says, and suddenly I know where this is going. 'She needs to be home, with me, and with Nathan. Your mother told me how well you were doing, living in Ashton now, and your husband being a solicitor. And she said to me before she moved, she said that I could call on you if ever I needed any help, dear. She gave me your number. This number and your mobile number as well, dear. So kind.' She falters a little now, and no wonder. 'So that's why I'm calling you, dear,' she says as if I hadn't got the message. 'I need your help.'

I feel a hard knot of anger tightening up in my stomach. But who is it that I should be angry with? Mrs Partridge for phoning me up out of the blue like this, or my mum, for telling her to? I can just picture it: my mum and Mrs Partridge in Forbury High Street. And my mum doing her Lady Bountiful act, for the benefit of passers-by. I picture her hunting in her bag for a pen and a scrap of paper, and scribbling down *both* my phone numbers and pressing the paper into Mrs Partridge's hand. *Do call Laura if you need anything.*

I picture this, and the knot tightens.

But even so, it was just a throwaway line, surely? Surely my mum didn't *mean* it? And what business has she got, giving out my mobile number to anyone, let alone Mrs Partridge? She could ring any time. She could ring when I'm in *yoga*, for God's sake.

I feel myself trapped; cornered and exposed.

'Mrs Partridge,' I say, 'I am sorry to hear about Heddy. But I really don't see that there's much I can do.'

'But your husband, dear. I thought if you spoke to him.'

'James is a property lawyer, Mrs Partridge. He doesn't know anything about hospitals.'

'He'll know about the law, though. He'll know about rights.' I hear the plea of desperation in her voice, driving her on. 'Perhaps if you'd just speak to him, dear—'

'Really, Mrs Partridge, I don't think he'll be much help.'

'But perhaps you'd ask him. And if I was to phone you again in a day or two ... '

'The thing is, Mrs Partridge, James is really busy at the moment. We both are.' I say this, but then the silence on the other end of the phone has me adding, 'But I will try.'

'You'll speak to him?'

'I'll do my best.'

I know I won't, though. Oh, I might mention it to James in passing, but it won't make any difference. I doubt if he'd know any more about hospitalization and patients' rights than I do. He doesn't have a magic wand that he can wave at every turn, dispensing legal advice like fairy dust. And more to the point, he doesn't have the time. 'Tell her to go to the Citizens Advice Bureau,' he'd say, 'or to her local solicitors.'

It used to happen all the time, people badgering him for advice over things like parking-ticket disputes or bothersome neighbours, especially when he was newly qualified. We'd go to dinner parties and as soon as people found out he was a lawyer, there'd always be someone bombarding him with their problems, or trying to catch him out with a trick question.

Of course it doesn't happen much any more. These days when we go to dinner parties the other guests are mostly lawyers, and wives of lawyers, or bankers, and wives of bankers. It's like a club we've sold up into. *People like us*, James said when we were thinking of buying this house. *People like us live here.*

And Mrs Partridge and Heddy, they are from a different world.

*

This is the quiet hour, before James comes home.

The children are in bed; the house is silent and the supper prepared. Normally I'd pour myself a glass of wine and curl up on the sofa and read for a while, cherishing the peace. But tonight I have no peace because Mrs Partridge has broken it. Mrs Partridge is in my head and Heddy Partridge is back in my life.

Helen Audrey Partridge. There, the girl is so under my skin that I can even remember her middle name. I can remember some moment from the juniors, years ago, when we all had to tell our middle names, and God help you if yours was something weird, something old-fashioned, named after a grandmother or something awful. God help you then, and God help Heddy. Hers wasn't the worst by any means, but it got the loudest laugh, the longest laugh.

Heddy Audrey Partridge. God knows why they called her Heddy instead of Helen, but everyone did. I can picture us all now, standing in the playground in a synchronized circle with Heddy in the middle, and reciting so carefully, so slowly, with all the movements perfectly timed:

> *I tells* (touch the eye, touch the mouth)
> *Heddy* (point to the head, of course)
> *Smells* (hold the nose, wave away that stink).

I was the genius who worked out that little rhyme, and how clever we all thought I was. I remember Heddy standing there and letting us sing this to her. I remember her bashful face, her hating it and loving it – loving the attention, however absurd.

I wasn't cruel. God, I hope I wasn't cruel. I was a *child*. She smelled of digestive biscuits. I said this to my friend, when we were tiny still, back in the infants, and she said it was because Heddy weed in her bed every night, and never changed the sheets.

'Then how do they dry?' I asked, and I wondered if it was true. I wondered it every time I was near her and smelled that smell. Nobody ever stood very close to Heddy in assembly.

'Heddy P smells of wee,' my friend said, and soon the boys started saying it too, and they went on saying it, right through the juniors.

Heddy Audrey Partridge. Pant-wetter extraordinaire. God, I could tell you a million things about that girl, but the thing that sticks in my mind most of all – the thing that makes me loathe her above all else – is the time she pissed herself at ballet. When I think of Heddy, I think of that. I see her plump body with its round belly and its mini-breasts, stuffed into her leotard and tights. I see her lumbering along behind the rest of us, slower than the rest of us. I see her getting her steps wrong and Madame getting impatient with her again. I hear Madame saying, 'Come on, come on, please try, Helen. We are a nymph, not a nincompoop . . . '

Then we were in our circle and Heddy was all over the place, feet everywhere, and Madame was getting crosser and crosser, and Heddy was getting clumsier and clumsier. Suddenly there was the sound of water hitting the floor, and we all looked at Heddy and there she was, standing with her feet somewhere between fourth and fifth position, with a stream of pee pouring down between her legs. She pissed like an elephant. Loads of it, coming straight down, while we all stopped our steps and watched, transfixed, horrified. I remember the embarrassment, turning my insides over. I remember Heddy's face, moon-shaped and blank, her eyes both bright and empty, like a rabbit's.

We were ten years old.

On and on it went, and we couldn't do anything until it stopped. Even Madame was caught in stone, her ceaseless instructions suspended. It started spreading out across the floor. The girl next to Heddy had to quickly move away and someone giggled. Madame regained her control, said *Okay, girls, class is nearly over* and carried on with her one two three, one two threes. We moved our feet and our arms, but we were all looking at Heddy. I was looking at Heddy, and I was feeling a loathing so strong that it shocked me. She stood still, feet planted in her puddle, with the wet patch visible on her leotard, a dark triangle at the top of her fat, wet thighs.

You could see the look of relief on Madame's face when she could dismiss us at last, and then the whispering started. Our coats were at the back of the hall, hanging up on pegs. Heddy's was an anorak. She put it on and it only just covered her bottom. Then she stood there looking back across the hall at the trail of footprints she'd left, and she waited for me.

'Pull your coat down,' I snapped as she got into the back of my dad's car. 'And make sure you're sitting on it.' I noticed exactly how much of her was covered by that anorak and exactly how much of her horrible self was in contact with the seat of the car, and I swore I would never, ever sit on that side again – not ever.

I hated that we had to give Heddy a lift to ballet, and to Brownies too. I wouldn't have minded so much if it had been Melissa or Claire, but why Heddy?

'Because she wouldn't be able to go if she didn't have a lift,' my dad would answer, irritated, for the umpteenth time.

Well, *good*, I'd think. I didn't want her at ballet or Brownies. I didn't want her always there, following along behind me like a lost dog. It was embarrassing. People might start thinking I was her friend. Just to make sure they didn't, I'd leap out of the car before Heddy, leaving her to say goodbye to my dad and shut the door, and I'd run on in to the Brownie hut or the village hall where we did ballet, and I'd ignore her for the whole time we were there. Pointedly. One hour at ballet on Saturday afternoons. One and a half hours at Brownies on Thursday nights. I'd see her standing on her own with her long, dopey face and I'd dismiss her; I was too cross with her to care. And when it was time to go home again she'd annoy me even more, hanging around me when I just wanted to chat with my friends and say goodbye.

I didn't see why we had to give Heddy a lift at all. I didn't see why we had to even *know* the Partridges. But my mum said that Mr and Mrs Partridge had always lived in Forbury and that Mrs Partridge had done a lot to help other people when she was younger, looking after other people's children and calling on the old people, that sort of thing, and now Mrs Partridge herself was in need of a bit of help. 'And I really don't think it's too much to ask that you try to be nice to poor Heddy Partridge, either,' she said, yet again.

Once, I dared say that it *was* too much to ask. 'But I don't like her,' I wailed. 'She's stupid and she *smells*.'

My mum flinched, visibly. And for a second I thought I saw something like pity flash across her face, and I thought that maybe I was getting somewhere, because I thought that pity was for me. But then she trussed her face back into its usual sanctimonious mask, closed the kitchen door so that my dad wouldn't hear and hissed at me, 'A long time ago Mr Partridge used to work for your father sometimes, fitting carpets. Well, for Grampy, really. Grampy was still in charge then. Your father was in the office, but it was still Grampy's business.' She spoke fast, as if she wanted to tell me and didn't want to tell me. And she stared at me, hard – like I was supposed to have a clue what she was going on about. On her cheeks there were red mottled splodges of anger. 'Mr Partridge was a good and loyal worker,' she snapped. 'And I really think that the least we can do is give that poor girl a lift sometimes.'

As if that was answer enough – which to me, when I was only eight or nine or whatever I was, it wasn't.

We used to own Forbury Floors, in the High Street. It was a family business; my grandfather set it up and then my dad took it over.

God knows what Grampy would say if he could see it now; it's a pizza takeaway. My dad sold up, before they went to Devon. I don't think he got all that much for it in the end; that's partly why they had to downsize. Though my mum would die rather than ever admit that, of course.

The Partridges lived near us, in the little road that separated our road from the council estate; Tin Town, we all called the estate, because the council houses were prefabs, slapped up after the Second World War. Heddy didn't live in a prefab, she lived in one of only two tiny cottages on their own, the only two houses in her street. Next to them was open space and overgrown bushes backing onto the reservoir, wasteland, fenced off, and next to that was Tin Town. Fairview Lane, Heddy's road was called, which is ironic, because there was nothing very fair about the view from her house.

She was never ready when we picked her up. We'd always

have to park up outside her house and my dad would send me to call for her, and I'd have to run up the pathway to her door while the dogs next door barked at me. They had a bell that chimed the first three notes of the national anthem, and those long, multicoloured plastic strips hanging down, just inside the door, like a curtain. Heddy's mother or her stupid lump of a brother would open the door and I'd have to go inside, and those strips would smack me in the face as I parted my way through them.

The house always smelled of eggs and the fat they were fried in. Heddy was never ready; she was always upstairs, hunting for a shoe or her scarf or something, and I'd have to go into the living room and wait while Mrs Partridge yelled up the stairs for Heddy to hurry up, as Heddy's brother slouched on the sofa and stared at me. They always had the TV on too loud and the gas fire up too high, for the benefit of Mr Partridge, who'd had to give up work because of his chest and now sat all the time in his chair, getting smaller and paler and more and more deaf. He died not long after we started at secondary school. My parents went to his funeral. And I remember looking at Heddy soon after, to see if she looked any different. She didn't. She looked just as dopey as ever.

Fleetingly I imagined how I would feel if my dad died, and panic spread across my chest – cold, terrifying. But it wasn't the same. You couldn't attribute the same feelings to Heddy.

And now poor Heddy is in a mental hospital, closed in, spent out.

It would seem that poor Heddy did have some feelings after all.

TWO

The next day I take Thomas to school and head straight on to nursery with Arianne. Tuesday mornings are always a rush; I've a yoga class at nine-thirty and the traffic is usually dreadful first thing.

The nursery is run by Carole, in a huge old house in Gloucester Road. It's actually called Les Petits Génies – there's a big sign out the front with the letters all in bright colours – but you feel just a tiny bit self-conscious saying that all the time, so we tend to just call it nursery or Carole's. Everyone in Ashton wants to send their children here, but only some are successful. There's a waiting list like you wouldn't believe, and then there's the interview to pass. I did hear a rumour that Carole is thinking of setting an entrance exam, which has got to be the world gone mad, though I wouldn't say that to my friends, of course. Nor they to me. Just like no one says it's madness to send three-year-olds home with homework every week, and to grade them at the end of term.

No, we don't say anything because we are the lucky ones, and everyone else can see our little darlings with their Petits Génies purple book bags and know that we are the lucky ones. As in all areas of life, it is better to be in than out. So

Arianne is in, on Tuesdays, Wednesdays and Thursdays, nine-fifteen until two with a good lunch included, and the odd extra hour here and there. Carole is flexible like that. With the fees she charges, she can afford to be.

Carole is marvellous; we say that to each other often, Penny, Tasha, Liz and I. Marvellous; the children are getting *such* a good start.

Penny pulls up outside Carole's in her Land Rover with Sam in the back, just as I'm pulling away. I honk my horn to get her attention. 'Speak to you later,' we both mouth simultaneously at each other through our windscreens as I drive past.

The traffic isn't too bad on the back roads, but once I'm up on the High Street I get stuck in the queue for the lights. It's always the same here. It can take ten minutes sometimes just to clear the lights. You'd be better off walking, if you had the time. I check my mirrors for police cars and phone Liz on my mobile to see if we can put coffee back half an hour, because I'm going to have to dash into town straight after yoga to get the stuff for Thomas's book-week outfit.

As it is, I still end up running late. There's a bit of a furore after the class because one of the women is thinking of buying a bread-making machine and isn't sure which sort would be best. Should she go for the top-of-the-range deluxe model with slow-bake and fast-bake, simulated kneading facility, plus an option for muffins and buns? Or should she go for the slightly smaller model, which doesn't do the muffins and buns, but does come in a stainless-steel finish and would therefore sit so well in her kitchen?

Honestly, you'd think she'd said she was planning to take a lover, the way the others react. Bags are dropped and sweatshirts and jackets abandoned half-put-on as they clamour around, almost shouting over each other in their efforts to get their recommendations heard.

Selina says get the top-of-the-range, definitely; you never know when muffins and buns might be needed.

Felicity says it's the bread that matters, not the buns. And so a debate ensues: do we want buns, do we not want buns? I find myself caught up in it all, strangely fascinated, and lose a good five minutes trying to escape.

'It all comes down to the rise,' Steph declares at last, and everyone agrees with this. 'Other features are all very well, but what you really need to be sure of is a good rise. Mine's excellent,' she says. 'I just bung in the ingredients before I go to bed and I'm guaranteed a nice, big, hot loaf in the morning.'

I never saw so much excitement after a yoga class.

Then when I finally get to John Lewis's haberdashery department I find all the grey fake-fur has gone, which sends me into a panic. I mean, why can't Thomas just go as Mowgli in a pair of red pants, for God's sake? Why does he have to be Baloo? Why does the school have to go and pick *The Jungle Book* for its theme this year?

The assistant suggests that I buy grey felt, and some white fake-fur to sew onto the tummy, but I'm not so sure about this. I can't remember seeing Baloo the bear with a white furry tummy, but she assures me it's what other people will be doing.

'There've been loads of them in since the grey fake-fur ran out,' she tells me cheerfully, 'and it's what I've suggested to all of them. Little bit of white fur on the tummy will make a nice bear.' And it would have to be just a little bit of white fur, because that's running low now too, and so is the grey felt.

John Lewis's haberdashery department is packed with women I recognize from the playground. We must keep the department in business, with all these costumes we have to make. If it's not concerts, it's book week; if it's not book week, it's hat parades. I sometimes wonder if the teachers do it for a laugh. Clearly they think we have nothing better to do all day than sit at home and sew.

I just have time to grab a sandwich from Costa, which I eat in the car on the way to Liz's because I'm starving, and I promised Arianne we'd go straight on to the playground when I pick her up from nursery, and Thomas has got a tennis lesson after school.

And in the evening James will come home to his supper and ask me how things are in Ashton. He loves to hear about the little social intrigues that go on here during the day. And the distance between the school playground and Sainsbury's can be quite a hotbed of domestic drama. There'll always be something to tell him, something to make him chuckle and smile fondly.

How easy it must be to look so affectionately upon the little world when you don't have to be in it all day.

To James, life in Ashton is a pleasant diversion from the real world where important things happen, the world of city finance and city law and city men. This is his little escape, his weekend retreat, and to listen to me recounting tales about my little day in my little world is easy entertainment indeed.

I didn't tell James about Mrs Partridge phoning last night. I didn't tell him about Heddy. Instead I told him about Belinda and her French songs and about the madness of French classes for three-year-olds. He laughed, as I knew he would. And tonight I'll tell him about the excitement at yoga over the bread-making machines, and he'll laugh about that. And he'll probably say something like 'Don't you ever get a bread-making machine', and then I'll laugh too. But sometimes, just sometimes, I think the laugh might be a tiny bit on me.

I'd like to say I don't even have time to think about Heddy and Mrs Partridge in my busy, busy day. I'd like to believe I've forgotten all about them. I've certainly convinced myself that Mrs Partridge won't ring back, but she does. On the dot of half-past seven. The phone rings and before I even answer I know that it's her, just as I know, then, that she won't give up.

'Violet Partridge here, dear,' she says. 'I do hope this is a convenient time?'

And what can I say to that? I think she's got it worked out already: seven-thirty, I'll be here.

She carries on, 'I was wondering, dear. Have you had a chance yet to speak to your husband?'

'Well, not really, no,' I say. 'Mrs Partridge, he is very busy.'

'Only I was thinking it might be better if I popped over. We could have a proper talk then, you know. It might be easier for you, dear.'

'Mrs Partridge, really, there's no need—'

'Oh, it's no trouble, dear,' she says. And then I stand there, frozen, with the phone clamped against my ear while she tells me how she's already worked out the bus route to Ashton and that she'll only need to change twice. 'It won't take me long, dear,' she says. 'Hour and a half at the most, and I'm used to the buses. So perhaps if you could just tell me your address, dear, and which day might be convenient ... '

I cannot imagine Violet Partridge on my doorstep, in my house. It cannot happen. Yet she knows my name, my phone number, the town in which I live. How difficult would it be for her to track me down? I picture her, walking the streets of Ashton, knocking on doors until she finds me. I picture this, and panic has me saying, 'No, Mrs Partridge, please. I'll come to you.'

And two minutes later I've arranged to go to her house, the following Thursday.

THREE

Violet Partridge's house is just as I remember it. I pull up outside in my car and sit there for a moment, looking at it.

I'm surprised at how nervous I feel. It's always odd, going back, revisiting the past, so to speak, but this is doubly unsettling because I never liked being here. I never wanted to come back here, to this house, in this dreary little road. I never thought I'd be here again.

Memory suddenly flashes up of the last time I was here, some twenty years ago now, but I force that memory back, right back. I just can't bear to think about it. And I can't bear to think about Mrs Partridge remembering that time too, though she does. Of course she does. That's why I'm here.

At least, that's part of the reason.

The house looks strangely empty. It's a bright, beautiful day already, but the windows are all shut and darkened by heavy net curtains in great need of a wash. The paint on the upstairs window frames is badly blistered and peeling; I can see it flaking from here. Both cottages are pebble-dashed, but the people next door have painted theirs an unlikely turquoise colour, in harsh, brutal contrast to Mrs Partridge's original, time-darkened grey. A large crack is spreading down from under the guttering, starting in the middle of the two houses and then veering off down Mrs Partridge's side. I try to remember if it was always there, but I can't.

It must be hard for Mrs Partridge to look after the house by herself. It must have been hard for her back then, too, when Heddy's dad was alive but sitting in that chair all the time, slowly fading away. I can't imagine Heddy's brother ever doing much to help.

There's a car outside next door, up on jacks, where the garden used to be. It's one of those big American cars, black and mean-looking, with its bonnet propped open and rusting, like a wide-open mouth. They've taken their half of the front fence away, to get this car in, but the gate post is still there, complete with gate standing closed and idle on its own. I wonder if their dogs would still bark at me, but when I open the car door there is silence except for the twittering of birds and the distant, dull hum of traffic.

Mrs Partridge's garden is overgrown; mostly it's concreted over, with a square patch in the middle planted with shrubs and bushes whose unpruned stalks have grown tall and thin and now thrust out at random, sparsely leaved, fighting for air with the weeds and stinging nettles. The gate is stiff and catches on the concrete when I push it open. I give it a hard shove and glance down, and see millions of ants swarming in and out of the cracks on the pathway, a shocking burst of activity in this unnerving stillness.

I press the bell at the front door, but it doesn't chime the tune I'm expecting, the tune I remember so well. Instead it just gives a short, flat buzz – as if it would have been a ring, only the batteries have worn right down.

She opens the door straight away as if she's been watching me, and this unnerves me even more. I'd half-convinced myself no one was home.

'Come in, dear,' she says and steps back, into the darkness.

The plastic strips have gone. I walk straight into the hall and it's the smell that hits me, it's always the smell. We had a boy next door to us when I was a girl, Andrew; two years older than me he was, and sensible. He went on to be a policeman when he grew up. Neighbours the other side of him left him in charge of their cat when they went away and he took me with him once to feed it. I remember how strange their house smelled, and how I didn't like it.

'It's just their family smell,' Andrew said. 'Every family has its own smell.'

Ours didn't, I was sure. I never smelled it.

Mrs Partridge's house smells of her whole life. You could pick it apart if you were an expert, some sort of smell-pathologist. You could trace every meal eaten, every circumstance, every celebration and counter-celebration. Every moment recorded by Mrs Partridge's cooking, the food and the odours from the people eating the food. The smell of their clothes, their hair and their bodies, the cigarettes they smoked. The smell of their emotions, of their stillness in rest, of their fear, all trapped within the closed-window timelessness.

I follow her into the living room. She's a thin, trousered figure, smaller than I remember and very slightly stooped.

'Do sit down, dear,' she says, gesturing to the sofa, and I get to see her face then, for the first time. It's just as it always was, only older of course, more wrinkled, the skin stretched paper-thin above the hollows of her cheeks. Mrs Partridge is one of those people who always look old. Her hair has been grey for as long as I can remember and she's still wearing it in that same short, rollered old-lady style. It's somewhat thinner now, though; I can see the white of her scalp through the curls. And there are angry red blotches on her forehead, looking sore, as if she's been picking at them. The eyes are just the same: dark, over-round. Like Heddy's, only sharper.

It's the same sofa, I'm sure it is. The same or nearly the same. Brown, everything is brown: the sofa, the carpet, the colour of the air. I bend to perch on the edge and the cushions give beneath me. I remember lying right here with my face pressed against the back of the sofa, I remember the dusty, biscuit smell of the material. I remember the shame, the terrible shame, and I feel it all over again, now.

I can't meet Mrs Partridge's eye. She hovers before me, bony hands busy, twitching, pulling her tunic top down over her thin hips, fussing, straightening out the cloth. She's staring at me. I half-expect her to say *My, how you've grown*, but isn't that ridiculous? Isn't all this ridiculous? She's as nervous as I am, standing there, pulling at her clothes.

'How are your parents?' she asks.

'Fine,' I reply. 'Thank you. The move went well. They're settling in nicely, enjoying the Devon life.' I ramble on, knowing I ought to be asking her back *How's Heddy?* But I can't, not in that flippant, chit-chat way.

Then she goes off to make coffee and I am alone in that room. Mr Partridge's chair is still there in the corner, just as if he might come back and sit in it sometime. The room is eerily quiet without his cough and the TV blaring out. The TV is still there, but it's been turned to face the sofa now. There's a little vase of plastic flowers standing on top of it. There are things everywhere, all sorts of things: a Spanish fan opened out, propped up behind an ashtray on the mantelpiece over the gas fire; a small carriage clock, not working, next to that; and a pair of china cats. And in between these things there are photos, so many photos. I push myself up from the sofa to look at them. They are of children, lots of children. Or are they of the same two or three children taken in different times, different places? It's impossible to tell. They've all got the same round, dark eyes. I look carefully at their faces, to try to link them. There's a school photo of a boy and a girl together, another one of just a boy. But that baby could be any one of those three or someone else; that toddler the same, grown now into the boy right next to him, captured at a different time, in school shirt and toothless grin. Other people's lives, captured in snapshots, but distorted too, misleading.

I can hear Mrs Partridge in the kitchen. She's a long time making that coffee and I move away from the fireplace to the sideboard, which is next to the small dining table, near the front window. The big photo there catches my attention, the one in the middle. It's of Heddy, unmistakably. Heddy on her wedding day. Heddy in a white puffy frock with her heavy hair pulled back from her face. She's smiling. Like the cat that got the cream, she's smiling. And next to this, among more pictures of unknown children, I find Heddy again, still smiling, though not as much, holding a baby in her arms. Her fat arms; I am shocked to see how fat she is.

I hear Mrs Partridge behind me, coming rattling into the room with a tray in her hands. I turn around, uncomfortable at being caught snooping.

'I was looking at the photos,' I say, somewhat unnecessarily. 'They're lovely.' I point to Heddy in her white frock. 'She looks lovely.'

'Yes, dear. Thank you, dear.' Mrs Partridge puts the tray down on the little coffee table, beside a big crystal ashtray, one of those old-fashioned round things with five or six ledges cut out around the edge, for communal smoking. There is one solitary cigarette butt in the middle of the ashtray, squashed down and fallen over, onto its side, in its little pool of ash. The milk is already in the cups with the coffee, but she's put sugar in a bowl and biscuits on a plate – custard creams – arranged in a circle. Instantly, I am embarrassed.

'She was very proud. We were all very proud,' Mrs Partridge says, and she rubs her hands up and down the front of her hips again. She gazes across at that photo, distracted for a moment, eyes fixed, thoughts elsewhere. On Heddy's wedding, probably.

I feel like I ought to sit down, but suddenly I'm not sure where to sit. Are we to perch, side by side on the only sofa, one at each end, and talk across the gap in between us? Mrs Partridge seems to pick up on my indecision; she snaps up her head suddenly and stares directly at me. 'He wasn't a bad man, John, Heddy's husband,' she says, and then she does something very odd. She goes over to Mr Partridge's chair and, with the force of her slight body behind it, she pushes it round to face the coffee table and the sofa. Then she sits in it, a tiny person, shrunk against the curved, high back. It's awkward, from that position, in that chair, for her to reach over across the table, but she does. She takes my coffee cup off the tray with her skinny arm stretching right out, and the cup clatters precariously in its saucer as she puts it on the table.

'Coffee?' she says and I sit down on the sofa, back where I should have been, where I should have stayed when she was out in the kitchen. 'Biscuit?' she asks.

The sofa has sunk so far beneath me that it's a struggle to wriggle forward and take one, but I have to; she's holding out the plate. I haven't had a custard cream in years and I couldn't eat one now; my insides are tight, plaited up. I take one and put it on the saucer and immediately I hate myself. What must she think of me, taking her biscuit and just sticking it on my saucer like that? What must she think of me?

What did she ever think of me?

What indeed? She watches me with her dark, knowing eyes.

'Yes, she got married.' There's an edge to her voice, a defensive edge. 'When she was twenty.'

My mind races back – did I know this, did I know that Heddy was married? I must have done. My parents would have mentioned it, I'm sure they would. But at twenty I was away at university, having one boyfriend after another, having a great time. Why would I have given a second thought to someone – anyone, not just Heddy – getting married? *Married*, for God's sake, at just twenty years old.

'He worked for the gas board.' She picks up her cup and saucer, then lifts the cup and sips. The coffee is way too hot still and her lips pucker. 'He was a good man,' she says, and I can tell she's said this a thousand times, if only to herself. 'A good man.'

I'm about to say something kind, something nice about the gas board, or about marrying young instead of going to university – not that Heddy Partridge would ever have gone to university – but she puts her cup back down suddenly with a clatter. 'She put on weight when Nathan was born. Before that. But it was hard to lose, you know. She always had trouble with her weight, always wanted to lose a few pounds.'

She is staring straight at me and I place my cup, still full, back down on the table.

'She was depressed.' She says it like she's been told to say it. Like she doesn't really understand the word, but she's practised saying it, over and over. 'She was pregnant before Nathan, but she lost the baby, late on, at five months. Awful, it was for her, awful.'

She rummages in the pocket of her tunic, agitated, and pulls out her cigarettes and a lighter. 'You don't mind, do you, dear?' she asks and I shake my head, though really I do mind. She sticks a cigarette between pursed lips, lights it and draws deeply, audibly. I try not to shudder. She leaves it in her mouth and it bobs up and down as she says again, 'She was depressed, after that. She wouldn't go out, not for ages. And she put on a lot of weight, just sitting at home all day. Then after Nathan was born we all thought she'd feel better, but she didn't. She became . . . *unreliable.*'

She takes the cigarette out of her mouth and taps the ash into the ashtray, taps it and taps it. 'She started doing things. To herself. Harming herself.' She shakes her head vigorously then and takes another long draw on that cigarette. 'I don't think she would ever have done anything to that baby, but . . . I made her go to the doctor. I took her there myself. He said she was depressed, he said it can happen sometimes – with the hormones, you know. He gave her some pills, but they didn't help, not really.'

Again she draws on the cigarette, and taps the ash while she exhales like a dragon, through her nostrils. I pull back a little, trying to avoid the smoke, though there isn't much point really. It's like a fog, wrapping itself around us.

'It wasn't easy for her, on her own all day. With a new baby.' She stares at me through the haze. 'John wasn't a bad man,' she says again, anxious that I understand this, 'but they bought that house. In Barton Village. A nice little house.' Another drag and a sip of coffee this time too; she sips as the smoke comes out of her nose. I pick up my cup again, grateful for something to do, even though it means half-standing for a moment from the dip of the sagging sofa. 'They had money worries. I don't blame him,' she says and her eyes are startlingly bright.

Don't blame him for what, exactly? And where is he now? Why isn't he looking after Nathan? There's more, I know there is. She's picking her words carefully.

'He did his best I'm sure,' she says, but I wonder if she really means it. 'It was hard for both of them. She was depressed,' she says, again and again. 'She was *depressed*.'

I can't break away from her stare. She's like a hawk, clinging on.

'She started doing things,' she says, and my mind is racing ahead, thinking *What things?* 'In public. With Nathan there too.' She sucks on her cigarette again and this time I notice that her hand is shaking. 'They took her in, once or twice, gave her more pills, you know, and she'd seem all right for a while, but then . . . She kept doing it. It got worse. She was . . . cutting herself. People don't like to see it, you know.' The ash has built right up again, but instead of tipping it, this time she grinds the butt into the ashtray, down and down until the shank bursts and frayed tobacco curls into the ash. 'Then they kept her in,' she says simply, letting go of the butt. 'That last time. They kept her in.'

I sit on that sofa, stricken. Stricken with the awful aware-ness that Mrs Partridge is on the verge of crying; stricken that I am there at all, hearing this stuff. I think of Arianne at nursery. I think of her learning her letters and her numbers. I think of her playing alongside Belinda's daughter, Tasha's daughter, and all the other daughters from our safe Ashton world. I think of Thomas at school, and of the cakes I have to make for the cake sale on Friday and of the new wellies needed for next week's school trip. I think of these things because I want them to pull me back into my own life, away from here, but it doesn't quite happen. Instead they just highlight the strangeness, the total surreality of my being here at all.

Desperately I try to think of something to say, to ease the tension.

'Are these all your grandchildren?' I ask, nodding towards the photos on the mantelpiece, and I would have got up and gone over to have another look at them, but I'm so buried in that sofa, and anyway Mrs Partridge doesn't suddenly perk up the way I'd hoped she would. She puts her cup back down with a sigh and gropes up her sleeve for a tissue, which she then screws up tight and rolls between agitated fingers. She doesn't even turn her head to look at the mantelpiece.

'Ian's children, mostly,' she says at last. 'He's got three. Two boys and a girl. Twins, the youngest two. And another one on the way. They live up near Birmingham. Near his wife's family.' She sighs again. 'I don't get up to see them much these days, which is a shame. It's good for Nathan to see his cousins, you know, to be with the young ones. To be part of a proper family.' She chews on the inside of her lip as she talks, and the tissue is getting twisted up so tight that bits of it shred off, onto her lap. 'But Heddy needs me here. I can't leave Heddy. Ian comes down when he can, does what he can, but' – she shrugs her thin shoulders, resigned – 'Linda's having a difficult time with the pregnancy. She needs him up there.'

I try to follow all this. I try to imagine Ian Partridge as a family man, but it's impossible. All I can think of is the big slob of a boy who used to slouch on the sofa gawping at me whenever I had to come in here to wait for Heddy. I can't imagine how anyone would want to get busy having his babies.

'This is Nathan,' Mrs Partridge says, 'Heddy's boy.' Still clutching that tissue, she put her hands on the arms of the chair and pushes herself onto her feet. She takes a school photo down from the mantelpiece and hands it to me. Of course it's Nathan. Of course it's Heddy's boy, with those eyes and that thick, dark hair.

I'm not sure what I'm supposed to say. *He looks nice* hardly sounds appropriate, so I say nothing and just look at the photo for a while, feigning interest. I'd have given it back to her, after a suitable time, but she sits back down again and gets herself another cigarette out and lights it, so I'm left holding the photo, left looking at Heddy reincarnated.

This is all too weird. And time is getting on; I'm supposed to be meeting Penny for lunch. I'm beginning to think that Mrs Partridge just wants someone to talk to, and I'm beginning to hope that the only help required of me is to sit here and listen.

'I worry for that boy,' Mrs Partridge says through a cloud of smoke. She leaves the cigarette in her mouth while she puts her lighter back in her pocket, and her lips purse around it, deep lines creasing downwards. 'Oh, I do my best for him. He goes to the school here, where you and Heddy went. He's settled in well, considering, but' – she takes another slow drag on her cigarette and holds it in for a long, long time before the smoke weaves slowly out from her nose – 'he hasn't seen his mother for two months. Two months.' Her eyes are bright with emphasis and I look back down at the photograph again to escape the glare. 'It's hard for him,' she says. 'Very hard.'

She taps the cigarette over the ashtray now, and keeps on

tapping it, after the ash has fallen. 'It's hard for Heddy, too. Stuck in that place. I took him to see her once,' she says, and I look up, curious, in spite of myself. 'But she'd trashed her room. Trashed it.' It's strange to hear a word like 'trash' coming from a woman like Mrs Partridge; suddenly I have this weird image of American TV, of rock stars, of guitars smashing against hotel mirrors. 'It was awful,' she says. 'Awful for him, and for her. They had to hold her down – I'll never forget how she screamed and screamed – they held her down and gave her something, you know, in her arm, to put her to sleep. He saw it all.'

She stares at me and I stare back now, appalled. I have the strangest feeling, sitting on that sofa, sinking into those cushions, that this is all some kind of mental sinking mud, gluing me in.

'I need to get her out of that place,' she says and she holds my gaze. I cannot pull away. 'I need to get her out, but the doctors, they just gave her pills and more pills. They *put* her in there. She needs to get out. She needs to be with her son.' She puffs on the cigarette. It seems as if more smoke is going in than coming out: two inhales for one exhale. I watch. I'm counting. I have to concentrate on something.

'I need to get her out,' she says again. 'But I can't do it on my own. I've tried, but . . . I need help. Your husband, he might know what to do . . .'

She knocks the ash off her cigarette, then grinds the butt into the ashtray, squeezing it out, dead. I think perhaps I'll quote James now, say *Go to the Citizens Advice*, and get myself off the hook, but then she stares directly at me and says, 'You'll help us, won't you, dear? You understand; you had a little problem once yourself, I remember. You'll help poor Heddy, dear, won't you?'

She sits there staring at me, letting me know that she remembers my little problem, as she calls it, making me remember it too, but I don't want to remember. Anyway, it's more an embarrassment than a problem. It's history.

I want it to stay history.

'Of course I'll help, Mrs Partridge, if I can,' I say, because what else can I say? 'But I'm afraid I really have to go now. I've got an appointment.'

Disappointment crosses her face, followed by panic. She shoots forward in her chair, sticks an arm out across the table and grabs me by the wrist. 'So soon?' she says. 'There's more, there's . . . other things.'

I'm not sure I want to hear these other things. I try to extricate my arm, but she's holding on to me, tight. Suddenly I can't breathe for the smoke and the gloom and the weight of Heddy's problems and Mrs Partridge's problems – and God help me if my problems are dragged up now, too. I have to get out. I have to get back into the real world, into *my* world.

But there's more, Mrs Partridge tells me. Much more. And I'll need to know it all if I'm to help. She's gabbling now, still clutching my arm with her bony fingers, and bombarding me with information about hospital dates and psychiatrist's reports and the downward spiral of medication. She shakes my wrist in her agitation.

'Perhaps you'd come with me, dear. See her for yourself. You could talk to them – to the doctors.'

Just the thought of it fills me with horror. I've got to get out of there, but she's still holding my arm. And she's staring at me with those dark, desperate eyes.

'Mrs Partridge, please . . . ' I manage to free myself from her bony fingers and I pick up my bag, getting ready to leave.

My heart is pounding now, hard. Carefully I start pushing myself out of the sofa. 'Look, I really have to go.'

She stands up too, jumping up quickly, and we almost bang heads. 'Tuesday,' she says. 'That's the doctor's day. Oh, they come and go on other days, of course, but always on a Tuesday ... '

She follows me out to the hall. She's too close. I'm afraid she's going to grab hold of me again and my skin prickles in the effort to get away.

'Tuesday,' she says again, as if I hadn't got the message. 'That's the best day for the doctors.'

'Mrs Partridge, I really don't know what I'm doing on Tuesday.'

'But if you have the time?' she insists. 'You'll come if you have the time?'

And just to get myself out of there I say, 'Look, I'll have to check my diary.'

FOUR

I practically fall out the front door in my haste to escape, and immediately I am hit by the brightness of the day after the gloom inside that house, and I have to squint against the sun. Mrs Partridge feels it too and cowers back into the hall, then peers round the half-closed door as I get into my car. I wish she'd go right inside and shut the door. I'd like to just sit there for a moment to clear my head before driving off, and I need to phone Penny, to confirm the time for lunch. But I can't do that with Mrs Partridge standing there watching, so I stick the key straight into the ignition. She's still there as I pull away; I catch a glimpse of her in the mirror, waving. I should have waved back, I suppose.

She didn't want to let me go.

I feel sorry for her now. She didn't want me to go, but I couldn't get out of there quickly enough.

I stink of Mrs Partridge's cigarette smoke. I can smell it on my hair, my clothes – horrible. I open the windows, all four of them, to try to blast the smell away, and the wind whips at my hair, fresh and spring-scented, blowing Mrs Partridge away.

Some bizarre curiosity sends me on a detour through Barton Village on my way back to Ashton. Barton Village is a 1970s conurbation on the north side of Forbury, about a mile and a half out down the long road that winds past the reservoir, the blackberry fields where the gypsies used to turn up every year, and the pig farm. The road always seemed like a divide, keeping the two places apart, and I'm surprised to see that it's like that still, that the blackberry field is still there, and that more houses haven't sprung up, closing the gap.

I haven't been down here for years and years. It's not just new houses. There's an old pub too, and a couple of sweet little cottages, the pretty bit before the rest begins. At juniors, I was friends for a while with a girl who lived over here, Kim. Whenever I came to her house I wondered how she remembered which one was hers. They all looked the same, still new back then, and neat, built in tidy rows. You love that sort of thing when you're young, that sameness. We played on the square of grass outside Kim's house with the other children on her block, and their mums could see us from their little front kitchens.

Kim seemed special to the rest of us in Forbury, because she had to come to school by car and be picked up again afterwards. Her mum was always there at twenty-past three, right outside the school gates in her little white Mini. Everyone else walked, but you couldn't walk all the way to Barton Village, and the bus into Forbury only came once an hour. In fact, if you didn't have a car you were stuffed. I picture Heddy living out here with a young baby, isolated. I picture her struggling with a pushchair and the shopping, getting on and off buses, red-faced and sweating.

There's a small parade of shops built under some flats, right on the corner of Kim's block, with a lay-by out the front. I pull in here quickly to phone Penny, and watch as one or two or maybe three people wander in and out of the newsagent's. I remember running round there with Kim to buy sweets, and a loaf of bread for her mum from the baker's next door. The baker's is gone now, boarded up, like a shut eye between the betting shop and the newsagent's. As I sit there, an oldish, fattish man comes out of the betting shop wearing a badly fitting brown suit and his slippers. Clearly it's been a good morning; he grins up at the sky and shoves a roll of money into his trouser pocket before shuffling into the newsagent's. As he goes in, a young girl comes out, pushing an angry child in a buggy. The man forgets to hold the door for her, and as he goes past her it starts to swing closed, bumping the girl from behind. She pushes it back open with her shoulder as she wrestles the buggy out, muttering furiously. Once outside, she uses her teeth to tear open a bag of sweets for the child and drops them into his anxious, clutching hands. Then she sticks a cigarette in her mouth and strikes up a match to light it, cupping her hands against the wind. She takes a long drag in, flicks the match into the gutter and leans forward, resting her weight on the handle of the pushchair for a second as she blows the smoke out of her mouth sideways, thereby avoiding her child's head. Then she's up on her feet again, clack, clack, clacking down the road in her black high heels, one hand pushing the buggy, the other holding the cigarette. She's dressed optimistically in a halter-neck top and a tight, short skirt that strains as she walks. She cannot be more than seventeen.

I wonder where Heddy lived. Naturally I picture her in a house like Kim's, with chipboard partitions for walls and open-slatted stairs going up from the living room. Those stairs would be hell for someone with a small child, a constant danger. Kim was small and thin, and her family were smallish and thin too – I remember them as modern and bright and stripy-clothed, like the families on frozen-food adverts; they seemed to fit their house, back then, when everything was new. Now, with my adult eyes, I can see a different scenario. I see Heddy, fat like in that photo at Mrs Partridge's, clad in the oversized clothes of post-pregnancy, too big for that house, too alone. I see her sitting on her sofa and staring at her reflection in the glass of the patio doors. I see the squareness of the room, of the windows, of the patio outside, boxing her in.

I hear the baby cry, I hear Heddy cry, and for a moment I shut my eyes.

Penny and I meet at Chico's in the High Street. Tasha joins us, last minute; she bumped into Penny earlier in John Lewis. You always bump into someone in John Lewis, it's guaranteed. We kiss the air beside each other's cheeks and I breathe in the heady scent of expensive perfumes and easy lives.

Tasha has a dilemma because she's just bought a house that needs renovating and can't decide whether to have wooden floors throughout, or just downstairs.

'What do you think, Laura?' she asks, pushing her blonde hair back from her face and staring at me with serious grey-blue eyes. She's had streaks put in her hair, red under the blonde, beautifully done at André's in the village, where we all go. The hand that pushes back the hair is newly manicured too, and thin; we are all thin, all exactly so.

We sit picking at our panini and discuss this, and other issues, such as Roman blinds versus curtains and whether a built-in fridge with ice dispenser would be better than one of those huge free-standing American things. We lean close as we talk and we talk fast, sometimes all of us at the same time. We talk about Tasha's house with the same level of enthusiasm as we talk about our children and the school, and our husbands too, sometimes, when we've had a glass of wine or two. And this talk is like a web that we spin around ourselves. I know this, and yet I sit there, I talk, I spin.

Penny has a funny story about Belinda. She looks behind her to check who else is in Chico's, then leans forward. We do the same, tight.

'Well,' she says in a stage whisper, and we're hanging on, Tasha and I, grinning already in expectation, 'you know that house they bought in Walpole Road? You know what a dump it was and how they were living in it when it was being done up?'

'Urgh! I could never do that!' I say.

'Me neither,' Tasha agrees, tossing her hair back over her shoulder to show her new streaks to full advantage, and we shudder in unison.

'Well, apparently it was really raining hard one day – you know, a total downpour – and Belinda was in the toilet when the weight of the rain caused the roof to cave in.' She pauses a moment, for dramatic effect. 'Right on top of her!'

Tasha and I slap our hands over our mouths, horrified.

'She got hit on the head by a plank of wood,' Penny says, and Tasha and I are collapsing into giggles behind our hands. 'Knocked unconscious. The builders had to get her out.' She pauses again, checks around the room once more, then shields her mouth with her hand, and says, 'Knickers still round her knees!'

We're beside ourselves now, Tasha and I, mortified on Belinda's behalf. Tasha dips her head to hide the laughter, letting her hair fall forward over her face. Then she tosses it back again, apparently oblivious to how it swings so perfectly into place.

Penny manages to keep her face straight. 'It wasn't funny,

you know,' she says, and tucks her own sleek, neat hair behind her ears in a perfect parody of Belinda, and we laugh even more. Penny's laughing too now and people are looking. We hope none of them knows Belinda, but for the moment we don't care.

'How did you hear that?' Tasha asks.

'Stephen told me. Belinda's husband Mike told him. He was at some old boys' do last week and Mike was there, propping up the bar apparently. You know what he's like after a few beers.'

I roll my eyes. 'James can't stand him. Thinks he's a total dickhead.'

Then we are back onto serious things again: weighing up the cost of decorators and discussing what Fiona Littlewood has had done to her dining room. And just then my phone rings. I fish it out from my bag, see it's a number I don't recognize and stupidly I answer it. It's *her*. Mrs Partridge.

'Laura?' she's saying. 'That you, Laura? Can you hear me?'

I can hear her and so will everyone else. I lean away from the table as far as I unobtrusively can and switch the phone to my other ear. 'What is it?' I hiss.

'It's Violet Partridge here.' Her voice is loud, too loud.

'Yes, yes, I know.'

I see Tasha glance at me, then at Penny, and raise an eyebrow.

'I wondered if you'd had time to consult your diary yet, dear. About Tuesday.'

'*What?*' I don't believe this. It's less than two hours since I left her house. Penny and Tasha have stopped talking now, and are both sitting there, watching me.

'About Tuesday,' she says again. 'Will you be free on Tuesday?'

Out of the corner of my eye I see Tasha mouth the word *Tuesday*.

'Yes, yes, that's fine,' I say, just to get her off the phone.

'You will?' I hear the surprise, the relief in her voice.

'Yes,' I say. 'Fine. I'll see you then.' And I hang up. 'Dentist,' I say to Tasha and Penny, who are both staring at me, expectantly. 'Change of appointment.' And I don't care right then if they believe me or not. 'Fiona Littlewood's wallpaper,' I say now, to stop them looking at me like that. 'Where did you say it was from?'

And so I steer us back into the smooth, benign conversation of our own safe, parallel world. And I do not mention Mrs Partridge, or the fact that this morning while Penny and Tasha were shopping in John Lewis I was trapped on that old sunken sofa in Mrs Partridge's cramped, dark front room. I do not mention this because I want to talk about the things in our world, our perfect world. I want to forget Heddy Partridge and everything to do with her. I want to forget her as I had forgotten her for the last however many years. She has no place in my life now; she never did. So I laugh about Belinda and I talk about decorators and kitchen plans, but still I can't help wondering what it was like for Penny and Tasha and Fiona Littlewood and all the other Ashton women when they were younger, *before* they were Ashton women. I wonder what it was like for them when they were at school. Were things always so smooth and easy? Do any of them know a Heddy or someone like her? Do any of them have a skeleton rattling around in their cupboard?

Do they?

Oh, I'm sure they must do, but no one will ever know. We meet, we chat, we think that we are the dearest of friends, but we all keep our cupboard doors firmly shut.

FIVE

She got breasts before the rest of us. That's the second thing I think of when I think of Heddy Partridge. After the ballet incident.

She got breasts too soon, before it was fashionable to have them. And we could all see them, two fat bumps inside her white school shirt, no matter how hard she tried to hide them.

'Heddy's got boobs,' we used to say, and the boys would run their hands up her back, to see if she was wearing a bra. Then they'd twang the strap and Heddy would pull away, embarrassed to the point of tears.

'Show us your boobs,' they'd chant, and she started standing with her shoulders sloping forwards, trying to hide them.

We had our own swimming pool at junior school, with changing rooms right by it: one block divided into two by a partition wall, girls on the left, boys on the right. The silly person who'd designed the changing rooms had put full-sized windows in, all along the front, so you could see straight in. So naturally the boys used to sneak out from their side of the building and dash across to ours to get a look at us when we were changing. We'd catch sight of their little faces peeping over the window frame and hysteria would break out; a mass of squealing and giggling and hiding behind towels.

Heddy didn't laugh, though. Heddy didn't squeal. Heddy was the only one of us with anything to hide, but she just carried on getting changed in the corner, her back to the window, struggling under her towel while the boys gawped. Her embarrassment was genuine, and we got a kick out of that, too.

We got a kick out of watching the boys looking at her in her big pants, and seeing her go red.

One day, somebody hid her clothes. Her skirt and her shirt and her big smelly knickers. We watched her hunting for them, groping about on the bench among everyone else's stuff while the other girls pushed her away.

'What you doing, Heddy Partridge?'

'Get off my things, Heddy Partridge.'

'You perv, Heddy Partridge, get off.'

She moved around the room, her face red and tearful and stupid. She was shaking, with the cold or with fear, and clutching that tatty towel around her body with one hand while her stringy wet hair dripped down her shoulders. Somebody started grabbing at her towel. Somebody else produced her clothes and started throwing them around – her shirt and her skirt – while Heddy lunged about trying to catch them, at the same time trying and failing miserably to keep her nakedness covered. And we shrieked with laughter. Shrieked and shrieked until the boys came creeping out from next door to see what was going on.

Nobody wanted to touch her knickers, though. They were thrown and landed on the floor with a flop, and everyone screamed and jumped away. And then they were kicked, and kicked again, back and forth across the wet floor, amid more screams, until the teacher eventually came and sent the boys packing, and then we all shut up, good as gold.

'For heaven's sake, what is going on?' Mrs Rogers demanded. And she looked at Heddy, who was standing there, quivering behind her towel. 'Heddy Partridge, why have you not even started getting dressed yet? Do you think you've got all day?' But she didn't wait for an answer. She marched off next door to sort the boys out.

And when she'd gone, someone quickly opened the door again and kicked out Heddy's soggy pants. They landed on the grass on the other side of the path, and that's where they stayed, for days and days, for everyone to see.

On Friday Arianne and I accompany Thomas into school, each of us carrying a tray of cakes that I iced but didn't make for the cake sale, each tray wrapped in a plastic bag because the unusually hot weather's broken now and it's turned colder and greyer and there's drizzle spitting in the wind, threatening real rain later, just when we don't need it. We like our cake sales outside, in the sunshine. We like to see the children rushing out at three-fifteen, grabbing their mummies and their mummies' money and crowding round the cake stall, eager eyes and eager hands, loading up. It feels timeless, like at a country fair, like we are doing what women are meant to be doing; dealing with children, with cakes, with pennies.

In the sunshine, it seems idyllic. In the sunshine, our lives seem idyllic and we like that, we like that very much.

At three-fifteen I am back again with Arianne, doing my bit for the class. The wind is getting up and throwing the rain into our faces in fitful bursts and smudging the icing on the cakes. There are four of us doing the selling. Juliet has an umbrella that she's tilting forward into the wind, trying to shelter the cakes – and us as much as she can – without poking the little ones in the eye with the spokes. Arianne is up close behind me, hanging around my legs and whingeing, 'Can we go? Can we go?', but we've another ten minutes of this at least. The children are still coming out, their mothers battling with umbrellas and lunch boxes and purses.

I stick more cakes out. Most of them are like mine: shop-bought fairy cakes with a bit of home-dyed icing squirted over them, and maybe a sweet stuck on top to make it look as if you'd made them yourself. You don't want your kids eating these. But you don't want your kids eating some of the real home-made ones either, when you don't know whose home they were made in. Thomas bought one once that had a long, long hair cooked inside it; it got caught between his two front teeth when he took a bite and I had to pull it free. I shudder to think of it. I shudder as the children arrive, swarming, fingers that have been busy poking at noses and bottoms now poking at the cakes, picking them up and putting them back again, looking for the ones with the most icing on top. I have the ones I've already picked out for my children put by in a bag behind the table; helper's perks. When Thomas comes bounding over, I hand him the bag and take a note from my purse and drop it into the kitty tin. Instantly Arianne lets go of my leg and turns her complaining to him now; it's all *Let me choose first* and *I wanted that one!*

Friday night children are the worst, always the worst. And tonight is James's football night, so he'll be in earlier than usual and he'll stir the children up just as I've got them wound down for bed. He'll stir them up, then he'll go out again, leaving me to deal with the fallout.

'James playing football tonight?' Juliet asks me after the

rush has gone, as if reading my mind. She smiles sweetly at me from under that umbrella – it's a *boys will be boys* smile. We shove what's left of the cakes into one tin, and Juliet pops one into her mouth and sticks a couple more into a bag. 'I'll take these for Andy,' she says, referring to her husband as though he was a seven-year-old. 'He never has time to eat much before football. You know what it's like. He dashes in, he dashes out. I have a sandwich ready for when he gets in from work, but I practically have to hold him down to make him eat it before he goes rushing off to his football.'

My husband plays football with my friends' husbands, every third Friday. And he catches the train with them every morning, and back again every evening. Oh, not the same ones, not every time. It does vary a bit. Some may go in ten minutes earlier some days, come home ten minutes later.

James will come home and say, *I saw so-and-so on the train today, and so-and-so.* And he'll tell me some little piece of gossip that he's heard: somebody's house sale's fallen through; somebody else is getting their loft converted so that the nanny can move in. Invariably I know this already. I talk to the women. He talks to the men, later.

I picture them all standing there on the platform at Ashton station. I picture them like cardboard cut-outs, like those wooden figures you used to get at fairs, years ago, the ones with no faces that you had to stand behind and stick your own face in the gap, either to be oh-so-amusingly photo-graphed or to be pelted with wet sponges. I picture them like this, those husbands. I imagine a certain number of basic cut-outs in place permanently, with only the faces coming, going, changing day to day. The conversation doesn't change; the conversation flows from one day into the next with barely a break in continuity. Each person comes, pops their head over the wooden collar and says their little bit. I imagine it flowing like a well-rehearsed play, an ongoing act, choreographed to perfection.

Sometimes, when I am feeling sour, I wonder what would happen if you stopped every one of these men five minutes after they left Ashton station in the evening, rewound them and sent them all back to the wrong home. I picture them scurrying along the streets, reprogrammed.

And sometimes, when I am feeling really, really sour, I think that they probably wouldn't even notice, and nor would their wives.

I pick clothes up off the floor where they have been dropped in random lines – socks, pants, shorts – and stuff them into the washing basket. At least Arianne has put her things in the basket, but no amount of nagging will get Thomas to do the same.

'Put your clothes in the wash,' I say every evening, and every evening I end up picking them off the floor. Sometimes I shout at him, sometimes I can't be bothered. Thomas thinks it's a game and he's right, it is. It's that little game called Let's See What We Can Get the Woman to Do for Us. He's practising for when he's older; he'll need to be good at that game when he has a wife of his own.

We like to joke that we are the ones with the brains, we women, and you only have to look at school-performance results to see that. Yet when I pick other people's dirty clothes up off the floor, I wonder about it. I wonder about it when I scrape the scraps off other people's plates into the bin, and when I wipe up the wee stains from around the loo. I wonder about it a lot. I wonder what happens to our brains when we get married, when we become mothers. I mean, look at me: would you believe that I organized events for a PR company in my previous life? 'We manage our families now,' Liz once said to me – she who used to manage an entire department for a major bank. But I don't feel like any kind of a manager right now. I feel a whole lot more like a fool.

I listen to my family laughing as I clear up their mess. They're tucked up in Arianne's bed, all three of them, with Daddy the Clown in the middle telling a quick funny story. Quick, because he'll be going back out in five minutes. He's got one eye on his watch already; can't be late for football. I know this and so do the children – there's a hysterical edge to their laughter now. I hear them getting wilder as I unplug the bath, hang up the towels. They're competing for his attention, getting louder, out of control, and I'm sure that James is loving it, this little burst of worship. But the children aren't loving it, not really. James thinks that they are, but he can't hear the tears creeping into their laughter. James can't hear how desperate they are to hang on to him, to entertain him, to make him want to stay with them a little longer.

But then James doesn't hear Thomas's plaintive little voice every night, calling down the stairs, 'When's Daddy coming home?'

And James doesn't have to listen to Thomas singing to himself, counting to himself, pop-popping his finger against the inside of his cheek to try to keep himself awake, hoping with all his little heart that he might see his daddy before he falls asleep.

I don't know which is worse: normal nights when James comes in too late to see the children, but at least the children get their sleep, at least they're tucked up and calm and there have been no tears; or this, this heart-breaking perform- ance every third Friday when he comes home early, winds them up full of excitement and then leaves them again.

Daddy the Clown is pulling away now; it's time to go. I hear the tone of his voice change instantly, so precise, so businesslike now. Playtime over. I hear Arianne's voice rising on a wail, I hear Thomas shouting, 'Dad, Dad, one more time ... '

But Daddy grabs his kitbag and is gone out the door, kissing me quickly on the cheek on his way past, smiling, oblivious to the chaos he leaves behind.

As soon as James closes the front door behind him it starts. Their little hearts are overloaded with disappointment and they turn on each other now. Arianne kicks Thomas to get him out of her bed. Thomas pinches Arianne. Arianne starts screaming, yelling, 'Mummy! Mummy!' Thomas calls Arianne a crybaby, Arianne calls Thomas Fatty Belly, Thomas calls Arianne Poopy Pants, and on and on it goes.

I walk into Arianne's room, bracing myself.

She is sitting on her bed, face red and squashed up with misery. 'Mummy!' she howls even louder now she sees me. 'Thomas called me Poopy Pants!'

'Poopy Pants! Poopy Pants!' Thomas taunts, jumping around the room, sticking out his bottom and blowing rasp- berries over his shoulder.

'Fatty Belly!' Arianne rises up like a cat, spitting out the words, and dribble spurts onto her chin.

'Ha-ha!' Thomas jeers, pointing. 'Dribble Chops! Dribble Chops!'

*

Some books tell you that the way to deal with this is to reason with them, to let them show their anger and to help them understand it, even though you're not allowed to feel any yourself. Some books say separate them, others say don't intervene.

I find the only way I can deal with it is to deaden myself inside.

Stop it, I say to Thomas; stop it, I say to Arianne. I put them in their separate beds in their separate rooms and close the doors, and I wish we didn't have to go through this every third Friday.

Once, my mother phoned, right in the middle of it all. And it was particularly bad that night; it must have been, for me to say anything. Both kids screaming away and me just about ready to join in.

'Whatever's going on?' my mum asked before I'd even said hello.

'It's James's football night,' I said, expecting her – stupidly – to understand. Expecting a little bit of sympathy maybe, a little bit of *Oh dear, I'm sure they'll settle soon.*

What I got was this disbelieving pause. And then she laughed, that short, shrill, committee-member laugh. 'Surely you can control your own children, Laura,' she said.

Funny that I should think of that now.

Downstairs in the kitchen I pour myself a large glass of wine. I can still hear the children grizzling away, but it's becoming intermittent now. Five times I've been called back upstairs, bringing drinks, finding teddies. Five times I've gone up, and each time I've said *I'm not coming up again.*

I sit at the table and sip my wine, and wait as the silence gradually eases down.

All day I have had the strangest sensation of going the

wrong way fast, like running backwards through a crowd. And all day I've felt that at any moment I might bump into Heddy Partridge. I keep getting the neck-prickling feeling that she's just behind me, that if I turn around she'll be there, moon-faced and rabbit-eyed, watching me.

This is so irrational. Heddy Partridge *makes* me irrational. I know she isn't going to come wandering out of St Anne's looking for me. I mean, just imagine it, big mad Heddy roaming the streets of Ashton in her hospital gown!

It's the girl she was that's haunting me. Not the woman that she is now, whatever that may be.

I have this image stuck in my head, of Heddy on her ninth birthday. Heddy coming down the stairs in her house, ridiculous as ever in her ballet clothes, stupid face open and hopeful as a baby's.

I didn't *know* it was her birthday. It was a Saturday, and there we were, picking her up for ballet yet again. My dad always let me sit in the front for the short distance from my house to the Partridges', but then I'd have to go in the back when Heddy got in the car, and sit next to her, because my dad said I had to be *nice*. So because of her I had to move away from my dad. The only time I ever got to be near him, to have him to myself, to feel like I was *special* maybe for a few minutes – and Heddy Partridge cut it short.

'Go on, then,' my dad said, and I got out of the car even more reluctantly than usual to knock on the Partridges' door, because that particular Saturday it was raining, hard.

The rain dotted grey spots on my pink ballet tights as I ran up the pathway, holding my coat up over my head. Halfway up the path there was a huge puddle. I jumped wide to cross it, misjudged, and clomped down onto the wet concrete, splashing puddle water across the tops of my feet and inside my school shoes.

'Stupid Heddy Partridge,' I cursed. 'Stupid, fat, *stupid* Heddy Partridge.'

You'd think she'd be ready when we came for her. You'd think a honk of the horn would do it and out she'd come, but oh no, up that pathway I'd have to go, come rain or shine. Up that pathway and into that house.

I rang the doorbell and listened to that awful chime.

'Come in, come in,' Mrs Partridge said, opening the door and ushering me through the plastic strips to stand dripping on the doormat. She pulled the door shut behind me, leaning over me, close, with her arm outstretched to do so. She smelled of the hard work of being Mrs Partridge, of cooking and sweat and cigarette smoke. I shrank into myself, appalled by her nearness.

'Heddy!' she called as the door clicked shut behind me, shutting out the sound of the rain. Her mouth was close to my face, her voice loud in my ear. I could smell her breath, a smell of cats and fish and dampened-out bonfires. I pressed my tongue against the top of my mouth and tried not to breathe, for far too long, and felt my heart thump.

'Heddy!' she called again, away from me now, shouting up the narrow stairs that rose steep and dark from the hallway into the darker beyond. I let out my breath and quickly took in another, through my mouth. 'Heddy!' Mrs Partridge yelled again and her voice caught on a gurgle and a cough. The cough rattled like water over stones, and as if in response Mr Partridge started coughing too, from behind the half-closed living-room door where he sat slowly, audibly dying. I wished I was safely back out in the car, next to my dad, who hardly ever coughed at all.

Mrs Partridge turned back round to me, a conspiratorial look on her face and said, 'It's Heddy's birthday today.'

I could smell her breath again. She grinned at me, triumphantly, waiting. 'Oh,' I said.

Then Heddy came down the stairs, at last, fat pink legs visible first, like butcher's sausages in her ballet tights, followed by the rest of her. Most of us wore pink leotards now. Mine was the exact same colour as my tights, with a thin belt around the waist, sewn on at the sides. Heddy's leotard was black and plain and cut low on the thighs with thick elastic bunching against her flesh, like old-fashioned knickers. She stopped at the bottom of the stairs and looked at me, all bright-eyed and expectant.

They were both looking at me, and waiting.

'Happy birthday,' I muttered, then I stood there impatiently as Heddy shoved her feet into her school shoes and took her anorak down from the coat rack. I'd got my hand on the door latch and, as soon as I possibly could, I pulled open that door and ran back down that pathway in the rain to the car, and my dad. I wanted to get in the front, right up beside him, but I didn't, because I had to be *nice* to Heddy.

I knew Heddy was following along behind me, but when I opened the door to the back seats and clambered in, I saw that Mrs Partridge had followed us too, come out in the rain holding a broken yellow umbrella over her head. She bent down to the front passenger window and tapped, and my dad started when he saw her, as if he'd had a fright, which would have made me laugh if I wasn't so angry. He leaned across the passenger seat to wind down the window, grabbing at the handle with a clumsy hand. And then he put on this stupid, gushy voice.

'Hello, Mrs Partridge, how *are* you?' he asked with way too much enthusiasm. I cringed on his behalf.

'Oh, good, good. Not so bad,' Mrs Partridge said back, and probably she was cringing too because there was this awkward pause then, as if neither of them knew what to say. And I sat there, thinking *Oh, just get on with it*, while Heddy stuffed herself onto the back seat beside me.

And then, 'It's Heddy's birthday,' Mrs Partridge announced, as Heddy bumped her big self up against me.

Oh, woopy-dee. Bring out the trumpets and put an ad in the paper. I wriggled across the seat to the far side and pressed myself right up against the door to get as far away from Heddy as I could. She smelled of wet dog.

'Happy birthday, Heddy,' my dad said, straining his neck to look round at Heddy in the back.

'Thank you,' Heddy muttered, and blushed, and looked down at her fat legs, flattened fatter against the seat of the car.

I thought Mrs Partridge would go away now that she'd made her grand announcement, but she carried on standing there with the rain running down off her crumpled umbrella and into the open window. Then, to my horror, she said, 'Would Laura like to come round later, this afternoon, for some cake?'

No, Laura would not, I wanted to reply, but my dad answered for me, gushing, 'I'm sure Laura would *love* to. That's very kind of you, Mrs Partridge.'

I sat the whole way to ballet staring out the window away from Heddy, and fuming. And when we were at ballet she seemed to think this unwanted invitation – and the extremely unwanted, unfair acceptance – somehow gave her the right to hang around me more than ever. When I hung up my coat with the others she was there, hanging hers on the next peg. I took off my shoes and left them under my coat and ran over to the bench on the far side of the hall where some of the other girls were sitting, to lace up my ballet pumps. I squeezed myself in between the other girls, deliberately, so there was no room for Heddy, thinking she'd get the message. But still she followed me across the hall, and stood there, totally ignored by everyone, until Madame clapped her hands for us to get started. Then Heddy tried to stand next to me when we did our circle exercises, so I had to dash across the hall at the last minute and butt in on the other side of the circle, just to get away from her. And then I was stuck with her stupid face opposite me, all hurt and bemused.

She was like a dog following me around all the time; she made me want to kick her. It wasn't my fault that she was too thick to know when to get lost. And it wasn't my fault that the only time I ever got to have my dad to myself – that is, when he was giving me a lift somewhere – *she* had to come along and spoil it.

She wanted me to tell the others it was her birthday. I didn't, of course.

I ignored her all the way home in the car too, staring out the window and not speaking to Heddy or my dad, so she was the one who had to answer him when he asked *How did it go, did you have a nice time?* And then I hated her even more for muscling in and talking to *my* dad when she shouldn't even have been in our car at all.

When we dropped her off, my dad said, 'Have a very happy birthday, Heddy. Laura will be along later.'

Before Heddy had even closed the car door behind her, and knowing full well she could hear me, I said, 'Dad, I don't *want* to go round there.'

And my dad turned around and snapped at me, 'How dare you be so rude! It's jolly kind of them to invite you.' And so I got another lecture all the way home, about how I mustn't be so selfish, about how I must make more of an effort, about how I must be *nice* to poor bloody Heddy Partridge. The injustice of it all was like a finger jabbing at my head, like Heddy Partridge was put on this earth just to make my parents forever disappointed with me.

If my dad liked Heddy Partridge so much, why didn't he go to her party? In fact, why didn't he have her for a daughter full stop, instead of me?

After lunch my mum gave me some money and made me walk to the shops around the corner to buy Heddy a present, even though it was still raining. I bought her a box of cheap bath cubes, like you'd give to your granny, from the chemist, and the worst card I could find, a hideous cheap thing with a bunch of old flowers on the front. It was my dad I was angry with, but Heddy bore the brunt of it. I spent the rest of the money on sweets, which I ate, though they stuck in my throat.

My mum made me get changed, too, into something nice.

'It's not a party,' I kept saying to her. 'It's just *cake*.' And mouldy cake probably, at that.

I sip my wine. Memory is a leech, sucking me back.

My dad walked me round to Heddy's house. I expect he thought I wouldn't go there unless he actually took me and watched me go in.

It *wasn't* a party.

It was just me, and the Partridges.

'Come in, come in. Come in out of the cold,' Mrs Partridge ushered me, all cheery-jolly, as she opened the door. Heddy stood right behind her, dressed in a purple, smock-type dress in some nylon material that had bobbled up, all down the sides. Hideous, absolutely hideous. And she'd got her heavy black hair pushed back from her face and held back by a gold slide. She didn't look any better for it. Some faces are best left covered up.

'Have a nice time,' my dad said behind me and then the door closed.

I felt like a Christian, thrown to the lions. Except, looking back, I know there was nothing very Christian about the way I thought, or felt, standing in Mrs Partridge's hallway.

I stood there, clutching Heddy's present in my hands, feet cemented to the doormat. Mrs Partridge and Heddy stood in front of me, leering at me. Then Ian Partridge came out of the living room and leered at me too.

'Well, don't just stand there,' Mrs Partridge said and moved forward, putting one thin hand on my arm, the other on the present. Instantly Heddy moved towards me too, eager hands outstretched, and took that present. She tore at the paper, and Ian sidled up closer to her, looking on. They looked like Tweedledee and Tweedledumetta. I didn't know how anyone could get so excited over a box of bath cubes.

'Thanks,' Heddy said, all bright-eyed, like she meant it.

'Go on in, then,' Mrs Partridge said, steering me away from that doormat. 'Go and say hello to Mr Partridge.'

Now I have to say here that the one thing I dreaded more than anything was having to go and say hello to Mr Partridge. He gave me the creeps. Normally I avoided him by staying in the hallway when I waited for Heddy to get ready for ballet or Brownies; sometimes I wasn't so lucky.

I could hear him behind that living-room door, rasping away.

'Go on, then,' Mrs Partridge said, with a big nod of encouragement. 'Go and say hello to Uncle Vic.'

Heddy and Ian stepped back, to one side, making a path for me. All three of them watched. I took a step forward, and another, towards that half-closed door. In my head I chanted the words of a rhyme we used to sing, tossing tennis balls against a wall and catching them again.

> Uncle Billy with his big hairy willy
> Uncle Bob with his big hairy knob
> Uncle Jock with his big hairy cock
> Uncle Vic with his big hairy dick.

I put my hand to the door to push it, and it caught on the carpet and stuck.

'Here,' Mrs Partridge said, leaning over me again. She gave the door a yank and a shove and it swung open. 'Look who's here,' she called to the shadow in the corner. 'It's little Laura Cresswell.' Then she dropped her voice again and half-whispered to me, leaning close so that I could smell her breath again, and feel it on my neck so that the skin prickled and cramped, 'Say hello to your Uncle Vic.' And she more or less pushed me into the room.

He wasn't my uncle, and I hated her calling him that. It made me terrified that he might try to give me a hug, like a real uncle. Or, worse still, kiss me. He had paper skin, and thin lips that disappeared into his teeth, and a great hollow in his neck that drew right in when he breathed. He can't have been that old really, but he looked it. He looked like death and beyond, and the only light in his eyes was the light of fear that sparked up every time he coughed. And God, how he coughed. You could hear the stuff coming up from his lungs. I don't know how Mrs Partridge, and Heddy, and Ian could carry on like normal, moving about their house with that cough as background music; it felled me into stillness. He caught me with his eyes as he coughed – brown eyes, dark, like Heddy's, darker still against his colourless skin.

There were three bags of sweets, quarter-pounds of something or other, wrapped up in paper and lined up on the arm of his chair.

'Can we have them now? Can we have our sweets, Dad?' Ian asked, his low, slow voice quickening only slightly, though he rocked from side to side, eyeing those sweets.

'We waited for you, Laura,' Mrs Partridge said. 'Ian's had his eye on those sweets all morning, but no, wait till Laura's here, I said to Mr Partridge. Didn't I, Uncle Vic?' She blustered up behind me, rounding us up like rabbits.

Uncle Vic.

He smiled and it made his skin look yellower. It was a horrible smile, spreading his lips across his teeth and making the fear in his eyes stand out, starker.

'Go on,' Mrs Partridge urged, giving me a little push. 'Ask Uncle Vic for some sweets.'

'Can I have some sweets, please, Uncle Vic?' I asked, automatically, trying not to look at his cavernous, grim-reaper eyes.

Heddy and Ian crowded up beside me. Mr Partridge lifted his hand above the sweets on the arm of his chair and, swallowing and swallowing, he croaked out the words, 'Help yourselves, children. Have fun. Enjoy yourselves!'

Have fun? Was he mad as well as dying? Heddy and Ian pounced on their sweets, stuffing them into their fat, wet mouths. Tentatively I picked up the last paper bag and held it, and listened to Mr Partridge's lungs collapse and gasp, collapse and gasp, as if there was some pedal-pump inside him, pumping him up like a lilo.

We played cards. Gin rummy and things that I thought were just for grown-ups. I wanted my dad, and my mum, badly. I wanted the loo badly too, but I was far too scared to venture up into the dark upstairs of the Partridges' house. We were sitting on the floor – not Mr Partridge of course, but the rest of us. I sat on the heel of one foot, finding it hard to keep still, until in the end I was fidgeting so much that Mrs Partridge said to me, 'Need the lavvie, Laura? Heddy'll show you where it is.'

Heddy showed me up the dark, narrow stairs where the air was much, much colder and smelled of old mattresses and damp. The bathroom was down the end of the landing, past the two bedrooms. Heddy flicked on the landing light, a dusty, solitary bulb hanging yellow and shadeless from the ceiling, illuminating the shadows and spooky corners. 'It's there,' she said, pointing at the bathroom door. 'Do you want me to wait for you?'

And I said *No*, in the way that we always said no to Heddy, as if everything she suggested was stupid, or weird, or both.

The light in the bathroom was one of those old-fashioned strips, worked by a cord. I yanked it on, and closed the door behind me. Bathrooms are intimate places. I remember laughing, recently, over someone's tale about a bathroom cabinet stuffed with marbles, so that when a nosy guest went prying the marbles came tumbling out, crashing all over the place, for everyone else to hear.

They had a really old-fashioned loo with a big, black cistern up above it, which looked as if it might crash down upon your head while you were sitting there; and a proper chain to pull, to flush it; and square sheets of toilet paper in a box, not on a roll like we had at home. The soap was on a little shell-shaped dish, and going soft underneath. I washed my hands and dried them on the big towel hanging over the bath. I wondered whose towel it was, and how they ever managed to have a bath when it was so filled with the washing basket, a cactus plant in a tub and Mrs Partridge's sewing machine.

Mrs Partridge had got the cake out when I came back down. She'd put it on the table and was sticking the candles into little holders balanced precariously on top. Heddy and Ian were standing by the table, watching her, both of them puffing their cheeks in and out as if practising their blowing-out skills. I looked over at Mr Partridge, still sitting in his chair. He'd fallen asleep, with his head tilted backwards and his mouth wide open.

I thought he was dead. I thought he was dead and no one else had noticed.

'There,' Mrs Partridge said, as she stuck the last candle in. She patted the pockets of her pinny, found matches and pulled them out. 'Now, what else do we need?' She glanced around the room, vaguely, her eyes passing over Mr Partridge. She didn't seem to notice that he was dead. 'Heddy,' she said, 'go and fetch some plates, and a knife.'

And Heddy went out to the kitchen, walking past Mr Partridge, and she didn't notice that he was dead, either. Soon she came back again, carrying plates with a big kitchen knife balanced on top. She watched what she was doing, so as not to drop anything. Still she didn't notice what had happened to Mr Partridge.

I didn't know what to do.

Ian was starting to jump about a bit now, excited at the prospect of cake. He'd see, I thought. He'd see that his dad was dead. But Ian didn't take his eyes off the cake, and now Mrs Partridge was striking up a match and lighting those candles.

'Come on, come on, gather round,' she said to me, but I stood rooted to the spot. '*Happy birthday to you* . . . ' she started up, and Ian joined in, and I tried to, but I couldn't stop glancing sideways at Mr Partridge. I wondered when they'd realize he was dead, and what would happen then.

Then, when they'd stopped with the 'Happy birthday' and Heddy was just about to blow out the candles, Mrs Partridge said, 'Hang on a minute now, don't want Mr Partridge missing everything.' And she moved over to his chair, put her bony hand on his knee and gave him a little shake. At once he gurgled and spluttered and coughed into life, and opened his eyes.

I cannot tell you how much I wished I was at home. I couldn't eat any of that horrible cake. And when my dad eventually picked me up to take me home, I got down their pathway and out through their gate and burst into tears.

'Why did you make me go there?' I cried. 'Why?'

But my dad just got angry with me and said, 'For God's sake, Laura, why can you not think about anyone but yourself?'

And worse, much worse than all of that, was that my parents went and invited Heddy to my birthday party, in March. No matter how much I cried and begged them not to, they said we had to return the invitation, we had to be polite. And again – why couldn't I just make an effort and be nice to poor Heddy Partridge?

*

I do not want to see Heddy Partridge again, ever. Heddy Partridge is gone, *gone*, like all the other mistakes made in childhood. What point is there in going back and revisiting nightmares? What could I ever say to her now? *Oh, I'm sorry I made your life sheer hell, and I'm sorry for any part I may have had in your current terminal gloom, but hey, let me have a little chat to your doctors and see if I can't put things right.*

I do not want to go back. And I don't want to even think about trying to put things right.

I moved on a long, long time ago.

She turned up at my party wearing that same purple dress, slightly shorter now, and tighter.

'Oh, it's you,' I said, opening the door and taking the present out of her hand, and then I ignored her.

We all ignored her. We made quite a game of it.

I opened my presents and said my thank-yous. Everyone crowded around to see what I'd got, except for Heddy, who stood glum-faced on her own. I opened her present last – it was a book, I think – and let it fall discarded to the floor with all the torn-up wrapping paper.

My parents gave me one of those make-up stations that opened out, all pink plastic and lit up inside, crammed with glittery make-up pots and hair things, and a dummy's head with long nylon hair to practise on. I let everyone have a go, except Heddy. And at teatime we wouldn't let her sit down. Whenever she went for a chair we'd all shuffle along, blocking her way. All the way round the table she went, red-faced and flustered, and round the table we went too, bumping along from chair to chair, until my mum came into the dining room and snapped, 'Laura!' in a shocked, angry voice. 'What do you think you are doing?'

And she made Heddy sit next to me, ruining my party entirely.

Later, when everyone had gone, my mum told me how disappointed she was with me. And when my dad came home early to see me, she told him how disappointed she was, and he got angry. Really angry. No *Happy birthday, Laura*, no *Have you had a nice day?* – oh no, nothing like that. Just straight in there, slamming his fist down onto the kitchen counter and raging at me.

'I do not want to hear this!' he shouted, his face gone all tight and grey. 'I do not want to come home from work to find that Heddy Partridge has been a guest in *my* house and that you – yes, *you*, Laura – have humiliated her!'

We had this huge row. Made all the worse because I was full of cake and sweets and lemonade and was riding too high on the innate belief that on your birthday *you* matter, *you're* the special girl, for the day.

He told me I was selfish and spoiled. He told me how ashamed he was of me.

I stood among the debris of my party – the wrapping paper, the crushed crisps, the ripped-up, tangled streamers – with the unfairness of it all boiling up inside my head, and yelled, 'But I didn't want to invite her! I don't *like* her!'

And my dad grabbed hold of my arm, tight, and glared at me right up close, with just this one muscle flickering under his eye, and said, 'Laura, I do not care whether you like her or not. *That* is not the point.'

But if that wasn't the point, then what was?

This morning's post is still on the table, unopened. I glance at it, and push it to one side. It's bills mostly, and junk mail, all after money, one way or another. One in particular catches my eye, although I don't want it to. It's a begging letter, a guilt letter. I shouldn't call it that, but that's what it is. There's a faint, grey pencil sketch of some poor starved child decorating the envelope. I've seen it now; the picture will be stuck in my head until I open it up, and pay whatever is needed to make the image go away. I get a lot of these letters.

I give money here, I give money there, I give it no more thought.

But the piece of me that Mrs Partridge wants cannot so easily be dispensed.

I have no intention of going to see Heddy Partridge. I agreed under duress, as James would say. And what possible use could I be anyway? What do I know about mental hospitals, for heaven's sake? What does Mrs Partridge expect me to do when I'm there? Have a good look round, say *This won't do*, and pack Heddy up and take her home with me?

The thing is, how shall I say no? It's always much harder, once you've already said yes.

The house is quiet now, and my glass empty. I stand up and take the wine bottle from the fridge, and pour myself another glass. And then I take the phone from where it's lying beside James's half-drunk cup of tea, and sit back down.

I'll tell her I'm too busy. I'll say, *Look, I'm really sorry, Mrs Partridge, I'd love to be able to help, but I just don't have the time at the moment.*

It'll be easier on the phone than face to face. She'll get the message. With any luck she'll just give up on me, and let me go. If she does still push me to come and see Heddy, I'll say I'm really busy at the moment and can't fix a date right now, but I'll call her, sometime soon. Ultimate fob-off. I've done it a million times before; I can do it again.

It's the best thing to do. I *don't* have the time. And at least on the phone I won't have to avoid her bird-like stare, imploring me.

I don't have Mrs Partridge's number and our phone directory doesn't cover that far out, so I have to phone up directory enquiries.

'Partridge,' I say to the operator. 'Mrs V. Partridge, One Fairview Lane, Forbury. In Middlesex.'

But the operator comes back to me and says, 'Sorry, we have no listing for that number,' and hangs up.

I sit there, listening to the dialling tone.

'Shit!' I mutter out loud and lay down the phone. Why on earth would Mrs Partridge be ex-directory?

This means I'll have go to her house on Tuesday, then, like I agreed. I don't have any choice now. But I'm not going with her to see Heddy. I'll go to Mrs Partridge's house and I'll tell her, straight away. I won't even go in, I'll ring the doorbell, say *I can't stop, I just wanted to let you know . . .*

I'll think of something.

I drum my fingers against my glass in annoyance; wine sloshes over the rim, and runs red across my hand.

There's no way on earth I'm going with Mrs Partridge to St Anne's Hospital to see Heddy.

SIX

On Sunday evening I am sitting on the floor with bits of grey felt and white fake-fur spread out all around me. I've cut out a big body shape from the felt, like a tabard, that Thomas can just pop his head through, and now I'm sewing on the arms. The legs were a problem, a big problem. I was going to cut out two long pieces of felt and sew them up sausage-like and then attach them to the main body, like I am with the arms. But then I realized that getting the outfit on would be impossible, and if I sewed the legs on while he was wearing it, he'd never get out of it again, to go to the loo. So I suggested that I just make the costume to go on his top half and that he wears his school trousers underneath – after all, they're grey. They'll do, I said.

Thomas went nuts.

'I can't wear my school trousers,' he cried. 'Baloo doesn't wear school trousers. Everyone will laugh at me. Everyone else will have proper legs.'

And everyone else will have a much better outfit. At least he didn't say that, though I expect it'll be true. Everyone else has a much better mummy who went to John Lewis before the grey fake-fur ran out, and who loves nothing more than to sit and sew perfect outfits for her perfect little darling to wear to school for just one day, after she's knocked up a batch of perfect cakes and produced a perfect meal for her perfect husband. I remember watching the film *The Stepford Wives* once, years ago, when I was about twelve. In the film all the women become robotized, all perfect, all the same. Good grief, I thought, that'll never happen to me.

Good grief indeed.

To sort out the leg problem Thomas and I agree in the end that I could sew felt onto his trousers, to make them match the body. I've still got this to do, and the tail. I snap off the cotton with my teeth. I hate sewing. I loathe it.

'Yes!' James shouts from the other end of the room and I glance up just as he punches the air. 'Chelsea are through!'

He's sitting cross-legged in front of the television, checking the football results. Fluff from the white fake-fur has spread itself across the floor and little clumps have stuck themselves to the back of his T-shirt. I should have sewn on the furry patch last, after I'd done the arms. I'll be clearing up white fluff for evermore.

The phone starts ringing. I am re-threading the needle to start on the legs and James is idly flicking through the tele-text. No one moves to answer the phone.

I look at James as I hold up the needle. My neck is stiff from leaning over and I flex it from side to side. The phone rings and rings. Looking at him, I wonder if he even hears it.

'James,' I say. 'James, I'm in the middle of sewing. Could you get it?'

He makes a noise that is half huff and half grunt and reluctantly gets to his feet. His socks are covered in white fluff. Still staring at the TV, still holding the remote control in one hand, he picks the phone up from the windowsill with the other and puts it to his ear.

'Hello,' he barks into the handset, then comes over and hands it to me. 'It's for you,' he says.

It's *her*.

Mrs Partridge's voice rattles down the line and I hold the phone close to my ear. For some reason I don't want James to hear. He's curious, I know; he looks at me as he goes out into the kitchen. He's looking at me still as he comes back again with a bag of pistachio nuts and a bowl. He stands in the middle of the room with the bowl at his feet and half-reads the teletext and half-listens to me as he splits open nuts with his teeth and spits the shells down into the bowl.

She's checking I'm still coming on Tuesday. She's upset; her voice is higher, louder than usual, and I press the phone against my ear to try to muffle it.

'Of course I'm still coming,' I say, because that is the easiest – the only – thing to say right now. But then she tells me Heddy's had a bad turn; she needs me to come and see her, she says. She didn't like to bother me so soon, and at the weekend too, but she hasn't been able to think about anything else.

'I see,' I say into the phone. I look at James and he raises his eyebrows at me as he drops another nut shell into the bowl.

'I've been worried sick, all weekend, worried sick,' she tells me, and I wish James would go away. 'I went to see her on Friday. I always do, you know, every day. Just in the holidays it's difficult, you know, with Nathan at home . . . but I always go when I can, always . . .'

I hear her sniffing, then she's gone for a second. James is losing interest now; he's flicked the TV back onto normal and is switching through the channels. When Mrs Partridge comes back on the phone, her voice is shaking, shockingly so.

'On Friday the buses were running late,' she says, 'I missed the connection in Fayle. I didn't get to the hospital until gone twelve. She must have thought I wasn't coming. She'd split open a yoghurt pot and cut herself with the plastic, all over her chest and her neck. I heard her screaming out when I got there. *Nathan*, she was calling, *Nathan*. Over and over. Heartbreaking, it was, heartbreaking.' She breaks off again and I hang onto the phone, frozen. 'They put her to sleep. She didn't know I was there, and then I had to get back again for Nathan, before she woke up. And I couldn't go back at the weekend, because I had Nathan to look after. I phoned them, but they tell me nothing on the phone. She's fine, they tell me, but she isn't. She isn't fine.'

James has stopped spitting out nut shells now. He switches the TV to standby, then drops the remote control down beside the overflowing bowl and goes out into the hall to get his BlackBerry. For a second I relax a little, but then he's back with it, walking around the room as he checks his emails.

'God, that's awful,' I say, and for the moment I mean it. And then I regret it.

James looks up from his BlackBerry and I avoid his eye as Mrs Partridge says: Could I come tomorrow? Could I, instead of Tuesday? Could I come tomorrow, come to St Anne's with her, because it's no good her going on her own, she can't make head or tail of what they're doing to poor Heddy.

'No,' I snap down the phone, and even James looks startled; poor Mrs Partridge is silenced. 'No,' I say again, softer this time. 'I can't – not tomorrow. I'm sorry, but I'm busy tomorrow, all day.' And I am. I've a full day lined up: I'm shopping first thing, then Arianne's got Tumbletots at eleven, and we're going back to Tasha's for lunch after that. Tasha's got some wood-floor brochures that she wants to show me. And Thomas has swimming lessons after school.

I don't tell Mrs Partridge all this. I don't see why I should. I listen to the silence now in my ear, and I try telling myself that I don't need to feel guilty, or to make excuses. I do have a life, and I didn't ask for the Partridges to come barging into it.

'It'll have to wait till Tuesday,' I tell her, and I'm too annoyed to feel any pity for her as she sniffs and sighs and mumbles her disappointed 'Yes, dear, thank you then, dear.'

'Shit,' I mutter as I switch off the phone and drop it onto the floor beside me.

'Well?' James says, and throws himself down onto the sofa, still looking at his BlackBerry. He'll be checking the football results again now; he always does this, as if they might differ from the results on the TV.

'Well, what?' I pick up my sewing and ram the needle into Baloo's tail.

'Well, who was that?'

'Family friend,' I say, sticking that needle in and pulling it out again; in, out, in, out. Family pain-in-the-neck, more like.

'Going to tell me what's going on, then?' he murmurs and I look up at him. He's not even paying attention, not really. I can see his eyes flickering as they read that tiny screen, his face intent, absorbed. I am a byline, a little extra on the outside, as usual.

I am not in the mood to be entertaining. I am not in the mood to talk to half a person. The annoyance I feel towards Mrs Partridge, and myself, transfers itself onto James now.

'Girl I was at school with is stuck in a mental hospital, and her mum wants me to help get her out,' I mutter and James laughs; it catches in his throat and comes out on a snort.

'Never thought of you as the altruistic type,' he says.

I stare at him. 'Why not? I helped that cat that got hit by a motorbike, remember? It was me who called the vet. And I do loads for the school.'

'Yes, I know, but that's animals and children. What I meant is I can't see you helping some nutter.'

His words make me flinch. The easy way in which he says them makes me flinch. They're throwaway words, that's all. I look at him sitting there with the foot of one leg propped up on the knee of the other, and one arm resting across the back of the sofa, bent at the elbow, hand thrust into his brown ruffled hair while the other hand plays away at that computer propped upon his thigh – his latest toy. I look at him and I wonder: when did we become so lost under the weight of our lives?

'I didn't say she was a nutter.' Something in my voice makes him glance up.

'You said she was stuck in a mental hospital,' he says.

'Yes,' I say, and I have the strangest feeling of something hollowing out inside me. 'But things happen, sometimes, to people.'

James is looking at me now, properly. 'I didn't mean to upset you,' he says. 'I'm just surprised you're getting involved, that's all.'

'I'm not getting involved,' I say, and turn back to my sewing, subject closed. I can feel James watching me, as if he's going to say something else, but I keep my head down, concentrating on my work. After a moment he gets up from the sofa and goes out to the kitchen. In the silence of the house I hear the click as he opens himself a beer.

I sit there on the living-room floor with felt and thread and fluff all around me and I am busy, busy, but my head is full of all the things that Heddy Partridge and her mother know about me, and James doesn't.

And I'm thinking about Heddy trying to cut herself up with the edge of a yoghurt pot. A yoghurt pot! A yoghurt pot would be plastic and flexible; you'd end up having to hack at yourself to get anything bigger than a scratch.

You'd never get a good cut with a yoghurt pot. And I should know.

Later, when I've given up on the sewing, I run myself a bath. I lock the door, which I don't normally, and wait in the steam as the bath fills up, then slide myself in.

I wish I could wash out my head. I wish I could wash Heddy out of my head, and Mrs Partridge and all the horrible stuff that comes with them. The past is the past – gone. When my parents moved away to Devon, I thought my ties with Forbury were finally cut, forever.

What was it Jane and I used to say to each other when we caught the bus and the train together to get to the tech in Redbridge, when everyone else just stayed on in the sixth form or quit school altogether? That's it: you can take the girl out of Forbury, but can you take Forbury out of the girl?

Can you indeed?

Heddy didn't go to college. Heddy left school at sixteen and got a job in the baker's down the High Street. I remember my mum telling me she saw her in there sometimes, serving behind the counter. And I remember thinking *I bet she ends up eating all the cakes*. I saw her once, one morning when

Jane and I were on the bus to the station to catch the train. She was walking along the main road to the High Street, bundled up in a short, thick coat that didn't quite cover her orange uniform. She'd got her apron on too, ready for work, and flat, black, old lady's shoes. Comfy shoes, just right for standing up in all day, serving cakes. She walked like she was in a hurry, head down, leaning forward slightly. Mustn't be late for work, I suppose.

I looked at her trundling along as Jane and I rode by on the bus. And I just felt so glad that she wouldn't be there in my life any more, watching me.

Because that is what she was always doing, watching me. At ballet, at Brownies, right through school – even secondary school, where we were in different streams, she'd be there at break, somewhere in the near distance, big eyes getting a look at my life.

She came into the toilets once when Jane and I were talking by the sinks. It was a private conversation. We were talking about our boyfriends. Actually we were talking about sex.

'Have you really done it?' Jane said, and right then Heddy walked in, big ears flapping. I sighed, Jane sighed, I folded my arms and we waited for Heddy to hurry up and go back out again.

'Honestly, some people have no consideration, butting in on a private conversation,' I said, and we stood there listening to Heddy trying to pee quietly. It seemed ages before we heard the scrunch of hard toilet paper and the resistant crank of the chain.

'She just wants to hear your answer,' Jane said.

So I bigged it up. I said, 'Oh yes, Paul's amazing. He goes on for hours. And hours. He can't get enough of me.' And so on. I said it just to shock Heddy. To see her red face when she came shuffling back out of that cubicle.

And she always seemed to be near the bins at lunchtime when I threw my sandwiches away. One bite we allowed ourselves, Jane and me, then into the bin with the rest. You'd think it was a crime from the expression on Heddy's face, if you ever made the mistake of looking at her. But you couldn't be as thin as we were and eat lunch – any fool knew that.

She was always watching us. I expect she wished she could be like us, but what chance did she have?

She watched us at break, when we pushed up our sleeves, to look at the cuts on our arms.

I close my eyes and her face is there inside my head. I open them again and she is still there, big eyes seeing too much.

We all used to cut ourselves in my group – Jane, Amanda, Cathy and me. It's just what we did; it was a phase, if you like. We started doing it in the fourth year; just little cuts, to our arms. We had quite an arsenal of weapons between us, stored in our pencil cases: razor blades, scalpels, drawing pins, and I had a big old metal compass with a long, sharp point.

We'd sit in maths or geography or biology, or whenever we were bored, and push back the sleeves of our cardies just a little way and dig away at the skin there, to pass the time. Small cuts, mostly; it becomes hypnotic, scratch, scratch, scratching away. You go into a sort of trance and the pain is a very fine thing, a very controlled thing, when drawn from you stage by tiny stage, each gentle movement of the blade or pin, or whatever, pushing just that little bit more into the soft, pink skin. It's a challenge, too, managing that pain – you know, resting that arm on your lap, hidden by the desk, cutting away and keeping your face totally blank. You cannot show the pain, ever; secrecy is a big part of it. We'd test ourselves, push ourselves. You cut, the pain rises, you keep your face calm, serene – to achieve this you have to stop breathing for a minute, then as the pain ebbs you can take in just shallow, small breaths, and then you cut again.

Cathy was brilliant at keeping her face blank. To look at her, you'd never know what she was doing under her desk, not at all. Then suddenly her eyes would fill with tears – big, blue eyes she had, like the Virgin Mary, and when she cried her face still stayed impassive, not a muscle flickered. Those tears just hovered on her lashes and rolled over.

Mostly we just did this in class, then at break we'd compare our work and describe the pain and all wish that we could be as composed as Cathy, and cry without having to sniff or get red-eyed. But I started doing it at home, in my bedroom. I'd sit cross-legged on my bed, in front of my mirror, and watch my face as I cut myself. It became quite an obsession, watching as my eyes registered the pain and absorbed it. I told myself I was practising. I wanted the perfection of an expressionless face; I wanted the power.

Once, I went too far.

Once, I was sitting on my bed and drawing a fine line along the inside of my arm with a razor blade, just up from the wrist, when I wondered what would happen if I pushed the blade a little deeper in.

Now I know there is a whole network of veins in there and I don't know which one I split open, but the blood rose up frighteningly easily. I watched it, pushing itself out, seeing how far upwards it came before it flattened out and ran. I held my arm out, keeping my hand down and turning it as the blood trickled in rivers over my skin. I cupped my hand to catch it, sickeningly warm, in my palm.

Calm, I was, at first; detached. I knew I wasn't dying. The blood was coming out too slow for me to be dying and the cut was too high up, too slightly off-centre. But then it dripped onto the floor, onto my nice cream carpet, and panic flashed through me.

I clenched my fist, feeling the blood sticky between my fingers, and ran downstairs. My dad was in the dining room; he'd got the Sunday papers spread out over the table. He looked up as I burst in. I shoved my wrist out in front of me and instantly he was on his feet, knocking his chair back to the floor, running after me. I turned and ran down the hall, out of the house, racing barefoot down the drive, and he was right behind me, chasing me, down the road and into Fairview Lane.

I ran as fast as I could for that little distance, swept up in my own hysteria, and then I stopped, right outside Heddy Partridge's house. My dad was right behind me. I wanted to be caught now. I wanted to see the pain and fear on his face, justifying my own, but when I turned I saw my dad's feet in just their socks and even though I wasn't dying, I felt as though I ought to be. I had to follow the drama somewhere and, as my dad reached out to me, the heat rose up my limbs in pins and needles, blackening into my head, and I let myself fall.

Instantly my dad was there, lifting me up like I was five, not fifteen. I heard his voice, but he was speaking to someone else, not me; he was saying, 'Let's get her inside', and someone else was muttering, 'Dear, dear, dear. Here, in here ...'

I felt myself laid down, on a sofa. I kept my eyes glued shut. I wanted to be dead, or nearly dead. I felt I owed it to myself, to everyone now. But the blood was drying on my arm, I could feel it, tightening up. Someone had got hold of my hands; they turned them, carefully. I kept my arms limp, not moving as cool water was washed over my stinging wrist, then a cloth pressed down.

'She's okay,' my dad said, and disappointment made me open my eyes.

I was in Mrs Partridge's front room. Heddy Partridge, her brother Ian and a pile of old newspapers had been moved off the sofa, to make room for me. The television was on, far too loudly, even though Mr Partridge was dead and gone now. Ian was still watching it, but Mrs Partridge, Heddy and my dad were all looking at me.

The drama was over now, and I was in the wrong place.

And my dad was saying these weird, out-of-place things now. He was saying, 'How are you, Mrs Partridge? How are you managing?', as if she was the one in crisis, right now, not me.

And she was saying back, 'We get by. We get by.'

'If there's anything that you need ...' my dad said and I shut my eyes again, tighter, wishing myself not okay, wishing myself dead in fact, but with the sunken feeling that even dead wouldn't be enough. I felt hollowed out, pared down to nothing.

My dad left me there while he went home to collect his shoes, my mother and the car. My wrist had been wrapped up in a yellowing old bandage. Mrs Partridge and Heddy soon stopped watching me, and started watching the television instead. Mrs Partridge perched on the arm of the sofa, by my feet. Heddy stood beside Ian, feet planted wide apart, stomach sticking out and arms folded, face blank. No one sat in Mr Partridge's empty chair.

I turned my face into the sofa to cut out the glare of the television and I wished I could cut out the sound. The material next to my face smelled of biscuits and socks. I was humiliated beyond belief. This was no place to die, or not to die.

My dad drove me to Casualty, with my mum in the front next to him; no one said a word. There we waited among the sprained ankles and chopped-off thumbs until a nurse taped together the edges of my pathetic little cut. A doctor told me that I would be referred to a counsellor, though I could tell no one was really worried about my mind.

Back home I felt 100 per cent like the silly drama queen I was. My dad settled down again to his paper, looking paler and tired and in need of a whisky. My mother fetched him one. Then my dad put down his paper again and looked at me, and my mum stood beside him, looking at me too.

'Why?' my dad asked. Just, *Why?*

Not *How are you?*, as he'd asked the Partridges. Not *How are you managing?* Oh no. For me just this, this one word: *Why?*

But I had no answer to give him, so I went up to bed and tried to block it all out in the dark.

I lie right back in the water and stretch my arms out, palms up. The scars on my arms are hair-thin. You'd hardly even notice them, unless you looked. I told James I got them in a childhood accident, falling through a glass door.

I had to go to see a counsellor in Redbridge for six weeks, standard-issue course for an attempted suicide. I went on

Thursdays, leaving school ten minutes earlier than everyone else to make sure I didn't miss the bus. I told my friends I was going to the chiropodist's, to get my insteps sorted out.

The counsellor was a woman with long, straight black hair, parted in the middle. She wore long skirts with matching long cardigans and pendants on chains that hung low down on her chest. We sat opposite each other on plastic chairs. She had a clipboard and paper on her lap, as if she was expecting to make a lot of notes.

'Why do you feel the need to harm yourself?' she asked, and I'd try to make up reasons.

It struck me as absurd that I was supposed to tell a total stranger what was going on in my mind.

The bath water is almost cold now and goosebumps are creeping out on my chest. I sit up and pull out the plug. The skin on my hands is swollen and wrinkled. I have been in here far too long.

Why did I do it?

To see who would care, that's why.

SEVEN

Arianne helps me in Sainsbury's, but it wasn't always like that.

Now she is three she likes to be grown up; she brings her own little pink plastic handbag and likes to help me by putting things into the trolley. She looks very sweet with her white-blonde curls and her pretty dress, and with her baby hands picking up apples one by one to put them in the bag. Old ladies stop and admire her. Arianne likes to be admired, now that she is three.

A year ago, she couldn't have cared less.

It used to be that the minute we pulled up in the car park the whingeing would start, and by the time we got to the trolley bay the foot-stamping would be under way. As soon as we got inside the shop, all hell would be unleashed. She wanted to sit in the trolley; she wanted to walk; she wanted to sit in the trolley again. She wanted to carry the bread, but then she'd throw it on the floor, scream. I'd pick it up, give it back to her, down it would go again. I wouldn't keep giving her back something just to have her throw it down again if I was at home or anywhere else, but in a supermarket you do anything to try to stem the screaming. You're powerless in a supermarket, and children know this, even at two. You open packets of biscuits as bribery, putting the rest of the packet carefully on top of your shopping so that people can see you're going to pay, you're not a thief. I never thought I'd end up doing that, but I did.

Once she wanted a banana, and I gave her one, keeping the skin to show the woman on the checkout. I expected the woman to charge me a nominal amount, whatever the average price of a banana might be, but I had to suffer the humiliation of the supervisor being called, and then I had two disapproving faces looking me over as bananas were weighed and a price worked out, while the woman in the queue behind me tutted and Arianne screamed. I expect all three of those women were mothers themselves, but it's amazing how quickly you forget what it's like.

I pushed Arianne back out to the car while she screamed and screamed, legs rigid, face on the verge of blue, and I unloaded her and the shopping from the trolley. Then I sat in the car and cried, with my hands over my face. She shut up then, satisfied at last.

The irony was that I only went to the supermarket for something to do. No one ever talks about that, do they – about how desperate you are for something to do when you're stuck at home with a small child all day, day in, day out? No one ever talks about the boredom, the loneliness. My goodness me, no. What with the rounds of coffee mornings and baby-gym mornings and music-time mornings ... how can it be that on the one morning of the week there's nothing on, you end up so desperate that you'd rather go to the supermarket and have your child scream there than be at home?

I didn't always shop in Sainsbury's. I used to go to Tesco, before Arianne was born. Thomas was good, so I thought.

He didn't scream the whole time. He'd sit quite content in his trolley chair, no bother at all, while I got on with the shopping. Sometimes I got strange looks from people, but I put that down to some bizarre sort of jealousy, or curiosity even; why wasn't this child howling when all the others were? But one day, as I was weighing out grapes, a woman whom I had seen in there often, herself the mother of girls, glared at me with a face profuse with outrage. She glared at me, then pointedly she glared at Thomas in the trolley behind me. When I turned round to look at him sitting in his trolley seat, he'd managed to wriggle his shorts and his pants right down and was pulling away on his newly nappy-free willy, perfectly happy.

I didn't go to Tesco again.

Now, of course, I get what I can delivered, but there are still always all those things you forget, or run out of unexpectedly. There are still those dark, pervading moments when domesticity sucks you up because you've run out of something, dishwasher tablets, peppercorns – something you didn't even think of when you put your order in. And it eats you up, the need for that run-out-of thing, as if the security of your whole little empire depends on it. So you think *I know, let's make a trip of it*, as if you're some numb-headed halfwit, lulled by the call of the fluorescent-lit aisles, the cloying, pumped-out smell of baked bread. And so you end up there again, back in the supermarket, pushing your trolley.

Today, as Arianne and I unload our things onto the conveyor belt at the checkout I can hear some child screaming. In fact, I've been hearing it for quite some time as we've been moving around the aisles. There aren't many people shopping on a Monday morning and sound really travels in these places. The screaming is getting closer now and the woman behind the till and I exchange a look. Her expression tells me that here comes yet another howling brat giving her a headache, and what wouldn't she do to shut it up! I cannot imagine what my face says to her.

The unfortunate owner of the screaming child appears from the frozen-foods aisle. Frantically she scans the tills for the shortest queue, and decides on mine. She's a young mother, with greasy hair tied back from her face and tired, numb eyes. She pushes the trolley one-handed, shoving her thin body against it for extra leverage, as she tries to still her child with the other hand. He's pinching at her arm, then he's throwing himself backwards as far as he can within the confines of the wire seat, twisting round, head flung back, and screaming.

The woman parks her trolley up behind me and mutters, 'Bloody pack it in, won't you, Connor?' Then she steps back from the trolley and stands, face turned away from her child and staring at the floor, eyes fixed on the tiles. If I was her, I'd be in tears by now. Everyone is looking at her. You can feel the disapproval rippling along from checkout to check-out. The woman serving me lets her breath out on a long, slow sigh as she passes my stuff across the scanner.

The child really is going for it. The pitch is unrelenting. Arianne stops helping me and stares at him. He's thrashing around in his seat, wrestling against the straps that are holding him in, trying to grab the sweets now, piled up in a dumper bin right next to him at the end of the checkout. In a burst of frustrated fury, his mother shoves the trolley, getting him away from those sweets; then she's back, arms folded, staring at the floor. Arianne jumps slightly and holds on to my skirt. I don't want to seem to be staring, so I try to keep my eyes down, as I pile up the last of my things onto the conveyor belt. As I look down and up, down and up, I can't help noticing the contents of her trolley: it's a sharp contrast to mine. There's not much in it, and no fresh stuff at all. Bread and tins from the economy range, a couple of pizzas, three jumbo bottles of Coke – buy two, get one free – some frozen chips and a multi-bag of crisps.

I have a sudden memory of something Liz said to me once, after some report had come out about the health divide between the well-off and the poor, and about how much of it came down to the food we eat. Liz has quite strong opinions on things; it makes the rest of us a little uncomfortable at times. 'It all comes down to education,' she said, and nobody liked to disagree. 'A packet of crisps costs the same amount of money as an apple. You need to be educated to choose the apple.'

Or an organic apple, in my case.

The last of my things are on the conveyor belt now, and the woman behind the till picks up item after item, scans each thing and packs it into a bag. Organic strawberries, organic mangoes, free-range chicken breasts, wild rice and Italian bread. She is positively flinching at the noise that child behind me is making, and her mouth is puckered, in badly suppressed disapproval. Handling my expensive goods seems to add weight to her umbrage, as if she assumes that just because I can afford high-quality foods, I will join in her silent condemnation of the poor woman behind me who can't.

'Thank you, madam,' she says to me with a strained, supercilious smile when I key in my PIN. Then she turns po-faced to the next load of haphazardly piled-up goods coming her way and shoves the stuff through quickly, as if too much contact might make her hands dirty. She is like those estate agents who act as if every big house on their books is theirs.

I push my trolley out to my car, disturbed. It's only food. We all need it. We all shove it in our shopping trolleys, shove it in our mouths. Our need for food should make us equal, that and the mind-numbing trek around the supermarket. You'd think we'd all be the same behind our trolleys, we women, we wives, we mothers. You certainly feel like every other woman, when you struggle with the wonky wheels and the monotony. What we stick in our trolleys shouldn't paint a picture of our lives, it shouldn't divide us.

But it does.

We're soul-bared in the supermarket. Soul-bared, purse open.

Everything is disturbing me today.

I can't even enjoy Tumbletots any more, since the other week on the evening news when there was some feature on early childhood development, and they showed a clip of some Tumble centre, just like the one Arianne and I go to. The clip showed the wind-down session, after the main tumbling time, when the women and the children join together in a circle to sing songs – songs that have movements to go with them. You know, 'The wheels on the bus' and that sort of thing. I'm sure there isn't a mother alive who hasn't 'Row, row, rowed the boat' down the godforsaken stream at some time or another, and perhaps we do feel a little bit self-conscious, silly even, at first. But it's just what you do, what we all do. We're all in it together, women and children in the bizarre, self-imposed world of women and children.

But the other night, when they showed that clip on the news, James was eating a peanut-butter sandwich and he nearly choked on it.

'Look!' he exclaimed, spluttering peanut butter everywhere, and pointing at the television where a group of women and toddlers were clapping together as they smiled and sang. 'Look!' He turned from the television to me and back to the television again, almost bouncing up and down on the sofa in his disbelief, as if it was the funniest thing he'd seen for a long time.

'That's what it's like, James,' I said. 'That's what we do.'

And he laughed even more, as if I'd said it just to amuse him. There is so much of amusement here, in the little world.

I take refuge from my thoughts at Tasha's house.

Tasha lives in a vast extended 1930s house built on a corner plot at the end of Chestnut Drive. Her husband works for an American bank. Tasha likes the idea of interior design and did a little course on it recently, not at the local college, but up in town somewhere – it cost a fortune, apparently – while Carole looked after Phoebe for her. When she was halfway through the course Tasha decided that she liked the planning more than the actual doing, that her forte was more in steering other people to carry out her ideas than doing it herself, and now she has a whole house to play with.

Wood samples are laid out along the huge, open expanse of the living-room floor, for me to look at.

'What do you think?' Tasha asks me, and both her voice and the heels of her shoes echo slightly against the wood flooring. The existing floor is parquet, dark little oblongs, all packed in, just like we had on the hall floor at junior school. Suddenly I picture us sitting on it – not Tasha, of course, but me and all those other girls and boys of thirty years ago, squashed up in rows, legs crossed and pink, fingers picking at the dried-on sticky bits and bogies, and at the unrecognizable remains of school dinners that gave the school hall its awful, unforgettable smell.

Tasha paces up and down, looking at the options, then she stops up beside me, one arm folded across her middle, hand supporting the elbow of the other arm that is bent, that hand up by her face, one finger extended and tapping against her chin. She is willowy elegant, Tasha. Always clad in black and grey, with just a flash of pink or red to lift things, and her nails always newly done, to match.

I switch my glance from the S-like curve of her figure standing next to me to the mirror opposite us, hanging above the great open fireplace. It's an enormous mirror; from this little distance it reflects us both, right down to the start of our thighs in our matching dark jeans. Looking in this mirror, I am struck by how alike we are. Oh, she is a good inch or so taller than me and I'm sure I don't have her incredible grace, and her hair is cut a little shorter and choppy now with those red streaks underneath the blonde, but still there are things, so many things. I realize that my stance is the same as hers, one hip lifting, one hand raised to the face in contemplation. I see our pale, serious faces with our pale, serious eyes and I think how similar we look, even though Tasha's changed her hair. She used to wear her hair like mine, like Penny's: highlighted blonde and falling straight to the shoulders. In fact, if you put Tasha and Penny and me in a row, you could pass us off as sisters. Liz too, though she fights against the grain a little by going about in her gym clothes half the time and letting her fair hair go wavy.

I stare at our reflections and I am unnerved. I wonder why it is that all my life I have chosen friends that look like me.

Tasha glances up, catching my eye in the mirror, oblivious to the way my mind is working. 'What do you think?' she says, frowning slightly. 'I'm torn between the natural and the honeyed oak. And should we take it upstairs? Rupert says not; he thinks carpet for upstairs, but I don't know.' She stares at me, serious, and I can be serious too.

I can lose myself in this.

We carry on considering Tasha's floor over lunch, which we eat at the dining table; through the double doors we can still see the samples on the living-room floor. Arianne and Phoebe chatter away at one end of the table while Tasha and I talk floors at the other. We won't make our minds up today. This is part of the pleasure – wallowing in choice.

It's like floating away on nothingness, and I want to float away.

Shortly after five on Monday my mum phones, from Devon. She asks after James, briefly, and the children of course, then she tells me about the trellis my dad is going to build over the patio, and about the vines they're planning to grow on it. You can get quite decent grapes down there, apparently, if the summer's kind. They have a very active garden society down there, in the village, she says; she's put my father up as treasurer. She'd do it herself, but she's busy with the church-renovation project fund-raiser and the Keep Our Village Green campaign. I listen as she talks breezily on, and wickedly I feel a little sorry for Lower Eddington. I picture the place: sleepy, time-warped and barely on the map. And I picture my mum and my dad descending upon it, with all the good that they no doubt will do.

I do not tell my mother about Heddy. I do not tell her, but I feel guilty just the same.

EIGHT

I cannot think what to wear.

I am up early as usual, and straight in the shower the minute James comes out. We get ready for our days around each other. He is standing in front of the mirror, looking at himself as he puts the cufflinks into his shirt and combs back his hair. I watch him; I can see both the back of his head and his reflection, an all-round view if you like, of James Hamley the lawyer, as he lawyers himself up. He tilts his head, from side to side and then down slightly at the front, peering up at himself, dark-blue eyes sharp under that dark, sharp brow. It used to amuse me, watching him practise like this. He runs through all his expressions: we have the considering look, the *I understand what you're saying, but . . .* look, the *Please, have utter faith in me* look, even the *This really hurts me to have to do this* look. We have it all. His whole self is exercised across his face as he primes up for the day.

It used to amuse me. I used to find this routine endearing until I realized he uses the same expressions on me.

James rounds off his routine with a smile – at himself, at his clients, I can't tell. It is a confident smile, a winning smile, worked to perfection. He is a winner, my husband. He knows it, I know it. The whole world must know it by now, surely.

Finally he pats a little cologne onto his cheeks and turns to me. I am standing, still in my underwear, with the doors of my wardrobe flung open, but I'm not even looking at what's inside. I'm looking at him.

'Not going to yoga?' he asks as he shrugs himself into his suit jacket. He gives me his cheerfully curious smile, the one that says he'd love to hear my reply, if only he had the time to hang around and listen.

'Not today,' I reply, and I wonder if I would have told him more, but he kisses me on the cheek and is gone, out of the house, before his children are even awake.

I cannot think what to wear because I have never been to visit someone in a mental hospital before. Hospitals of the ordinary kind are bad enough. You feel the dirt jumping onto you, the germs, the promise of death. Especially on the floor. The floor is always the worst.

The year before last my father was in hospital for a week after a knee operation. I visited him twice. I wore the same clothes each time, kept them in a sealed bag between visits, then sent them to the dry-cleaner's when he came out. I wore the same pair of shoes too, and then I threw them away.

I do not want to waste a pair of shoes on Heddy Partridge.

In the end I decide on a pair of last year's trousers and a top I don't often wear because the colour isn't exactly right on me. I know I'll never wear them again. And I'll wear the suede mules that I bought last week in town, and tomorrow I'll go and buy myself another pair to replace them.

Mrs Partridge is standing on her doorstep, waiting for me to arrive.

I am late, for the obvious reason that I do not want to be

here at all. I chatted to Penny in the playground, long after the children had gone in. Chatted while Arianne pulled at my clothes, saying, 'Mummy, Mummy, come *on*.'

Chatted until Penny said, 'What are *you* doing today?' She skimmed her eyes over my clothes, curious.

'Oh, boring stuff,' I said, grabbing Arianne by the hand. 'Dentist. That sort of thing. Must dash.'

On my way out of Carole's I bumped into Tasha.

'Fancy a coffee after yoga?' she called, unloading Phoebe from the back of her car. Then in seconds – milliseconds – she'd clocked me head to toe and said, 'Oh. Not going to yoga?'

Curiosity is a big, big thing around here. Lives are built and ruined on it. The slightest little thing out of the ordinary will not go unnoticed. Today it will be my life under scrutiny; I do not fool myself otherwise. It will not be Tasha and me having coffee, it'll be Tasha and Penny and Liz instead, and I'll be the subject of discussion for today. And for many days to come if I'm not careful, if I don't nip this thing in the bud, so to speak. They're probably on their phones already, speculating.

And so it is that I am late arriving at Mrs Partridge's. Late according to her plan, that is. As far as I'm concerned, she's lucky I'm here at all.

She's looking out for me, twittering and fussing on her doorstep like an agitated penguin. It's a warm day, but she's buttoned into a thick, quilted jacket that makes her head look tiny poking out the top, and her legs even thinner. She watches me as I park up the car, and I think, as she is clearly ready to go, she will close the door behind her and come and get straight in the car, but she doesn't. She darts back into the house, swallowed up by the darkness, and I wait where I am. I am not going to be hurried. I am not going to be blustered into some false sense of urgency. It is essential that I remain detached, for both of us.

I think I might check my phone for messages, perhaps make a call, just to make my point, but before I do Mrs Partridge reappears, anxiously gesturing for me to come inside. I don't like being beckoned like a child, and I get out of the car slowly, irritated.

Once again I am walking up that pathway, and into that house.

She disappears inside the house once I'm halfway up the path, and so I have to follow. I feel as though I've been tricked.

She's got a bunch of papers in her hand, seemingly pulled from the big plastic shopping bag at her feet.

'This is the man,' she says, without even a pre-emptive hello, thank you for coming. 'This one here.' She waves a letter at me, pointing at the signature. 'Dr R. D. Millar. He's the one you need to talk to.'

Do I, indeed? And what, exactly, do I want to talk to him about?

'You don't want to bother with the rest,' she goes on, and I hear in her voice the weird mixture of inherent suspicion and isolation that some people – old people, especially – seem to have when faced with anyone in authority. 'Dr Millar, he's in charge of Heddy.'

She prods her bony finger against the papers as they flop in her hand. She's not looking at me. She's staring at the writing, as if everything that matters is there in the black-and-white print. She seems to have shrunk since Thursday, and she's looking very, very tired. 'Dr Millar,' she says again, to herself, not me. 'Dr Millar.'

She stuffs the letters back into her bag, wedging them down the side of all the other things that she's squeezed in; you'd think we were going for a week, not just an hour or so. I watch as she checks the contents of that bag. There's a rolled-up towel in there, sticking out the top, a washbag and sandwiches wrapped in tin foil.

'Only ham, dear,' she says. 'I didn't know what you'd like.'

I haven't the heart to tell her I'm planning to be back long before lunch.

Then she's patting her pockets, feeling for her keys, fussing, looking around for anything she might have forgotten. Finally she takes a deep breath and lets it out on a sigh, and I see her brace her tiny shoulders inside her coat. Suddenly I find myself feeling very sorry her. Heddy is her daughter, after all.

On the way to the hospital Mrs Partridge talks non-stop. She tells me how normally she takes the bus, two buses in fact. The one that comes only once an hour and goes up through Barton Village and all the way to the airport eventually if you stay on it. She gets off before then, by the junction on the Great West Road, and catches another bus, the 911, that takes her right through Hounslow. The whole journey takes her about two hours, she says, and she does this every day, when Nathan is at school. Two hours there, two hours back, one hour with Heddy. It's not so bad. The 911 stops almost right outside St Anne's, and she normally makes herself up a sandwich to eat on the way home. And she gets a good hour with Heddy, if the buses run to time. Long enough to brush her hair and give her a bit of a wash.

Dread uncurls itself inside me. I hope to God I don't have to have anything to do with washing Heddy Partridge.

We drive through Barton Village and I glance sideways at

Mrs Partridge, keeping one eye on her, one eye on the road. I am dead curious to know which road Heddy lived in, and I expect Mrs Partridge suddenly to turn her gaze, to look sideways in a poignant way, marking out the spot, but she doesn't. She carries on staring ahead, and she carries on with the endless stream of nervous chat.

'I did go, yesterday,' she says, and by the tone of her voice I can't tell if she's criticizing me for not coming with her, or reassuring me that she went on her own. 'They'd put dressings on her neck, you know, where she'd hurt herself. And they'd given her something.' She pauses, for just a second, and sighs, and when she speaks again I can hear the helplessness in her voice. 'She wasn't in any pain,' she says, but I can tell that isn't the point. Pain is there, whether you try to numb it out or not.

'It's Nathan she wants,' Mrs Partridge says to me. 'She's pining for him. But what can I do?' She waits, as if she expects me to have the answer. I cannot think what to say so I say nothing, and concentrate on the driving. 'Straight across up here and then left, at those lights,' she directs as we come into Fayle, and I realize that we are following the bus route, and that we've probably added twenty minutes or so to our trip in the process. Sure enough, she says to me, 'You go on up here, dear. That's where I normally change buses.'

'What about Nathan's father?' I ask. 'Where's he?'

'Oh, we haven't seen him for a long time,' she replies, breezily, far too breezily. 'He sends the odd card, you know, at Christmas. And a bit of money, when he can. But we haven't seen him. Not for a long time. They moved in with me, Heddy and Nathan,' she explains, 'when they had to sell that house. John, Heddy's husband, he made other arrangements, and we haven't seen him since. Poor Heddy, she was in a very bad way. It was a terrible time, a terrible time.'

Suddenly she leans forward and turns on me, anxious. Her seatbelt catches and yanks her back. 'It wasn't me that put her in hospital,' she says, and I can feel her staring at me. I keep my eyes fixed on the road. 'I'd never do that. We were managing all right. Heddy had her problems, but we were managing. I did my best.' Her voice is small and shrill and insistent. 'She was out. Gone on the bus to Fayle, when Nathan was at school. Next thing I know there's a policeman knocking on my door telling me they'd picked Heddy up outside the shopping centre. They'd had to call the ambulance. It was a terrible to-do. She'd smashed a bottle on the ground and cut right down her arms with the glass.'

The skin across my shoulders prickles, cold.

'It was help she wanted, poor Heddy. Breaks my heart to think that I couldn't help her, my poor girl. They took her into hospital and then they moved her to St Anne's. Nothing I could do.'

Mrs Partridge leans forward now and rummages in her bag. She comes out with tissues, one of those handy packs. Out of the corner of my eye I can see her hands shaking as she pulls out a tissue and blows her nose. I cannot think of anything to say.

'It wasn't the first time, see,' she says in a thin voice. 'They'd taken her in before. Nothing so bad as that last time, but . . . Thing is, you can't go doing things like that in public. People don't like it, do they?' There's a tight, bitter tone to her voice now. 'Of course they don't. It's not what they want to see when they do their shopping. My poor Heddy. It was a cry for help, that's all. It's always a cry for help, isn't it, dear?'

Mrs Partridge's words are weaving a strange and cloying magic inside my car. I feel misplaced, as if I'm caught up in somebody else's nightmare, trapped in one of those journeys that go on and on, going nowhere.

Is it always a cry for help? Is it?

Heddy Partridge and I, were we crying about the same thing? Did we feel the same things as we hacked ourselves up with our House of Hammer, kitchen-sink torture tools?

I try to take myself back, to remember what I was feeling that long-buried and newly dug-up day.

I remember the challenge. I remember pushing the blade down into my wrist, seeing the skin peeling back as it split, and watching the slow rise of blood.

I remember the voice in my head, saying *What if, what if?*

Thick people don't have feelings.

I have a sudden flash of my nine-year-old self, hands on hips, imparting that little gem of wisdom to my friends. *Thick people don't have feelings.* You can tell them to get lost and call them names and make them the brunt of your jokes – they may not like it much, but that doesn't matter because they don't have feelings, not proper feelings. They don't have the brains, so how can they feel? How can they know how to hurt?

Heddy always reminded me of a cow, a big, slow cow, fit for nothing more than chopping up and eating. Even more so in her Brownie uniform. Then she was a big, slow, brown cow.

On saints' days we were allowed to wear our Brownie uniforms to school. We liked that; it showed everyone else we were special. There were only about three of us in my class that went to Brownies, three of us and Heddy. Now a Brownie uniform is not the most fetching of outfits, but if you were thin and dainty with nimble arms and legs you could wear the dress pulled in at the middle with a belt and look quite sweet. Heddy's uniform was a hand-me-down, too short, too tight, too straight-up-and-down and with no belt round her big middle.

We rounded on her at playtime.

'What are you wearing *your* uniform for?' I demanded, outraged.

'It's St George's Day,' Heddy mumbled, staring at the ground.

'Well, St George doesn't care about *you*.' I looked her up and down. 'You're a disgrace.'

'And we don't want you trying to copy us,' Claire said. 'Or following us around.'

Heddy carried on staring at the ground, her white face going slightly pink.

'You shouldn't even be in the Brownies,' I told her. 'You're far too fat.'

'And stupid,' Jane said.

'You're a fat, stupid cow.' I made my eyes big and pulled a long cow face. 'Moo,' I said.

'Moo,' said Jane and Claire.

Now I think of Heddy, wanting herself to be dead.

Again, I remember her watching us at school, when we were older, when we cut ourselves for kicks. I remember her spying on our private world of self-inflicted pain. I think of the criss-crosses under my sleeves, and the constant threat of *what if?*

I see her face, her dark, still eyes looking down on me as I lay bleeding and trying to die on her mother's brown Dralon sofa on that otherwise very dreary Sunday afternoon. Was that a cry for help? What did I have to cry about except the constant emptiness, gnawing away inside?

Didn't I hear it all the time, how lucky I was, how fortunate I was, how grateful I ought to be? I think of my mum, at every opportunity, telling everyone how good Laura was at dance, at English, at maths, at everything ... *Bragging*, if you like, painting her perfect picture of her perfect family. And I went along with it. I thought it had to be so.

And yet, and yet.

I think of my dad, always so distant, and always so slightly disappointed. And I think of my childish self, so very far from perfect, and of the terrible things that I did.

Mrs Partridge falls silent as we pull off the road and into the concrete grounds of St Anne's, looking for the car park, which turns out to be not a car park at all really, but just lots of parking spaces squashed in here, there and everywhere in the network of roads and small empty spaces that weave their way around the hospital site. St Anne's is an old, grey sprawling building built way back in the Victorian age, and it's long overdue for demolition. There are letters about it sometimes, in the local paper, which I read occasionally when I'm really bored. *Save St Anne's*, someone pleads, but no one takes any notice; why should they?

Eventually we find a spot tucked away at the back of the hospital, between the bottom steps of a black iron fire escape and the kitchen bins. I open my door to go and buy a ticket from the machine. Mrs Partridge is horrified and flaps and blusters, digging her purse out from her carrier bag and hunting for change, which I do not take. It's a big purse, with lots of compartments, some zipped, some clipping together.

'Never thought you'd have to pay,' she says, flustered with outrage. 'To visit a hospital? It's disgusting.' She's still flapping when I come back with the ticket. 'Shouldn't have to pay to come to a hospital,' she mutters, fussing with her bag now, and her coat, as she gets out of the car. She looks worryingly frail as she bangs the door shut, and anxiety is pulling at the muscles in her face. 'How do people manage?' she says. 'Shocking, it is, shocking.'

'Really, Mrs Partridge, it's okay,' I say, to try to calm her, but she's still muttering as we try to find our way to the Arthur Mitley Wing, where Heddy is.

Mrs Partridge knows her way from the main entrance, of course, which is where she normally comes in from, off the bus, so first we have to find our way round there, which takes a while in itself. The place is a maze of covered walkways that seem to go on forever. God knows how you find your way back out again. One corridor leads on to another and then another, through plastic, swing-shut doors. The sound of our shoes clack-clacking on the concrete floor echoes off the walls, and the deeper in we go, the hotter it gets and the more I can smell the horrible hospital smell of disinfectant and boiled cabbage, masking the sweeter, sickly smell of human decay. It's like an invisible gas, choking out the air.

Walking along those endless corridors, it suddenly occurs to me: how will Heddy feel about seeing me?

I've never given a thought to how she must feel towards me. I think of all those times I was mean to her and of all the cruel things that I said. She never said anything back, ever. I never gave a thought to how she might feel about me.

And now here I am, turning up in her life again, just like she's turned up in mine.

Heddy Partridge must hate me, surely. Way more than I ever hated her.

Mrs Partridge sticks her finger on the buzzer outside the Arthur Mitley Wing and presses hard. Through the blue of the window I can see a nurse sitting at a desk writing up notes. Slowly she rises to her feet to tap in the code to let us in. It reminds me of the maternity ward where Arianne was born – there was keypad security there, too, but just to keep the dodgy people out. Not to keep them in.

'I've brought a visitor with me today, dear,' Mrs Partridge says, to explain my presence. 'And we'd like to see Dr Millar, if we may.'

The nurse looks from Mrs Partridge to me and back to Mrs Partridge again. She's about my age, with mousy blonde hair scraped back from her world-weary face. 'I'm not sure if Dr Millar's available,' she says.

'No, dear,' Mrs Partridge says and I'm surprised by her assertiveness. 'He wasn't available yesterday, but he will be today. That's what the nurse here yesterday told me.'

The nurse keeps her face carefully blank. 'Dr Millar's a very busy man,' she says. 'He has a lot of patients.' She fiddles with her pen, flicking it between her fingers. 'But I'll see if I can find him for you. It's Mrs Partridge, isn't it?'

'Yes, dear. Thank you, dear,' Mrs Partridge says, and then, to my total embarrassment, she adds, 'And this is Mrs Hamley, whose husband is in the legal profession.'

Heddy's in a room on her own. There's a small round window in the door, which I'd have liked to look through before going in, as a sort of easing-in measure, but the window's too high for Mrs Partridge, so she pushes the door right open and in we go.

She smells of shit, faintly. That's the first thing I notice when I walk into Heddy's room, that and how fat she is. How incredibly fat. Puffed up and bloated and swollen. There's a large piece of gauze taped onto the flesh where her neck would end and her chest begin, but on Heddy they all blend into one, chin, neck, chest. The back of the bed is tilted upwards so that she can sit, propped up by pillows. Yet she gives the impression of being boneless, of sinking into herself. The dressing on her neck serves to hold up her face, else it would slide down into the rest of her, and her body's held in place by the blanket tucked up tight around her. It's a big baby blanket, yellow and holey, pulled tight across the mass of her body. Her arms are out on top, lying straight down, as if they've been placed there, as if they have no movement of their own. The fat cuffs her wrists in folds. All down her arms there are crisses and crosses, much like my own, only newer, redder, more clumsily done. How bizarre that we should wear the same pattern on our skin, Heddy Partridge and me.

Mrs Partridge goes to the side of the bed and takes hold of Heddy's fat, limp hand. 'I've brought someone to see you, dear,' she says, patting that hand with her own skinny one. 'Look,' she says, 'here's Laura Cresswell. You remember Laura Cresswell, don't you, dear? Of course you do.'

I stand at the end of the bed and I pray to God that Heddy Partridge *doesn't* remember me. 'Hello, Heddy,' I say, kinder than I've ever said it before. But I do not know if she hears me or even sees me; Heddy's eyes are open, but she is some-where else. Her eyes are wide, stark, like a rabbit's before it dies.

There's a bit of dribble, bubbling out at the corner of her mouth. Mrs Partridge takes the tissue from her coat pocket and dabs at Heddy's face. It's a tender act; I watch, transfixed. While she's there, up close, she checks the fixings holding down the dressing on Heddy's neck, the strips of plaster stuck onto her flesh. She loosens her gown a little, easing it away from Heddy's skin where it is starting to chafe, along the edge. It's a hospital gown. 'She's got nighties, of course she has,' Mrs Partridge tells me, 'but this is easier, you know, for washing her, and tending to her needs.'

Heddy's breasts roll down her body underneath the cotton, like the vast slide-down of a cliff, one mound barely discernible from the mound beneath. I have never seen anyone so fat. Not in real life. Not outside of magazines and modern-day freak-show documentaries on TV. And then how superior we feel, looking on, how *oh-my-God-how-awful* titillated and gloriously repulsed. I mean, how could anyone let themselves become so obscene?

By sitting out endless days in a hospital bed, that is how. Unable to move. Body static, dead but not dead.

Mrs Partridge is busy now, unpacking the contents of her bag, the towel and the wash-things, and placing them on the small wheeled table at the end of the bed. She takes a hairbrush from the washbag and starts to brush Heddy's lank, greasy black hair away from her face and over her shoulders. Lovingly she brushes it, as if it wasn't plastered flat and unwashed to her head at all. She brushes it much the way I brush Arianne's hair and the similarity shocks me, horrifies me. She pushes that brush just as I would through Arianne's springy, baby-soft curls. I baulk at the tenderness. How would I feel if this was Arianne – in however many harsh and damaging years' time – numbed out and bloated by the life I'd given her, worn out, yet still my baby?

Suddenly, ridiculously, the effort of not crying overrides everything else. There is a lump in my chest the size of a washing basket and I feel my whole head about to dissolve. I cannot believe I am here, pulled up like this, made witness to this tragedy.

At eleven-thirty lunch arrives on its white plastic tray. Mrs Partridge takes it and mashes it up with the fork, like baby food. Shepherd's pie it is, apparently, and carrots and potato. She mashes it up and spoons it into Heddy and, like a good girl, Heddy gobbles it up. There's sponge pudding for afters, with custard. Heddy gobbles this up, too. Mrs Partridge scoops up the spill that runs down Heddy's chin and spoons it back in, just like she's feeding a baby. Heddy eats it all up, loose mouth sucking it in. She registers no difference in taste.

And then comes the toileting, as Mrs Partridge calls it. The minute lunch is finished, the tray is put aside and it is all hurry, hurry; a bedpan is found and there is much shifting of blankets and much shifting of Heddy. Mrs Partridge is panting from the exertion. She calls for a nurse, but the nurse doesn't come. I should help. I know I should, but I can't stand it. I just can't stand it.

Heddy flops over as she moves sideways, off the bedpan, and she moans then, a low guttural sound. I go to Mrs Partridge's aid, I have to – she's struggling to put the bedpan aside without tipping it, and at the same time trying to hold on to Heddy. I go round to the other side of the bed and push Heddy back up into the middle. She's very heavy, and her skin is warm and soft under my hands. I think of all the times over the years when I have avoided – successfully – having to touch Heddy Partridge.

Mrs Partridge presses the bell to call the nurse again, twice. 'It's always the same,' she complains, red in the face, anxious. 'Always. They don't have the staff, that's the trouble. Poor Heddy would be left to herself half the time if it wasn't for me.' She rearranges the pillows as I hold on to Heddy; between us we get her back in place. I'm still holding on to her shoulders when she makes that moaning noise again and looks up at me. She seems to be coming round, coming back from wherever she's been, and I can feel her trying to place me. Her eyes are close to mine, filled with fear and confusion, and I pull back.

'Nathan?' she asks and her voice is deep, not at all as I remember it. But how would I remember it? When did I ever hear Heddy say anything? Our shared childhood whizzes through my head and all I can hear is my own shrill voice, sneering, jeering, putting her down.

'Nathan?' she calls again, louder, and she's staring at me, as if I might have Nathan hidden behind my back, ready to produce him at any moment.

I stare back at her, helpless. Mrs Partridge is at her side, shushing her, and stroking back her hair and tucking it behind her ear. Then the nurse does come in, carrying a tray bearing a little dish with two pills in it with one hand, and checking the watch pinned to her dress with the other.

'Nathan!' Heddy barks, at the nurse now, and Mrs Partridge hushes her again. And water is poured into a cup and the pills popped into Heddy's mouth, followed by the water, which spills out a little, over her lip.

'Oh dear, oh dear, these pills ... I don't know, I don't know ...' murmurs Mrs Partridge as she mops up Heddy's mouth. The nurse is inspecting the dressing on Heddy's neck, peeling it back, peeping inside, and sticking it down again.

Then she's checking Heddy's pulse, fingers probing Heddy's swollen wrist, her lips moving silently as she counts out Heddy's heartbeat against her watch. Heddy is starting to cry in short, snuffling sobs. Thin tears slide out of her eyes and snot bubbles up from her nose. It makes me feel sick to look, but I can't turn away. I am useless.

I am useless as Mrs Partridge fills a dish with warm water from the sink and gently washes Heddy's face and hands with the flannel from her bag, and pats her dry with the towel. I am useless as, between them, Mrs Partridge and the nurse shift Heddy forward a little and loosen her gown and things are done with talcum powder. And all the time Mrs Partridge murmurs soothingly, a comforting stream of *There, there, dear, hush, now, dear* and *All better now, all better*. I listen to Mrs Partridge's words, wanting them to comfort me. My arms hang like heavy weights from my sides; I cannot lift them. I cannot do a thing. The lump in my chest has grown to the size of a laundry room. I can barely breathe, I certainly cannot speak.

Finally they are finished and Heddy is settled back down, tucked up. The nurse yanks the pole on the side of the bed and Heddy is horizontal, willed into sleep. All three of us watch her for a minute, looking at her waxy face and closed eyes, as if waiting to be sure they don't open again. It is like looking at a corpse, checking to see that it's dead.

Then Mrs Partridge starts rolling up her towel and gathering up her hairbrush and things and putting them in her bag. The nurse mops something off the floor with a length of blue paper towel yanked violently from the dispenser by the sink. There's a bin by the door, a bright-yellow bin bag suspended inside a metal frame; she stamps her heavy black shoe down on the pedal at its base and the lid flips back with a clank. In goes the paper towel. Then she rips off another sheet, smaller this time, and drapes it over Heddy's bedpan. She stacks the bedpan on the brown tray alongside the plate and bowl and cutlery that Heddy ate her lunch from, and starts heading for the door.

'Wait!' Mrs Partridge snaps. The nurse stops at the door, tray in hand, and I am startled out of my mute and horrified stupor. 'I want to see Dr Millar now, please.'

The hard mass in my chest vanishes and my heart kicks off on a fast, panicked tattoo. I glance at my watch. It's twenty to one. I don't want to see the doctor now. I just want to get out of here and go home.

'Dr Millar's not available,' the nurse says, and relief flushes through me. The nurse turns back to the door and raises her free hand to push it open.

'Now listen here,' Mrs Partridge says, and there is a sharp crackle to her voice. 'This lady' – she points in my direction, jabbing at the air with her bony finger – 'has come all this way specially. We're not going till we've seen the doctor.'

I feel a scene coming and I don't want it. I just want to go. 'Really, Mrs Partridge, it doesn't matter. I'm sure—'

'It does matter,' Mrs Partridge interrupts me. She's starting to tremble; I can see it, her little body vibrating inside her clothes. My racing heart starts racing even faster. 'You've been so good to us, all of your family. Always been so good to us. Now here you are, given up your time. I can't have you going home without talking to the doctor.'

Something like guilt, only thicker and deeper and disturbingly cold, builds inside my stomach. The crackle in Mrs Partridge's voice has turned into a crack, and the muscles in her cheeks and around her mouth are quivering and twitching at a startling pace.

The nurse watches Mrs Partridge, and me, that tray balanced on her arm as if she is a waitress. Her face is carefully impassive. 'Well, you can't see Dr Millar,' she says. 'It's his day at the Mordon. Dr Wolf's doing Mitley today. He's down the corridor. You can talk to him if you like.' And out the door she goes.

I imagine her pasting a smile on her face, gliding among non-existent white-linened tables and serving up the dish of the day from that tray upon her arm.

We find Dr Wolf down the corridor, just as the nurse predicted. He is writing up his notes, having just finished with the patients who are awake and who are walking round and round, or sitting, or rocking, in the two glass-walled lounges at the far end of Mitley Wing. To get to him, we have walked past a few closed rooms like Heddy's, and one main ward with many beds, some with discernible lumps in them, some without.

He is a tall man, blond, with floppy hair that falls down into his eyes. He is young, too young, as far as Mrs Partridge is concerned. I can tell this by the way she starts muttering and mumbling as we approach him.

'Always the same,' she whispers to herself. 'Always the same. Not enough staff. Nobody cares. What am I to do? What *am* I to do?'

The clack of our shoes echoing on the tiled floor alerts him to our approach. He raises his head from his notes, tilting it to one side, and smiles a tired doctor's smile.

'Mrs Partridge,' he says kindly, putting out his hand. 'And you are Mrs—?'

'Hamley,' I say, and one by one we shake his hand, then follow him back down the corridor to the small office at the start of Mitley Wing. He walks in big strides with his doctor's coat flapping out behind him, and Mrs Partridge and I trot along like lambs in his wake.

Inside the sparse, unkindly, drab office Dr Wolf perches on the edge of the chipped teak desk and Mrs Partridge and I sit in the only two chairs, instantly at a disadvantage.

'Ladies,' he says, and then he pauses, pretending he's got time for us, when I can see in his eyes that he hasn't. 'How can I be of help?' He has a faint accent: German, I think, or maybe it's Dutch. I was never any good at accents.

'We wanted to see Dr Millar,' Mrs Partridge says to Dr Wolf's knees, which are only a little below her eye level. Her voice is quiet, perfectly audible but pinched, halfway to being defeated.

Suddenly I see how professional and how subtle it is, this smooth intimidation of troublesome little old ladies.

'I am Dr Millar's colleague,' he says. 'Please.' He gestures with his hand for Mrs Partridge to speak. His face is all sympathetic encouragement, the frowning eyes, the smiling mouth. Mrs Partridge opens her mouth to speak, but then his bleeper goes. He looks at it to read it, spends a moment pressing in a quick reply, pops it back in his pocket, then he's back with us again, frown and smile sliding simultaneously back into place.

'I want to take my girl home,' Mrs Partridge mutters, and then she clamps her mouth shut tight, sticking out her chin, like there's nothing more to be said.

'Of course you do,' the kind doctor says, and both the frown and the smile deepen. 'That is only natural. But we must do what is best for Helen.' He pauses for a second, then adds, 'That is what we all want, is it not?'

I am finding him increasingly irritating. 'When do you expect Helen to be ready to go home?' I ask. It feels strange to call her by her proper name. She's always been Heddy to me. As in *Heddy P smells of wee.*

The doctor raises his shoulders and his hands in an exaggerated shrug, as if such knowledge is beyond him. He drops the smile, too, and backs up the shrug with an extended bottom lip. He has very full lips for a man – some people would think them attractive. 'That depends on Helen,' he says enigmatically.

'What do you mean?' I ask.

He stares at an area above my head for a moment, concentrating hard as if searching for words that I might understand. When he's found those words he looks at me and says, 'Helen's cooperation is vital to her recovery. At the moment we do not have that cooperation.'

'She wants to go home,' I say. 'It's obvious she does. She wants to be with her son.'

'It is not just a matter of patching Helen up and sending her home again,' Dr Wolf says, as if I was so stupid as to think it was. 'Helen has issues that need to be worked through.'

'How can she work through anything if she's sedated all the time?' I can hear myself starting to sound fractious. He is infuriating me with his controlled patience. Now he nods his head to one side as if conceding my point, and is about to reply when Mrs Partridge butts in.

'We were managing all right at home,' she mutters, to no one in particular.

Dr Wolf raises his eyebrows at this, and there is a short, uncomfortable silence. Then he looks at his watch. Pointedly, I look at mine too. I am in just as much of a hurry as he is.

'We need to be sure this will not happen again,' he says and there is a definite full stop after his words. We are being dismissed. He stands up from the table; we stand also. He puts out his hand; in turn we shake it once again, and then he opens the door and holds it for us as we trot out after him.

'Try not to worry,' he says with a last, economic smile. 'We are doing our very best for Helen.' And then he is off, marching back down the corridor with his coat flapping out behind him.

We stand in that corridor, Mrs Partridge and I, and watch him disappear. When I turn to look at her, she is still staring into the distance, coat zipped up to her chin, shopping bag in hand, just like she's waiting for a bus.

'We have to go,' I say. 'The children . . . '

'Yes, dear. Of course, dear,' she says, and turns and starts hurrying towards the exit, so that I have to walk quickly to keep up with her. I was afraid she'd want to go in and see Heddy again, before we left, but she pushes straight out through those swing doors and back along the endless labyrinthine passages towards daylight. She doesn't speak again until we are outside, both of us flinching as the brightness spears our eyes.

'Thank you, Laura,' she says then, and she says it so formally I wonder if she's been rehearsing it in her head as we walked. 'For all your help, for your kind interest in Heddy—'

'It's nothing,' I interrupt, wishing she wouldn't go on. But she does, of course.

'For bringing me here, and giving up your valuable time. You have always been most kind to Heddy, you and all your family.'

III

She is so sincere and I am so ashamed. 'Really, Mrs Partridge, it's the least I could do,' I say, and for the moment, at least, I mean it.

On the way back Mrs Partridge lights up a cigarette inside my car, and I haven't the heart to tell her to put it out. It'll take me days to get rid of the smell, and James will do his nut if he notices. I open my window and try to breathe sideways.

There is something I just can't understand.

'Why does she do it?' I ask. 'I mean, if she knows they're going to stick her in hospital, away from Nathan, why does she do it?'

'My Heddy's been unhappy for a long time,' Mrs Partridge says quietly, breathing out smoke on a dragon's sigh. 'Since long before Nathan was born.'

This isn't the answer I'm after. Heddy's unhappy face was a fixture of my childhood, as predictable and as necessary as Christmas. The guilt would knock me over if I let it.

'But why does she do these things if it means she is taken away from her son? Why make herself even more unhappy?'

'Hormones,' Mrs Partridge says and I try not to notice as she tips her ash onto the floor. 'First she lost the baby. Then it took such a while for Nathan to come along. We thought that would make things better, but there was the post-natal depression, see, and the bereavement still, from the first baby. And the money worries.' She sounds like she's making a list. It could be a shopping list. One hundred and one things to buy so that you, too, can be like Heddy Partridge. 'Then her husband left her, just when she needed him most. That came especially hard to Heddy, after losing her father so young. And she was never happy about her weight.' She stops. She's run out of reasons.

'But surely she's just making it worse for herself,' I persist.

'Yes, dear,' Mrs Partridge says. 'She is. But she can't help herself. She doesn't know what else to do.' She looks around her and finds the unused ashtray in front of the gear stick and grinds out her cigarette. 'It's all just too many things for one person.'

And that's the truth of it. Too many things. One of which was me.

NINE

The minute I get home I close the front door behind me and take my shoes and all my clothes off in the hall, and leave them there. Then I run naked up to my shower and stand under it before the water is even running warm. I don't stop to take my make-up off first, and I can feel my mascara running into my eyes, stinging them. I clamp them shut; I want the water all over my face, all over every inch of me. I feel I need to be washed, and washed again, before I can even begin with the soap. I start on my head first, groping for the shampoo bottle without opening my eyes and tipping far too much out. I scrub and scrub until my scalp feels scratched raw. Then I move on to my body, working my way down bit by methodical bit so that nothing gets missed. I even soap my face, which I never, ever normally do, and my skin tightens in objection. Then under my chin, in my ears, across my shoulders and down.

And as I wash I am mentally retracing my steps, going over in my head everything that I have touched with my hands before I got in the shower. The handle to the bathroom door. The inside of the front door where I closed it behind me, the outside where I pushed it open. My keys. The car door handle; *both* car door handles. The steering wheel.

The gear stick. I will have to go over them all with Dettox, and then I will throw away the cloth. I try to think where Mrs Partridge's hands have been and I remember her searching for the ashtray; the whole dashboard will have to be sterilized.

The thought comes into my head to get out my steam cleaner and clean the car seats. But I haven't the time before I have to pick up Arianne from Carole's, and I wonder if that might perhaps be going just a little bit far. The thought stays there, though, and I know I'll end up spraying the seats with Dettox, just in case.

Even though my hands have been washed, as they've washed the rest of me, I now wash them again, paying attention to every groove and line between fingers and around knuckles. Hospital germs and bugs get everywhere; I can almost picture them, burrowing into my skin. I do not have a nail brush inside the shower, so I press my nails into the soap and dig hard, feeling it clog up underneath them, right down, where the germs might hide.

The bathroom is thick with steam when I turn off the shower. I rub myself dry, then wipe a clear patch on the mirror and see the awful mess the soap has made of my make-up. By the time I've cleaned my face properly and got dressed, I'm really running late. There isn't time to redo my make-up or dry my hair.

I hesitate over the clothes in the hall. For just a second I wonder if I should take them to the dry-cleaner's, in case I need them again.

I take the optimistic route, and chuck them all in the bin.

I make it to Carole's on time by the skin of my teeth.

Penny is just coming out of the gateway with Sam perched

on her hip when I get out of my car. In one glance she's taken in my wet hair, my bare face, my change of clothes. As unobtrusively as possible I try to peel my shirt away from my back where it is sticking to my skin, damp from the Dettoxed car seat.

'Got time for a quick coffee?' she asks casually, lowering Sam to his feet.

'Sorry,' I say and, borrowing from James, I pull an *I'd love to stop and chat if only I had the time* face. 'I've got a splitting headache.'

Penny's eyes are almost popping with curiosity. She's about to speak and I'm racking my head for quick excuses, but then she is distracted and I am temporarily saved, by Belinda, who is just coming out of Carole's front door.

'Laura!' Belinda calls, rushing up the pathway towards us, Molly following at her heels. 'I've been waiting for you.'

'Lucky you,' Penny mutters quietly, under her breath.

I can feel Penny's gaze slipping away from me and wandering down to Belinda's rather wide feet, which are clad in a pair of navy-blue loafers. Between these unfortunate shoes and the too-short trousers are what look suspiciously like popsocks, in a worrying shade of beige. Out of the corner of my eye I notice Penny stick out one of her own mock-crocodile-skin boots, pivot it on its pin-thin heel and make the comparison.

'You haven't got any make-up on,' Belinda accuses me, gawping at my face with undisguised horror.

'I know,' I say. 'I'm running late.'

Belinda proceeds to make me even later. 'I want to talk to you about French classes for Arianne,' she says, of all things. 'There may be a space coming available soon in Molly's class. I could put a word in for you, if you like.'

I stare at her hamster face staring at mine. French classes are the last thing on my mind right now.

'And I wondered what you thought about the girls doing flute lessons together,' she carries on. 'They're starting them at St James's Hall in September. I've put Molly's name down already.'

'I'll leave you to it,' Penny says to me, taking Sam by the hand and somewhat reluctantly letting me go.

And so I am off the hook for now, but a juicy story gets all the juicier for the waiting. I am well aware of this. My naked face on its own would be enough to bring empires down, around here.

My mother phones again that evening, when the children are eating their tea. Twice in one week is not like her at all. I hear her voice and I wonder if there is some mother–daughter telepathy thing going on along the psychic airwaves. I hear what she has to say, and I know it.

'Laura,' she says, without preamble. 'There's something I've been meaning to tell you, but I keep forgetting. Just a day or two before we moved I bumped into old Mrs Partridge in the High Street. You remember the Partridges, don't you, darling, from Fairview Lane?' She doesn't pause long enough for me to reply, which is probably just as well, but carries on, 'Well, it seems poor Heddy's had some kind of a breakdown and has had to go into hospital. Mrs Partridge had been having a terrible time. I did feel sorry for her.' Hesitation is slipping into her voice now, slowing her down a little. 'I gave her your phone numbers, just in case things got too bad. You don't mind, do you, darling?'

'No,' I say, keeping my voice as level as I can. 'Of course not.'

'Only I did feel so sorry for her. For both of them. They've had a very hard life, the Partridges.'

I can hear the pity in my mother's voice, but also something else, much more disturbing. And it's something directed at me, I can feel it.

'It's probably something and nothing,' she says, brightly now. 'I'm sure she won't need to call you.' The pity is jollied away on a light little laugh, but the something else is still there. I can hear it. And then she says, 'But if she does call you, you will try to help her, won't you, darling? You will do what you can?'

And I think I know what the something else is. It's doubt. My own mother thinks me incapable of being nice.

I tell James later, but he's not that interested. He's had a hard day at work and he finds the description of Belinda's footwear and her bumptious enthusiasm for all things French or musical much more entertaining.

'God, she is one pushy mother,' he laughs, twirling spaghetti carbonara around his fork and swigging back his wine.

But when I tell him about my trip to St Anne's I see his face shut down a little. He is quiet as I speak; he shovels pasta into his mouth with his head tilted slightly to one side as if I have his full attention, but I know he is not really listening. He's thinking about work. I know this because of the politely fascinated expression on his face. I see this expression a lot. Sometimes it tempts me into telling him something totally wild, such as that a family of badgers has taken up residence in the study and used his Chelsea programmes for bedding, just to catch him out. But not tonight.

Tonight I tell him there is this poor old woman who travels four hours a day on buses just to spend one hour with her mentally ill daughter. I tell him that the daughter, a woman of my age, is someone I was at school with, though I don't tell him what a bitch I was to her the whole time I knew her.

'She's trapped inside herself, drugged up and shut away,' I say, and I wonder where all this compassion is coming from.

'Right,' James says, curling spaghetti round his fork.

'I mean, it's a downward spiral.' I can hear myself talking in clichés. 'It could happen to anyone. You get depressed, you go to the doctor, you get put on pills. But pills don't sort out the problem and you end up needing more pills, and before you know it you're caught up in the system and can't get out.' For a second I wonder what on earth I'm talking about, and I shut up before James asks me the same thing.

He doesn't, though. He carries on eating, twisting up his spaghetti and cutting off any unruly tails with the side of his spoon.

'It's terrible that this should happen to people,' I finish lamely.

'It's a tough old world,' James says, which is a safe thing to say, when he clearly hasn't been listening to a word I've said.

I can't get over the cuts all up her arms.

The more I think about it, the creepier it is.

I lie awake in the darkness with my eyes wide open and there are a million questions firing in my head. I listen to James snoring away beside me and I wonder why it is that Heddy watched us at school all those years ago, cutting ourselves. Did she just want to be like us – pretty, popular, blonde, *included*, all the things Heddy Partridge could never be? Or was she trying to pick up tips on technique from the master cutters so that she'd be better able to copy us one day, when her own time came? I stare into the dark and I see Jane, Cathy, Amanda and me huddled together in the playground, close, each of us in turn rolling up our sleeves and baring the soft, latticed skin of our inner arms, and I see Heddy, always there, hovering close by, trying to catch a look.

When we cut our arms it was a very private thing, or so I thought. Something between just the four of us, binding our friendship. But all performers need an audience, don't they, and now I wonder: did we need Heddy? Did we need her just so that we could tell her to get lost, just to make our need for secrecy more intense?

Did I need her, just to make myself look and feel better?

I turn on my side and close my eyes, but the thoughts won't go away.

I remember my English tutor at college telling the class that if you hate someone, it is because you can see in them that something you dislike about yourself. What nonsense, I thought.

Heddy Partridge and I are aeons apart in our lives and in our heads, surely?

Surely?

She is like a shadow that just won't go away.

What was she thinking when she watched us, all those years ago? And what was she thinking when she stood looking down at me as I lay on her mother's sofa with my wrist so half-heartedly slit? I squeeze my eyes tight shut, but I can still see her blank, emotionless eyes, giving nothing away.

And when she so publicly cut up her own arms, what was she thinking then? Not of me, surely. Not even for a second. That would be just too creepy for words.

I press together the inside of my arms, inner wrist against inner wrist. I remember how it felt to peel back the woolly sleeve of my cardigan, the anticipation, the thrill. I remember it so well I can almost feel it. The prickle and the tingle of the blade scraping away at my skin, the pop as it burst through. The adrenaline, shooting out and making my heart race while I kept my body oh so still. And the pain, the secret, glorious pain, beating in time with my heart.

I remember all this, though I want to forget.

I will help Mrs Partridge. I will do whatever I can to help get Heddy out of St Anne's. I have to, otherwise they will be on my back like clawed beetles forever, dragging me down.

Sure enough, there is a message on the answerphone the next day, when I get back from town with my new shoes. It's the third message after the one from Tasha confirming coffee on Thursday and Liz's *Hello, how are you? Didn't see you at yoga.*

'Mrs Partridge calling,' she announces in a semi-shout, as if answerphones were the newest of the new and just too baffling for words, rather than simple taping mechanisms that have been around for years and years. 'Violet Partridge calling. For Laura Cresswell. Phoning to say thank you, dear, for all your kind help. Will try again later.'

Please don't, I think, as I wipe off the message. Please don't try again later.

But she does, of course. This time, thankfully, I am busy bathing the children, and again I don't answer. So she calls me on my mobile. I hear the distant ring of it from my handbag, down in the hall.

And I see my life, opened out and crawling with beetles, eating me up and pulling me down.

*

James and I have sex scheduled in on Wednesday nights. Obviously if he's away on business or working late, then we can't do it and then there's the nightmare of rejiggling diaries to see if we can fit it in on a Tuesday or a Thursday instead, but more often than not one of us is either out or busy. And there's always the Saturday slot to fall back on.

Tonight James is at home, we are on the bed and he has been working on my left nipple for quite some time now.

I started off with good intentions, but I just can't concentrate. I just can't relax. I mean, how can I, with Heddy Partridge and her mother permanently stuck in my head? It's like they're here, in the room with us.

I sigh, and James seems to take this as a sign that he's getting somewhere at last. His fingers speed up the twiddling, and he starts rubbing himself against me, and kissing my neck.

'I've got to help them,' I say, and James grunts into my neck. 'I've got to.'

James grunts again, lets go of my left nipple and moves his hand across to start on my right.

I stare at the ceiling. 'But how? What can I do?'

James's fingers stop twiddling, and start drumming on my breast instead, a sign of impatience, I think. 'No one can be held against their will unless they're a danger to themselves or to others,' he mutters into my hair.

I turn my head and we are nose to nose. 'You make it sound like she's in prison!'

'No,' he says, finally giving up on my breasts altogether and taking his hand away, 'you make it sound like that.' He props himself up on one elbow and looks down on me. 'You know, I think I preferred you when you were selfish,' he says.

He means it as a half-joke, but it isn't even half-funny.

Tears rush into my eyes, and sex is definitely off the menu. 'I am still selfish!' I cry as James stares at me, startled. 'Believe me, I am.'

I arrive at Chico's at twelve-thirty on Thursday to meet Tasha and, surprise, surprise, Penny and Liz are there too. I see them through the glass before I open the door, heads together around the table, chatting very animatedly. The chat stops, of course, when I walk in, and they grin up at me, hungry as wolves.

Coffee is ordered for me, and more coffees for them. They've clearly been here for quite some time, though they quite ridiculously try to pretend they've just arrived and that it was a coincidence, them all bumping into each other like this.

I sip my coffee and wait, and they wait too, all eyes upon me, blatantly voracious.

'Well, go on then,' Liz says at last. 'You know we're all dying to know what you've been up to.'

'Yes, and it better be something good for you to keep us in suspense like this!' Penny quips, and I notice she sounds just the tiniest bit miffed.

'Teenage lover, at least,' Tasha drawls, manicured fingers stirring her spoon around her coffee cup with artificial ease.

'Well, actually,' I say, looking at each of them in turn, 'I've been to see a girl I knew from school, who's stuck in a mental hospital. I was wondering if any of you'd know how I could help get her out.'

All three of them stare back at me, mouths open, eyes wide.

'Oh, my God, what did she do?' gasps Penny. 'I mean, what kind of mental?'

'Do you mean mad-mental or is it just some kind of breakdown?' Tasha asks, and when she says mad she shakes her head a little, and crosses her eyes, cartoon-like, lest I should doubt her definition of the word. 'Who is the girl? Do we know her?'

'No of course not. And she's not a girl now; she's a woman. She's a mother.'

'Oh, my God,' says Penny again. 'Now that is awful. You shouldn't go having children if you're, you know—'

'What? *Mental?*' I ask and my voice is tight and dry. 'Well, maybe she wasn't then.' And square up before my eyes rises that image of Heddy Partridge trapped in her box-house in Barton Village, beaten down by her life, new baby in her arms. Suddenly, mortifyingly, I'm going to cry, and I have to dig the nails of one hand into the other to fight back the tears.

I see Penny look at Tasha, and Tasha look at Liz.

'Where's the hospital?' Liz asks.

'St Anne's. Other side of Hounslow,' I say, over the lump in my throat.

'Why would you want to get her out?' Penny asks. 'I mean, I'm sure she wouldn't be in there in the first place unless there was a very good reason, Laura.'

I can't answer this. Again, I see them all exchanging glances.

'She might be *dangerous*,' Tasha suggests, and Penny nods, vigorously, in agreement.

They're waiting for me to tell them more, but I can't. I should never have mentioned it at all. I should have stuck to clothes and houses and children and the general bitching with which we normally amuse each other. My throat is burning, the skin under my hair prickling up with heat.

Tasha shivers slightly, and pulls her cardigan a little closer around her. The silence drags on.

And then Penny suddenly sees someone she just has to wave hello to across the other side of the room, and Tasha remembers it's at least five minutes since she checked her phone for messages. Liz picks up her cup, stares into it for a long moment and eventually notices that it's empty, again.

'More coffee, anyone?' she asks stoically, breaking the silence.

'Oh, yes,' Tasha says, 'good idea', and the relief is palpable.

'Me, too,' Penny says and, turning towards Tasha, and away from me, she says, 'I've been dying to ask: how is your floor coming along?'

And swiftly they are back on floors, and wall coverings, the debatable progress of the children's book-day costumes and the new summer collection already appearing in Flavia's in the village, as if I had never done anything so gauche as to throw a nutter into the conversation.

It's a while before I can join in. It's a while longer before any of them can meet my eye again.

TEN

Mrs Partridge catches me in the next time she phones.

We are just in from school, with Thomas tearful and angry inside the sad remains of his Baloo outfit. I'd be just the tiniest bit angry myself if I didn't feel so sorry for him. He's torn his school trousers trying to rip the felt off them, and the white furry patch on his tummy is covered in dirt from rolling around on the ground, fighting. The tail is gone altogether, thrown around the playground apparently, until it got stuck up a tree.

'There's been some silliness,' Mrs Hills said when I went to pick him up. She kept him back with her as the rest of the class dispersed, always a bad sign. She kept Milo Littlewood back too, at her other side, which was doubly worrying as we were supposed to be going back to the Littlewoods' for tea.

'Oops,' Fiona Littlewood whispered into my ear as we waited, as required, until all the other delightful little *Jungle Book* characters had been claimed.

Oops, indeed. Thomas was sporting a scowl that would sink battleships on his tear-stained little face. Milo, who was clad in a Baloo costume worthy of a stage production, was sporting two large red scratches on his.

The silliness turned out to be fighting and name-calling and all manner of inappropriate behaviour, rounded off most effectively by Thomas digging his nails into Milo's milky-white cheeks. Naturally, Mrs Hills hoped never to see such behaviour again, and certainly not during book week.

I felt like a six-year-old myself, and thoroughly told off. This I covered with a profusion of apologies on Thomas's behalf in a voice slightly lower than my normal tone. And Fiona Littlewood graciously accepted my apologies with vocal and smug generosity. Although she did go on to say that perhaps the tea arrangements might be postponed as the children seemed a little tired after their rather exciting day. She smiled as she said it – a smile at once superior and understanding – and for just a second I wondered how she would look with a couple of scratches to match Milo's on her beautifully maintained face.

And so we came home, Thomas, Arianne and I, with Thomas and me feeling, I imagine, equally deflated and Arianne piping up every two minutes, 'Has he been naughty, Mummy? Has Thomas been naughty again?'

'They kept calling me a rat,' Thomas cries when we are home, and he is clinging on to my legs and pressing his face into my tummy, just above the belt of my jeans. 'They said I looked like a rat, not Baloo.'

He lets his tears bubble up, and I hold him. He cries, and I cry too. Soon Arianne is holding on to both of us, and joining in. Thomas is crying over the humiliation of his bodge-job Baloo outfit. Arianne is crying over Thomas. And I am crying over a million things that I couldn't even begin to explain, not even to myself. And so we launch ourselves off onto a family crying jag. And this is how we are when Mrs Partridge phones, and catches me in.

The annoying thing is, if Thomas hadn't scratched Milo's cheeks, if Milo hadn't been wearing such a sick-makingly perfect Baloo outfit and if there hadn't been such a tortuous annual event as book week in the first place, we'd have gone back to the Littlewoods' as planned and I'd have been out and have missed her call, and believe me, I'd have had my mobile switched off.

I loosen myself from my children's arms to pick up the phone and have to listen to her thanking me again for my time given up and my most appreciated concern. I feel like God is having a laugh at my expense. Then she gives me a full unwanted update on Heddy's progress, or rather the lack of it, since my bountiful visit to St Anne's. Right now I couldn't care less.

She falls short of asking me outright what I'm going to do, but the question is there, hanging in the long pause, when she finally shuts up.

I feel a deep tiredness, which I think you might call resignation, sinking into my bones.

'I have given it some thought,' I say, which is true enough. 'We need to get her out, back with Nathan. That's the main thing.' The children loosen themselves from my legs and stare up at me, intrigued.

Mrs Partridge remains quiet on the other end of the phone, waiting for me to tell her something she doesn't already know.

'It seems to me that Heddy's caught in a cycle. We need to break that cycle.' I am talking complete rubbish. I can tell by her silence that Mrs Partridge thinks this too. Even the children have forgotten their tears and are starting to giggle now. I'd laugh too, if the joke wasn't on me.

I tell her I'll help. I tell her I'll do whatever I can. I say it just to get her off the phone, but it's true. I have no choice. It seems to me that on one of his particularly boring days above the earth God decided to make the Partridges my problem, and so I am stuck with them unless I can sort them out and get rid of them for good.

The first thing I do is write a letter to the local paper. Not just my local paper, here in Ashton, but all the local papers around here that get printed out of the same office. So we have a pretty large area covered. I am surprised at how easy it is to write your own little feature and get it into print. In fact there's no writing involved at all, I just phone the central office number and speak to the nice guy on the phone and he writes it all down for me.

'Mental illness is still a social taboo,' I tell him, 'and the trouble is that people like these become lost in the system. They don't have the confidence to stand up for themselves, or, frankly, the brains. Their social status marks them out as victims; it is incredibly unfair.'

I feel quite pleased with myself. I am a pioneer for the working classes. I find myself quite liking this role and the easy sleep it brings, until I see my article in print, one week later.

I have been completely misquoted. Every 'they' I said has become 'we'. I read the article with drop-dead horror. '"Mental illness is still a social taboo and people like us get lost in the system," says Ashton mum Laura Hamley. "Just because we don't have the confidence or the brains to stand up for ourselves, we're marked out as victims. It isn't fair."'

Embarrassment settles over me like a heavy blanket. The local paper is posted through every door, in every street, in Ashton.

James thinks it's hilarious. He half-kills himself laughing when he reads it. 'Oh dear, oh dear,' he says, 'what will the ladies of Ashton do, now they know they've got a nutter in their midst?'

Nobody says anything. That makes it worse.

I feel like all of Ashton is looking at me, and I wish someone would say something, make a joke about it at least. I wish I could make a joke about it. I would, if they'd give me the chance.

I get kind looks in the playground, if I get any looks at all. Mostly people are suddenly very busy, dashing here, dashing there. I find myself painfully invisible. No one is pushing for coffee, or lunch, or tea, later, with the children. Even Penny, Tasha and Liz are suddenly unavailable when I call, but I'd bet my bottom dollar they're not unavailable to each other.

It is a strangely quiet week. Whatever we three do, we do alone. Tennis lessons, swimming lessons, after-school recorder practice. All the things we normally rush to and from are suddenly so much less of a rush when there is no tea to be fitted in before or after; no tea, and no chat. It seems to me that for days I speak to no one but my children, and my husband – and he, obviously, doesn't count.

'Oh, Laura,' James laughs, oblivious of his place at the very bottom of the list of those I would like to chat to, 'how are the ladies of Ashton going to get over that one?'

Tasha makes the first move, to break my exile.

After Tumbletots on Monday, when we have each sat and clapped and separately applauded the musical, balancing and all-round marvellous performing skills of our children,

Tasha turns to me with a generous smile and says, 'Hi, Laura. How *are* you? Haven't spoken to you all week – I've been *so* busy.'

'Me too,' I reply, as required, although we all know that Coventry isn't the busiest of places when you're sent to it.

'Listen,' she says, 'I'm having drinks at my house on Thursday night, for the girls. Rupert's away, on business. You will come, won't you? I've got something exciting to tell.'

'I'll have to check my diary,' I say, which is what we always say. 'But that should be fine. I'd love to come.'

My smile is at least as big as Tasha's, so wide it's almost cracked out into my ears.

Oh, what it is to be relegated to second-rate invitee rather than first-rate planner in this powerful, powder-puff world of ours.

I arrive latish, so no one feels compelled to talk to me before the action gets under way. Tasha is holding court already, tippy-toeing about so that her heels don't dent her new, soft oak floor. Everyone else is doing the same; I walk in and see this and it occurs to me just how de rigueur it is, this funny indoor walk, and how I'd laugh and point it out to them all if I wasn't in enough disgrace already.

I myself am wearing flats tonight.

'Laura!' Tasha trip-trips over to me and kisses the air on each side of my face. 'So glad you could come.'

And so I am greeted all round, and so I greet back. Everyone is here tonight. Tasha's star is clearly in the rising, whereas mine has plummeted to earth. No one mentions my dreadful faux pas with the local paper.

Now we're all on our second glass of champagne, and we're all starting to get just the tiniest bit ditzy. Tasha herself is rosy-cheeked and starry-eyed, but not from the champagne. She has pointedly kept one hand placed over her glass all evening.

'Girls,' she announces now, after trilling one nail against her glass to get our attention. 'I know you're all dying to know ... ' She lets her words trail off as she coyly smiles around the room, and then she extends her free hand, waggles her manicured fingers and slowly pats her incredibly flat stomach.

The room erupts into squeals.

'Oh Tasha, you're not!'

'Tasha, how could you keep it from me?'

'Oh Tasha, you dark horse – I knew it, from the moment you went off coffee!'

'And gin!'

And so we crowd around and we gush and push and shove in our efforts to be favourite friend. My new position in the back row makes the viewing of this social zoo all the more entertaining.

After enough of a fuss has been made of Tasha, and a little more champagne has been drunk, we start on the obligatory tales of pregnancy and childbirth. We all have a stack of such tales, to be brought out on occasions like these. It's the one thing we all have in common, I suppose – that and our love of shoes.

Fiona Littlewood starts it off, telling us all how she spits them out, like shelling peas. Personally I don't actually think this is something to be proud of, especially as she goes on to give them all such ridiculous names. *Minka*, she called the last one, for God's sake. I suppose that's what comes of having too much energy left over after pushing, and not enough decorum. The harder the push, the plainer the name, that's for sure.

I mean, look at Penny.

'It took me days to have Joe, and I mean *days*,' she states and though we have all heard this story several times before, we are all ready to hear it again, curling up our toes and our noses in anticipation. 'Forceps, suction, cut from here to here,' and she holds up her hands in what I sincerely hope is an exaggerated estimate of the distance down below. 'It was years before I could have sex again, and I mean *years*. And then look what happened. I got Sam. Same thing all over again.' She shudders, and we all shudder too, glorying in the delight that at least there is one couple out there having sex less often than ourselves.

'Well, I went through all that and still ended up having a Caesarean,' Juliet squeaks, pulling a poor-me face and crossing her eyes.

'How awful,' we all say, sympathy itself, 'imagine it, all that pain for nothing.'

'And in the days before tummy tucks!' someone laughs, and we all laugh too, though terribly politely of course. I mean, no one would actually suggest that Juliet could have done with a tummy tuck.

And meanwhile Tasha sits there, centre stage, touching those beautifully painted fingernails to her mouth, her forehead, her stomach in a parody of anticipated dread. 'Bang go my Joseph trousers,' she moans now and again. 'And as for my new Prada skirt – why on earth did I buy it? What have I done? I'm ruined.'

I have my own little repertoire of ever-so-amusing stories from the arena of childbirth and I'm wondering which little ditty I should share tonight.

There's the one about my first day at the NCT group where the group leader handed around picture cards to the eight of us in her group. On these cards were pictures of women, in various types of attire. Well, I say various, but mostly they were of a type, what you might call the comfy type – dare I say it, the mumsy type – make-up-less, hairstyle-less, clad in joggie bottoms and sweatshirts and their husbands' big denim shirts. Clothes I would not be seen dead in. All of the women in the pictures were like this except for two, who between them were wearing lipstick, decent highlights, cute jackets and heels.

'Now pick out the images that most represent you,' our leader said to us, as if we were imbeciles. I thought she was checking to see if our brains had all gone with the arrival of our bumps.

Naturally I picked out the two women wearing the lipstick, the decent highlights, the cute jackets and the heels; after all, that's how I dressed for work every day. And even though I wasn't going straight back to work – my job in PR meant erratic hours and too much travel – I assumed I'd still carry on dressing the way I liked.

But, 'Oh *no*,' our leader admonished, shaking her head, and the other women all shook their heads too, like over-sized puppets. 'You can't go around looking like *that* when you have a new baby to look after. You won't have time to put on make-up, or worry about your hair. You'll be lucky if you manage even to get dressed in the morning.' All around there was a general murmur of agreement, and relief. Obviously no one else had been so stupid as to think they'd carry on being themselves, after they'd had their babies. 'And *smart jackets*,' she added, with a good deal of contempt in her voice, she herself most definitely being someone who did not go in for such frivolities, 'don't look so smart with sick all down the lapel. This is what you'll be wearing,' she finished, jabbing her finger at a picture of a washed-out woman in a sweatshirt so hideous it might as well have been covered in sick, 'when you're a mum.'

The girls always love to hear that one. They think it's hilarious, they love to imagine my horror. Of course when I tell that story I paint myself as the rebel, the one that got away, the one who did sit up in bed and ask for her lipstick and a mirror, the minute her stitches had been sewn.

I never tell them how isolating it was to be told, in effect, that you might as well just give up on yourself once you became a mother. That just wouldn't be funny.

Or there's the one about the time I took Thomas along to the clinic to be weighed, when he was just a few weeks old. I went along to the clinic a lot when Thomas was tiny, just for something to do, and to have the nurses tell me my little boy was fine, though I didn't see how he could be fine when he cried all the time. Thomas hated being weighed. He hated having all his clothes taken off and being placed on the scales, much like a bunch of bananas in the greengrocer's. He'd scream as soon as the cold metal touched his skin. One time, as he lay on the scales, screaming, his little willy popped up and sent out an arc of pee, right across the room. It hit one of the nurses, square on the chin. She screamed in surprise, making Thomas scream all the more and wriggle about, thus sending the arc across the other side of the room and squirting another nurse, also in the face. He was like a high-powered garden sprinkler, spraying around the room. Soon everyone was screaming and trying to dodge his fire.

But today I decide to tell them about the cabbage-leaf woman.

'Oh no, not the cabbage-leaf woman!' squeals Penny, who's heard this story before.

Oh yes. The cabbage-leaf woman turned up as guest speaker at one of our antenatal classes, come to talk to us about breast-feeding. She was a very curious-looking woman, somewhat round in shape and squeezed into an all-in-one green jumpsuit, the sort of thing I vaguely remembered being fashionable way back in the 1980s. And she'd obviously had it since the 1980s – it was fraying a little around the ankle hems, just above the straps of her red Jesus sandals. She had very pale skin and wore no make-up except for two matching bolts of electric-blue eye-shadow applied midway between her eyes and her overplucked brows. Her hair was a shocking frizz of yellow curls cut to just below her ears, in such a style that it seemed to be the same length all over, as wide as it was deep as it was long.

I found myself unable to stop staring at this hair, and was busy trying to decide if the colour was natural or accidental when she introduced us to her bag.

'This is my bag,' she said, patting the very large weekend holdall beside her. 'In here,' she proudly told us, 'I have everything you will ever need for breast-feeding.'

Now I was a little surprised by this because I had been under the impression that I already had everything I would ever need for breast-feeding, right there, inside the front of my shirt. After all, surely one of the big, big advantages of breast-feeding is that it doesn't need any paraphernalia or gadgets at all. But the cabbage-leaf woman had other ideas.

Out of that bag came a large packet of circular pads – sanitary pads, in effect, for the leaking nipple. And let's face it, once baby was born, there were going to be leaks springing out from all over. Next came a plastic sombrero-type cap, much like the one the Mexican mouse in *Tom and Jerry* wore on his little head, which we all passed around to get a feel for. This I was to wear on my nipple, should baby and me not much like the flesh-to-mouth contact. Then there was the ice-cube tray for us to look at, just in case any of us were not familiar with such a thing. This we were to fill with our expressed milk, which could conveniently be frozen and stored, ready to pop out and defrost when required. Naturally one would have to take care not to pop a cube out into one's husband's gin in place of the ordinary ice, but the cabbage-leaf woman did not deem it necessary to mention this. The contraption for getting the milk out of the breast and into the ice-cube tray still ranks at about 8.5 on my list of real and imagined torture implements: the breast-pump, with its candy-pink plastic trimming, a bit like a sex toy, but with a nasty twist. The funnel went over the nipple, the pump went in the hand, the bottle hung off at an angle, waiting to be filled, all worked by vigorous battery.

'I had one of those!' laughs Juliet. 'I used it all the time!'

'I didn't need one,' boasts Fiona. 'I expressed perfectly well by myself.'

'Well, I just couldn't get the hang of it,' I say. 'I clamped it to my nipple and I pumped and pumped with my hand rattling from the vibration, until my whole breast was pointed and twisted like a Mr Whippy ice cream. And after half an hour of agony I'd squeezed out only a dribble of milk. It'd take me a week to fill one cube in the ice-cube tray.'

The girls are laughing simultaneously now, and cringing, and begging me to stop.

'The woman was like a travelling salesman,' I say. 'She got these bras out of her bag next. Honestly, you should have seen them.'

Now everyone knows that you need a decent maternity

bra, but would it be too much to hope for one that was even slightly attractive? Apparently so.

The cabbage-leaf woman had two choices in design to recommend to us. God knows where she'd got them from. The first was designed to cover you up from just below the neck to a good few inches down the ribcage, and was done up at front and back by a series of hooks and eyes, much like an old-fashioned girdle. The bucket-like cups allowed room for natural expansion, and the front hooks could be undone, with patience, for what the cabbage-leaf woman took for easy access.

The second bra was similar in material and coverage, but involved a series of straps that had to be tied around the body so that the bra was fixed in place all day, with just the front flaps being opened and shut when feeding was required. The positioning of the straps meant that you could not put this bra on unaided. You'd have to enlist your husband's help with the strapping in the morning before he went off to work, and the unstrapping in the evening, when he came home. And I presume that you just had to hope for the best that he didn't notice too much the difference between this gargantuan ensemble and the lacy black items that he had previously helped to remove.

As she showed us these bras, I felt a little hormonal hysteria bubbling up inside me. I saw my womanhood flying out the window, my femininity and my sexuality competing in the race to escape my new lot.

And if by any chance your marriage did manage to survive the keep-off scream of armour-thick nylon, the cabbage-leaf woman had one final trick up her sleeve. You've guessed it: the cabbage leaf.

'Oh no, not the cabbage leaf!' squeals Juliet.

Well actually, she had a whole cabbage in her bag. It was

a big, light-green one with the outer leaves curling away slightly, though I imagine any variety would do. She took the cabbage out of her bag and held it in the palm of her hand, as if weighing it.

'This,' she announced, 'is what you need for engorgement.'

'But it works!' interjects Fiona.

'I thought she was going to tell us that we had to eat the cabbage,' I say. 'Which would have been bad enough, and I was thinking that perhaps a few lightly dressed salad leaves would do the same job. I didn't realize you had to put it inside your bra!'

'Not the whole thing!' cries Fiona. 'Just a leaf!'

I look around as the girls erupt into laughter, and I laugh too. After all, what is the point of such experiences if one cannot turn them into entertainment for one's friends? In this moment of social success I am almost tempted to believe that they might have forgotten my unfortunate appearance in the local paper. Almost.

'I can just picture your face!' Tasha shrieks.

'I know it's supposed to help with engorgement,' I say. 'But can you imagine it? Your husband comes home from work to untie you from that hideous contraption of a bra, and finds you smelling of sour milk and cabbages! What would that do for your marriage?' I sip my champagne. 'And really, what kind of woman tells another woman to stick cabbage leaves in her bra?'

'Oh, all those sleepless nights!' Tasha moans now. 'I'm dreading it.'

'You'll have help, won't you?' says Fiona. 'You'll get a nanny or something.'

And Tasha says, 'Rupert says we'll get a live-in, now we've got the room.'

'I wish we'd had a nanny,' Juliet says. 'We could easily have put one in the loft. But Andy wouldn't have it. Didn't want to have to stop walking around naked in the mornings.'

And so we move on to talk about our husbands. We all have them, even those who we all know would rather not. It is better to be dead than divorced in some circles.

It's a competition, like everything in our lives. Strip away the fancy tops and the highlights and we'd be vultures in any other jungle. Tonight we're vying for the wittiest-story award, and social success is such a sweet prize. I eat my large piece of it, choking myself up on the sweetness, so nearly lost.

And if I remember what it was really like to feel so alienated by women bearing cabbage leaves, I keep that very much to myself. I keep to myself also how I started crying the minute I got home from that final NCT meeting, and carried on crying, on and off, for a worrying time after Thomas was born. They ripped him out of my body in the end, two weeks after he was supposed to come. Scissors and knives and pliers and forceps and weird rubbery suction pads and every implement known to medical man was used to separate Thomas from me. The shock of it still haunts me.

For months I walked round and round my house with the horror of it eating me up. I'd have my lipstick on when James came in from work, but Thomas would be crying, either in his cot or in my arms, and I would be crying too. I felt like I'd died and was stuck in that last inch of purgatory before hell. My self was lost. My self was ruined and ripped out with the baby.

I wanted James to understand. I wanted him at least to acknowledge what I'd been through. But he pulled away, and

I felt like I was letting the side down with my endless tears.

'Do you think you should see a doctor?' he said to me. 'Maybe you could get some pills.'

Tonight I laugh along with the girls, but there is a lizard of chill up my spine. I didn't go to the doctor; instead I shut up crying eventually and shoved my mask back into place. But imagine if I had, imagine if I'd done as James said and got some pills to blot me out.

I could be stuck in St Anne's now, side by side with Heddy.

ELEVEN

Of course Mrs Partridge gets the local paper, and sees my little piece.

She phones up, about a week later.

'Don't often get a chance to read the paper,' she tells me. 'It comes through the door, but mostly I just save them up and give them to next door for the guinea pigs. Mrs Day told me we were in it: knocked specially, she did, and showed me. I must say I was most surprised.'

I can tell by her tone that she's trying to sound pleased, but then she pauses for a moment and I am so embarrassed I can't think what to say. I mutter something about people needing to know about Heddy, and people like her, but I feel like a complete fool.

Then Mrs Partridge carries on, and says, somewhat tentatively, as if she doesn't want to offend me, 'But do you think it'll do any good, dear? Do you think they read the *Recorder* over at St Anne's?'

The thing is, how to help without actually being involved?

I don't want the Partridges' problems becoming my problems. It isn't fair and it just isn't possible. I need to find a way of helping from a distance, as it were. Though, really, I don't see there's much I can do. People have to help themselves, in the end.

I decide to write a letter to the doctor. Not to the doctor we saw at St Anne's that Tuesday, but to Dr Millar, as he's supposed to be in charge of Heddy. It must be down to him in the end, what happens to her.

My desire to be free of the Partridges makes the letter all the easier to write. I tell him quite simply that a mother's place is with her child and that to keep Heddy separated from her son can only be making things worse. After all, that is what seems to be the most immediate problem: Heddy's combined longing and inability to be a mother to her child. Surely that longing could be used as an incentive? Couldn't it be made clear to Heddy that if she behaved in whatever way she was supposed to behave, she could soon be back at home, with Nathan?

It seems to me that she is in the worst kind of vicious circle at the moment, and that cannot be sustained indefinitely. Something has to change. So I write to the doctor and say that, for Nathan's sake, something must be done while the child *is* still a child.

It makes me feel actually sick to think of him yearning for her, and her yearning for him. I try not to think at all, and get back to practicalities.

I ask what is actively being done for Heddy, in the long term. What is the prognosis, so to speak? When will it end?

I half don't expect a reply, but I get one. Almost by return of post.

Dr Millar is delighted and encouraged by my interest in Heddy, but all cases are confidential, he tells me, and can only be discussed with next of kin.

He does, however, assure me that his aim is to have Heddy back at home as soon as possible and that he and his staff are working 100 per cent to achieve this. He understands my concerns, but her welfare, as his patient, has to be his primary concern. And he is sure that my support will be of great benefit to Heddy.

Obviously any letters will have to be written through, and signed by, Mrs Partridge in future. I can feel them all, sucking me in.

Still, I have other things to tend to, right now.

My cleaner has decided to quit, which means I have to spend the entire morning cleaning the house myself. Nothing is guaranteed to piss me off faster than scrubbing my own bathrooms and sweeping my own floors, especially as I was planning on spending the morning shopping. But the place is such a tip that it has to be done.

Tasha and Penny are sympathetic over lunch. This is, after all, the kind of problem they can relate to.

'You've *got* to have a reliable cleaner,' Tasha says, all understanding. 'I'd offer you mine, but I know she's all booked up. I could ask her if she knows anyone.'

'I'll ask around too,' Penny says. 'It's one of the three essentials in life: a good cleaner, a good hairdresser, and a good bra.'

'Talking of which,' Tasha says, subtly patting her enviable breasts, 'these little fellows are growing already. At least there's one advantage to being pregnant.'

'Yes, I'm sure Rupert's very happy about that,' Penny says, and we all giggle for a moment, behind our hands.

'And talking of hairdressers,' I say, 'I'm getting my colour done soon, and I was thinking of going for something a little warmer this time.' I pull a few strands of hair forward towards my face, so that I can see them. 'A little more honey-coloured, perhaps. What do you think?'

Thus I launch us into the endlessly riveting topic of hair colour, which leads us on to skincare, and then shoes, and fashion in general. And so we lose ourselves in the saccharine conversation of the fortunate ones, and everything is giddily fine again, so long as I keep to the rules and steer clear of mentioning nutters.

But mention her or not, the nutter and her mother are there, hooked onto the inside of my life like a pair of circus-grade tapeworms. An irritation, I tell myself. An irritation, nothing more.

It is the Monday of half-term. I've just dropped Thomas at Fiona Littlewood's to play with Milo. Arianne and I are going out to buy new ballet shoes, and we've just popped home to pick up the old pair, to compare them for size. In the few minutes we're home, the phone rings and, like an idiot, I answer it.

It's Mrs Partridge, in a total panic. I can barely make out what she's saying. Arianne is coming down the stairs swinging her ballet shoes by the ribbons and singing 'Old Macdonald' at the top of her voice. I shush her to be quiet and take the phone into the living room.

'She wouldn't take her pills,' Mrs Partridge wails into my ear. 'And she'd got hold of the ring pull off a Coke can. Said she'd slit her wrists if they made her take her pills. And I feel so wretched ... all my fault ... I took her in that Coke ... always so careful to take away any rubbish; I have to be, you know . . . don't know how she got hold of the ring . . . They've sedated her, you know, in her arm, but she made a terrible fuss . . . '

Arianne has followed me into the living room and is staring at me with wide blue eyes and swinging her ballet shoes round and round above her head like lassoes.

'I've got to go and see her,' Mrs Partridge is saying and I'm cursing myself for forgetting to take the old ballet shoes out with us in the first place. We should have gone straight to the shops after dropping Thomas, and then I'd have missed this call. 'I've got to see her, but I've got Nathan at home . . . Asked Mrs Day next door if she'd have him for a bit, but she's got to go out herself at eleven. I'll never be back by then . . . Don't know what I should do . . . '

'I'll have Nathan.' The words are out before I even think. There is definitely some god playing chess with me.

'Oh, would you, dear?' Mrs Partridge erupts into gratitude. 'I could get the bus if I go now . . . Mrs Day can have him till eleven, if you could—'

'I'll pick him up from there. I'll leave now.'

And that's it, sorted.

'Damn!' I snap as I put down the phone.

Arianne stops swinging her ballet shoes and her eyes grow wider.

'The ballet shoes will have to wait,' I tell her, and before she can start protesting I add, 'Nathan's coming to play.'

'Who's Nay-fun?' Arianne asks. And I reply with the first thing that comes into my head.

'He's my friend's little boy.'

And so it is that Arianne and I go to collect Nathan from the turquoise house attached to the Partridges'.

I have never had to knock at this house before and I cannot tell you how nervous I am. When I was a child, this house was even more frightening to me than Heddy's. I never knew who lived here, I only knew that they had the most vicious-sounding dog on earth locked behind their front door. And no matter how quietly I crept up the Partridges' pathway to call for Heddy, that dog would hear me, and bark and growl and slaver like mad, hurling itself at the inside of that door, trying to break out and get me.

I do not even know if it's the same people who live here now, and there's no sign of any dog so far. Even so, as I walk up to the front door I'm tense, on the alert, waiting for the dreaded thud of animal against wood, and for the attack to begin.

Arianne is oblivious to my fears. She's fascinated by that awful car stuck up on jacks, never having seen such a thing before. She's crouching down in the weeds, trying to get a look underneath it.

'Don't touch,' I say, but she finds herself a stick, and starts poking it in the rust holes around the wheel arches.

The doorbell doesn't seem to work, so I do my best to rattle the letter-box flap instead; it's stiff and I have to really force it back and slam it down for it to make any sound at all. It occurs to me how farcical this whole situation is. I could not have dreamed it up, not in the weirdest of dreams.

The door is opened by a plumpish woman of uncertain age, whom I presume to be Mrs Day. I have to say she doesn't appear to be in too much of a hurry for someone who is about to go out. She's wearing a quilted pink housecoat buttoned down to the floor and there are heated rollers hanging in the ends of her lemon-yellow hair. She's smoking a cigarette, which she must have stuck in her mouth while she opened the door, and now she takes it out and smoke clouds out of her face and into mine.

'Poo!' says Arianne, who has stopped poking at the car and come to see who's opened the door. She jumps up and down between me and Mrs Day, flapping her arms around to disperse the smoke.

'Mrs Day?' I say. 'I'm Laura Hamley. I've come for Nathan.' I give her my most charming smile because she looks as though she needs it. She doesn't, however, return it, possibly because Arianne is still jumping about, trying to wave the smoke back inside the house and running off a stream of observations, out loud.

'That lady's got her nightie on,' she says, pointing, 'and it's got tatty round the end.'

'It gets a bit much, all these last-minute emergencies,' Mrs Day says, through another puff of smoke, as if this is somehow my fault. 'I do have commitments of my own.' Then she tips her head back slightly while still looking at me and calls out, 'Nathan!'

Out of the shadows behind her comes this small boy. I find myself straining to see him better and realize I know nothing about him. He skulks in the darkness behind Mrs Day's pink form; from what I can see he is no bigger than Thomas.

Arianne is intrigued. Children are always curious about other children. She pushes herself round the side of a some-what affronted Mrs Day, to get a better look.

'Is that Nay-fun?' she says to me.

'I think it must be,' I reply. And to the little boy I say, 'Hello, there.'

He creeps a little nearer, until he is up beside Mrs Day. She doesn't provide much refuge, but steps to one side, leaving him exposed to our stares. He's a stocky little thing, with black hair falling over dark, solemn eyes.

'Well, here he is, then,' she announces with some displeasure, and it is very plain that she wants to be rid of us all.

I think he might have some things with him, things he might need for the day, but he doesn't. There's just himself, in his football T-shirt, jogging bottoms and trainers.

'How old are you, Nathan?' I ask cheerily as he gets into the back of the car, beside Arianne.

'Seven,' he says, and sits staring at the seat in front of him while Arianne prods him and tugs at his sleeve.

'I'm three,' she tells him proudly. 'And Thomas is six.'

In the mirror I watch as he ignores her. Poor little boy; he doesn't know who we are.

'Thomas is Arianne's brother,' I tell him. 'You might meet him later.' I watch for his response in the mirror – there is none. 'He's out at a friend's today, so we're having pancakes for lunch. They're Arianne's favourite. Do you like pancakes, Nathan?'

He shrugs, but says nothing. His hair is in bad need of a cut, hanging right in his eyes and making him blink. It's thick, black hair, forward-falling, like Heddy's. Designed to hide the face. He scratches his head a lot, the sides, the back, the top. I see him scratch in the mirror, and my heart sinks.

And he smells slightly, it's a biscuit smell, like Jacob's cream crackers. I can't help noticing it, in the confines of the car. It reminds me of Heddy, and the names we called her. I think of their bath, with the cactus plant and the sewing machine in it, and I think of wet beds.

And again, I wonder how on earth I ended up in this nightmare.

*

Arianne is a very sociable child. She shows Nathan her marble run and her farm and lets him play with her Duplo. He sits on the floor with his legs crossed and lets her boss him around. He's got a Duplo horse in one hand and a little house in the other. He puts the horse in the house and takes it out again, then in again, then out. And every few seconds he lets go of the horse altogether, and scratches his head.

I sit on the sofa and watch them. And every time one of them leans forward too much and it looks like their heads might touch, I find myself acting like a jack-in-the-box and leaping between them to keep them apart.

After lunch, which Nathan eats quickly and without saying a word while Arianne chatters away non-stop, we have to go and get Thomas from the Littlewoods'. The Littlewoods live a short drive away, just off the High Street. This time I put Nathan in the middle seat in the back of the car so that Thomas can just hop in beside him. But then I find myself checking in the mirror every two seconds that his head isn't too close to Arianne's.

Normally Arianne and I would go into Fiona's house for a while, and perhaps stay for a quick coffee and a chat, but today I leave the children in the car outside. I can feel Arianne's little face staring at me, somewhat miffed, as I walk up to the door.

Fiona opens the door, immaculately clad in unrumpled linen. The baby Minka is clamped to her hip and sucking on a carrot.

'Come in, come in,' she says. 'The boys are in the play-room.'

'I can't, I'm afraid,' I tell her. 'I'm in a bit of a hurry.'

'Oh,' she says, hoiking Minka up a little. 'Where's Arianne?'

'In the car.'

Fiona peers past me and looks at the car. 'Doesn't she want to come in?' She jiggles Minka, who is struggling dangerously with that carrot. 'We were looking forward to seeing Arianne, weren't we, Minky-Mink?'

Minka appears to be holding her breath and is going a little blue around the mouth. Suddenly she shudders and retches and shoots out a large lump of carrot, which Fiona deftly catches in her free hand.

'Well done, Minka!' Fiona applauds at this very strange achievement. To me she says, 'It's so important to give them finger foods, I think. Helps them to learn how to eat.'

So long as they don't die in the process, I think, but I smile in agreement. The colour is coming back into Minka's somewhat dazed face in raspberry-pink blotches.

Then Fiona says, 'Who's that in the car with Arianne?'

'I'm looking after a friend's boy,' I lie, and to stem her curiosity I say, 'Look, thanks for having Thomas. I really ought to be going.'

'Oh,' Fiona says, curiosity not stemmed in the least. 'Right. I'll call the boys, then.' She has another quick look at the car, then calls down the hallway, 'Thomas! Mummy's here! Milo, Julius, Cornelius, come and say goodbye to Thomas.'

Thomas, Milo and the three-year-old twins, Julius and Cornelius, come bounding from the playroom dressed as Robin Hood, a wizard, a cowboy and Captain Hook, respectively. There is no end to the wonders of the Littlewood dressing-up box.

'Darlings, how wonderful!' exclaims Fiona as they screech and whoop up and down the hall. 'Oh, they've had such fun! Haven't they, Minky-Mink? They've had such fun!'

I try to find this sweet, but really I just want to get going. I can't leave the others in the car forever. Agitatedly I wait as Thomas gets back into his own clothes, finds his shoes and the goodbyes are said. I can't help noticing that there are still faint lines on Milo's cheeks where Thomas scratched him. Funny how the most embarrassing wounds always take the longest to heal.

'Who's he?' Thomas demands as he gets into the car.

'This is Nathan,' I say in my jolliest voice. 'He's come to play with us.'

'Why?' Thomas does up his seatbelt and stares at Nathan suspiciously. Nathan stares down at his knees.

'We're looking after him today,' I explain, patiently as I can, as I start up the car.

'Why?' Thomas says again. 'Where's his mummy?'

This is just the sort of question I was dreading. I decide to take the honest route. 'Nathan's mummy is in hospital,' I say brightly, making it sound like a fun day out. 'She's not feeling very well at the moment.'

I look in the mirror and think perhaps I shouldn't have said that. Nathan is still staring at his knees and his face is almost completely hidden by his hair. My children are both staring at him and I'm wondering what they're going to say next.

'Has she got a sore tummy?' Arianne asks. 'I went to hospital when I had a sore tummy.'

'And I went to hospital when a bee stung my cheek,' Thomas boasts proudly.

'Did a bee sting your mummy?' Arianne asks Nathan.

Nathan says nothing. I glance in the mirror again as he lifts up one hand and starts scratching his head.

Nathan is playing with the Duplo again, putting that horse in and out of the house.

Thomas has set up a race track for his cars, with bridges and bends and all kinds of hazards, and he's whizzing his cars one by one to a spectacularly noisy end. Arianne has built an entire village out of Duplo and her little people are heading home now after a busy hour or so at the shop, the park, the school. But Nathan just sits on the floor and puts that horse in and out of the house.

He seems closer to Arianne's age than Thomas's, but really he is worlds away from either of them. He's Heddy's boy all right. I look at him and I see it, the same slow blankness.

It's nearly six o'clock. I've given the children tea and soon I will need to put Arianne and Thomas to bed. I watch Nathan sticking that car in and out of that house and I think it can't be much longer before Mrs Partridge phones and I can take him home again.

By seven o'clock she still hasn't phoned and I am getting anxious, and more than a little annoyed.

The toys are tidied up, Thomas and Arianne are getting tired and fractious, and Nathan is still holding on to that horse, though I've told him he'll have to give it back before he goes.

I am toying with the idea of returning Nathan to Mrs Day's, though that does seem a little unkind, and of course she may not even be in. But I want to get my children to bed, and James will be home at eight-thirty. I decide to phone the hospital, to see if I can find out what's going on. I've just got out the phone book to look up the number of St Anne's when, at last, the phone rings.

But it isn't Mrs Partridge. It's Ian.

'Laura!' he calls down his crackly mobile, just like we

were old friends. 'Ian here, Ian Partridge. I'm on the M40, just past Oxford. Mum phoned me from the hospital, said Heddy's in a bad way. Headed down, straight from work. Should be there in an hour or so.'

His voice is tinny in my ear. I picture him as a boy, pudding face salivating at the prospect of sweets, or cake, or a better look at me.

'Mum says you've got Nathan,' he shouts over the crackle. 'I'll pick him up later, when I take Mum home.'

Sheer horror forces me to think quickly. I cannot have Ian Partridge and Mrs Partridge turning up here at God knows what hour. I'd have to invite them in. I cannot bear it, the thought of them here, in my house.

'Well, that'll be late—' I start to say, but he butts in.

'What? Can't hear you,' he shouts in my ear. 'The line's breaking up.'

'It'll be too late,' I shout back, determined to be heard. 'Nathan can stay here. I'll bring him home in the morning.'

'You sure?' he yells at me. 'That's great then, Laura. Thanks a lot.'

I put down the phone slowly, reeling from the shock of yet another Partridge barging into my life.

They're in the playroom, all three of them squashed onto one sofa, watching TV.

'Guess what?' I say, like I have fantastic news. 'Nathan's staying tonight!' I say it like it's the biggest treat since Christmas, but they all look at me with tired, doubtful eyes.

'Where's he sleeping?' Arianne asks.

'In the spare room,' I say. 'He'll be nice and cosy in there.'

'Where's his pyjamas?' asks Thomas.

'He can borrow some for tonight,' I say in my cheeriest, jolliest voice, knowing what's coming next.

Sure enough, 'He's not borrowing mine,' Thomas says, scowling at Nathan.

'We've got plenty of pyjamas,' I say. 'I'm sure we can find a pair for Nathan.'

I wish I'd anticipated this and got Mrs Partridge to pack him a bag of clothes, just in case. But if I had anticipated it, there's no way I'd have ended up in this situation at all.

I've only an hour before James comes home, so I put Thomas and Arianne in the bath together, to save time. Nathan watches from the doorway, seemingly fascinated as they splash and play. Then the bath is emptied, and refilled, and it is his turn.

I leave him to it as I see Thomas and Arianne into their pyjamas and beds. I find spare pyjamas, plump up the pillows on the bed in the spare room next to Arianne's, then whip Nathan out of the bath, even though he seems to be having a lovely time, wallowing on his front and making whale noises into the water. I wrap him in a towel and rub him dry. The skin on his body is white and slack already; in a year or two he'll be fat.

Then James phones. Fortunately for me, his train has been cancelled and he is stuck at Waterloo. This means I can gather the children into Arianne's room and read them a story, which is fine until Thomas notices that Nathan is wearing his Superman pyjamas.

'He's got my pyjamas on!' Thomas accuses in outrage, pointing his finger at Nathan, who is sitting on the floor with his legs crossed and staring at his knees.

'He's just borrowing them for tonight,' I say placatingly, but Thomas will not be appeased.

'No he's not!' he storms. 'I want them back!'

'You can have them back tomorrow,' I say. 'Now let's get on with the story.'

'I want them back now!' Thomas yells, and throws himself into a full-scale rage. He launches himself off the bed and at Nathan, and starts tugging at his pyjamas.

'Thomas!' I shout, pulling him away from poor Nathan, who just sits there, bending his head down further, his face turning scarlet.

'He's stinky!' Thomas yells. 'And he doesn't live here. I want him to go home!'

'Enough, Thomas!' I know he doesn't mean it. He's just a child, he doesn't mean to be cruel. But as I drag him out of Arianne's room and put him into his own with a thorough telling-off, I don't know who I am most embarrassed for, Nathan or myself.

Amazingly, the children are all asleep by the time James eventually gets home. I hear his key in the lock, then he swings open the door and flings his briefcase down in the hall, breaking the silence.

'Bloody trains!' he says, by way of greeting. He shrugs off his jacket and more or less throws it at me, as if I were a coat hook. 'I have had a bloody hard day and I do not need to finish it waiting at Waterloo station for nearly an hour because of some stupid signal failure!'

He continues moaning throughout supper. I watch him eat and listen to him complaining. Then he goes into the living room and watches the TV, and falls asleep the minute the news is finished. He comes to bed after me. I hear him padding up the stairs, and listen to the pause as he glances first into Thomas's room and then into Arianne's, oblivious to the fact that we have a visitor fast asleep in the spare room.

I wake in the night, hearing something.

James hears it too. 'Oh, what now?' he moans and turns over, dragging the duvet up around his ears.

'One of the children,' I whisper. 'I'll go.'

Quickly I slip out of bed and out of the room, closing the door behind me. The landing light is on, turned down low on a dimmer switch. I turn it up a fraction and see Nathan, standing in the doorway of his room. He's crying, his little shoulders jerking up and down inside the borrowed pyjamas as he sobs. He's making an awful noise, crying like only a boy can, from low down in his throat. He sees me, and cries louder.

'Sshh!' I whisper, thinking he'll wake the others, but already Arianne's door is opening wider and out she comes, dragging her beanie doll behind her.

'What's the matter with Nathan?' she asks, her voice thick with sleep, and loud.

'Sshh!' I say again, to her this time. 'I don't know.'

I'm thinking he's probably wet his bed or something, which is the last thing I need, but when I bend down nearer to him I see his pyjamas are dry, thank God. But there's a huge snot bubble growing out of his nose.

'What's the matter, Nathan?' I ask him quietly, but he just keeps on crying, and the snot bubble is getting bigger. I can't stand to look at it, so I take him by his hot little hand and lead him into the bathroom.

Arianne follows us and watches, squinting in the bright light as I tear off a strip of loo roll and wipe his nose. 'Go back to bed,' I say to her. 'He's probably just had a bad dream.'

She stays where she is and stares at him, not convinced.

'Go on,' I tell her. 'He'll be fine in the morning.'

Reluctantly, she goes back to her room. Now Nathan's face is clean I can touch him; I put my hand against his forehead. He's hot from crying, but there's no temperature. I'm pretty sure he isn't ill and so, as he isn't telling me what's wrong, I tell him.

'Just a bad dream,' I confirm.

He's still crying a bit, but it's under control now and, armed with a length of tissue, I take him back to his room. I pull back the duvet and obediently he climbs into bed.

'You'll be all right now,' I tell him, wanting just to get back to bed myself now. I'm about to leave him when at last he speaks.

'I want my mum,' he says, and the crying starts up again, even harder.

I sit down on the bed beside him.

'I want my mum!' he wails again, and his little body is jerking up and down on a torrent of tears. Somewhat rigidly I put my arm around his shoulders; instantly he yields and turns his face into my body. Shocked, I hold him. His arm comes up and clings to my neck; soon he is on my lap. With one hand I stroke his hair, with the other I hold him to me. Gently I rock him.

'Sshh,' I say, 'sshh,' as I stroke his hair.

He cries into my breast and I hold him. I hold him until he cries himself to sleep, this poor, poor little boy. I rest my face against his head and I am crying, too. I hold him long after he is asleep, then I tuck him into his bed and kiss him goodnight.

*

James is up early in the morning, and out, before the children are up. He is completely unaware that we have had Nathan to stay.

Now that we are taking him home and therefore it is certain that he is not a permanent fixture, Thomas finds it in his power to be a little nicer to Nathan. He especially can't wait to see the big black car with no wheels.

'Look, there it is!' squeals Arianne, frantically pointing as we pull up outside numbers One and Two Fairview Lane.

'Wow!' Thomas gasps in total awe, and tries desperately to whistle through his lips.

'Wait,' I say as I let them out of the car. 'Nathan lives next door.' But they line up in a row, all three of them, staring at that hideous old banger as if it was a spaceship down from the sky.

They are still there when the door of number One opens, and Ian Partridge comes out and walks down the path.

Would I have known it was him, if I hadn't seen him here, now? I don't know. He's tall and wide and carries his weight with a confident swagger. His black hair is thinning at the front and brushed back, and he's dressed in aged jeans that do up tight below his belly and a check shirt. He thinks he's gorgeous. I can tell that just by the way he moves.

'Laura,' he says. 'Good to see you again.'

He puts his hands on my shoulders and makes the bold move of kissing me on the cheek. I hang between his hands like a wooden doll. I do not know if he's learned a few cosmopolitan manners since he grew up or if he's just taking advantage.

'You're looking good, Laura,' he says as if his opinion should matter to me, and his smile is just as leery as it ever was. Then he calls over to Nathan, 'All right, mate?'

Nathan looks at him and grins; it is the first time I've seen him smile. I've the feeling he would run over to his uncle, but he's enjoying the success of being with the others, looking at that car.

To me, Ian says, 'Those yours? Kids are great, aren't they? Got three myself, and another one on the way. They're hard work, but worth it.'

I agree wholeheartedly and watch the children, which is infinitely better than making eye contact with Ian Partridge.

'It's hard for Mum, looking after Nathan on her own,' he says. 'Wish I could do more. He's a great kid. Needs his family, though.'

'He needs his mother,' I can't help saying.

I sense, rather than see, Ian shrug his shoulders beside me, but I hear him sigh clearly enough. 'It's a sad old business with poor Heddy. Can't see an end to it, somehow. And you're right, the boy does need his mother.' He clicks together his teeth, then sighs again. 'But it's Mum I worry about most. She's not as young as she used to be and it's too much for her, looking after Nathan and going back and forth to the hospital every day. Took her back over this morning, I did. Worn out, she is, worn out.'

'And what about Heddy?' I ask. 'How's she?'

'Oh, she's all right,' he says. 'Well, as all right as she can be, stuck in that place. Drugged up.' He pauses. 'She cut her arms with a Coke ring. Didn't do too much damage. It's the fallout that's worse, you know. The upset.'

'I can't understand why she'd want to make things worse,' I say.

'That's the trouble,' Ian says. 'She doesn't see it like that. She's caught in a vicious circle. Can't see how to get out.'

'Well, she's not going to get out if she keeps cutting herself,' I say, perhaps a little sharply.

When I leave he gives me his business card. *Ian Partridge*, it says, *Painter and decorator. No job too small.*

'You can call this number any time. Always got my mobile on.'

I put the card in my bag, quite sure I'll never need it.

He leans against the car door as I get in, then stays standing there right by the kerb so that I feel obliged to open the window as I start up the engine.

'Thanks, Laura, for all your help,' he says, bending down and sticking his face in the open window, uncomfortably close. 'Be in touch.' Then he pats the roof of the car in farewell, much as I'm sure he'd like to pat my bottom, given the chance.

As I drive away, with Thomas and Arianne giggling in the back, I think of poor Nathan crying in the dark for his mother, and I feel an anger towards Heddy Partridge far greater than anything I ever felt in the past.

TWELVE

Later that same day Tasha, Liz, Penny and I are sitting on Tasha's new wrought-iron chairs on her newly laid patio. This patio is bigger than most people's gardens; it is semi-circular in design and staggered in three tiers, each tier being wider than the last, with the widest one opening out onto the huge lawn. From here we can observe and contemplate the vast expanse of grass bordered in the distance by an eclectic assortment of interwoven and overlapping hedgerow; honeysuckle, hydrangeas, you name it and it's out there, all strung together like loosely and fulsomely braided hair. The lawn is interspersed here and there with trees: apple and pear, and something else we can't quite make up our minds over.

It is a fine day, and in and out and around these trees our children play like wingless fairies. Distractedly, we watch them. We are busy with the dilemma of Tasha's proposed swimming pool. She has the plans, laid out on the table, and lifting slightly in the gentle breeze. She'd called us all up in a panic, and round we all came. The thing is, should the pool be at the end of the garden as planned, or would it be better situated on a raised area to the left and midway down, thus breaking things up a little, without intruding on the space?

'It could be a real feature, then. You know, with steps leading up to it and maybe decking around the edges.'

'You are lucky,' Penny says, 'to have a garden like this, so close to London.'

'Mmm,' Tasha hums, in that tone that only the truly fortunate dare adopt – that tone that lets you think that, to them, it's all something and nothing. 'It'll be a pain to maintain, though,' she says, meaning either the pool or the garden, or both.

We all nod and sympathize, making it quite clear that we're not jealous – no, not at all.

'That's the trouble with big gardens. And big houses, too,' says Liz, who's still living in the house that she and Tim bought when they first got married, now with three kids and one bathroom between them. 'They're a lot of work.'

'I just wouldn't have the time,' agrees Penny a little too eagerly.

'I was thinking of getting some sort of marquee,' Tasha says, 'for our house-warming party. What do you think? And I'll need a couple of decent-sized patio heaters. Some of those really big industrial-sized ones.'

'You know, they're really bad for the environment,' I say, and it comes out too sharply, not because I'm a perfect saint about such things, but because I'm feeling prickly. It's been creeping up on me all afternoon, all through this fawning session. Penny and Liz look at me aghast. Tasha looks out across the beautiful garden towards her beautiful daughter with a slightly hurt expression on her face.

'Well, they are,' I say, in defence.

'Rupert and I actually take a lot of care to offset our carbon emissions,' Tasha says a little huffily, still without meeting my eye.

'Of course you do,' Penny jumps in, then she says to me, 'And anyway, it's only *once*, for heaven's sake.'

'Yes, Laura,' Liz says, so they're all rounding on me now. 'It's not like she's going to be using them *all year*.'

And who am I to dare criticize Tasha? I stick a sweet smile on my face and back-pedal fast. 'Of course not. Now and again can't hurt. And anyway we don't want to freeze, do we?' I laugh, remembering too well how it felt to be in exile, and knowing how easily I could end up there again. 'Didn't Fiona Littlewood have one of those at her garden party last year? I'll ask her where she got it from, if you like. I'm seeing her on Saturday.'

They all look at me curiously now, Tasha included. They know that I can't stand Fiona Littlewood.

'Dinner,' I say, flatly. 'The Littlewoods, with Juliet and Andy. Our turn.'

'Poor you,' Penny says, and the others murmur sympathetically.

You know how it is, you get into these rounds and rounds of dinner parties and the whole thing becomes like a roulette game: who did you have last time, who the time before, who have you been to, and who with whom? And then when you've sorted out the right guests so that you don't offend anyone, and fixed a date when everyone's free, you have to get the food.

I loathe cooking, the hours spent ploughing through recipe books, then trawling round Sainsbury's in search of obscure ingredients upon which your whole ensemble depends. I hate it, whenever; but more than anything I hate it when I'm cooking for Fiona Littlewood.

The girls know this, and they understand why. Not for Fiona Littlewood some impromptu pasta dish washed down with copious amounts of Sauvignon. Oh no. Fiona Littlewood is the benchmark of domestic perfection by which we all measure ourselves. Fiona Littlewood is the perfect cook. Dinner at Fiona's is an invitation to be received with honour and returned with dread. She is the sort of woman who can stuff a live lobster as if it were a pepper. There is a section in her wardrobe devoted to pinnies, in a variety of fabrics and colours, to go with every outfit, including evening wear, and I have never, ever seen her get one dirty. Even afternoon tea with the children at Fiona's house is a full-blown Aga affair with pinwheel sandwiches (home-made bread of course), scones and three-foot-high cakes, effortlessly produced. Never did a fish finger cross the lips of a junior Littlewood.

'That woman is a marvel,' Tasha drawls. 'Do you know, she did the catering for the Christmas fair almost entirely single-handedly. Six hundred mince pies.'

'Sickening,' Liz says. 'I don't know how she has the time. And with all those children, too. What's the latest one called?'

'Minka,' I say.

'Minka!' Liz screeches. 'Oh, for God's sake!'

'So what are you cooking?' Penny asks.

'I'm not,' I reply. 'I'm having it catered.' My voice drops like a stone into water. They stare at me, wide-eyed, as the ripples roll out. 'Well, I haven't even got time to go shopping. I'm going to my parents' tomorrow and I won't be back till Friday.'

Penny's mouth has dropped open. Tasha's perfectly pale face is looking a little flushed. There is something dangerous in the brightness of Liz's eyes. I observe them, strangely detached.

'Who's doing it?' asks Liz, and there's a slight disapproval in her voice. Mostly I think it's just jealousy that she didn't think of doing it, or wouldn't dare, but there is also the slight sense that you're not a real woman unless you do your own hostessing.

'Nicola Blakely,' I say. 'Lives on Barlow Road. You've probably never heard of her. I hadn't till I looked her up.'

'I *have* heard of her!' Liz exclaims, and Tasha and Penny are both leaning towards me now, nodding their heads in frantic agreement.

'She had a child that went to Carole's for a while – don't you remember?'

'Weird child, wasn't it? Funny eyes.'

'Weird mother.'

'Fiona can't stand her. Didn't they both do the same cookery course once?'

'It was college, wasn't it? Weren't they at college together?'

'Don't you remember them at the nursery Christmas party, bitching about each other's vol-au-vents?'

I don't, but I can't think anyway. Can't think of anything but Nathan, seated on my lap in the dark and crying for his mother.

'Oh, this is so hilarious!' Penny squeals. 'You mustn't tell Fiona. She has to think you did it all.'

'I can just see it now. *This chicken supreme is wonderful*,' Liz mocks. '*You must give me the recipe.* Oh, Laura you mustn't tell her.'

'I won't,' I say and my voice is so cold it would freeze lesser beings. Not these women, though; they are too knocked out by the joke to notice the chill. 'The food will arrive half an hour beforehand. Back door, of course. And the plates will be collected in the morning. No one will know.'

They are staring at me like schoolgirls, hiding their thrill behind their hands. Yes, Tasha's hand is actually up there, against her mouth, perfect nails coyly displayed. You'd think I was doing this for their entertainment. You'd think I'd found the cure for ageing, or for the boredom of married sex; for something important, you know, in our little world. I look at their faces and I see that I have. I see my kudos rising up and shooting through the metaphorical roof.

'Oh, this is brilliant,' Tasha says through her fingers. 'Fiona *mustn't* know.'

'Just imagine,' Penny says, 'if Fiona Littlewood thinks there's a better cook in Ashton than her!'

'How will she cope?' laughs Liz, and so they go on, thrilled with my wit and daring.

I find myself looking away. I cannot be bothered to laugh, or not to laugh. There is a commodity much like cement settling itself in the space between my stomach and my heart. I watch the children play and I think how they run around on Tasha's huge lawn as if they owned the world. I try to picture Nathan running around with them, in and out of those trees, and I can't. I can only picture him seated on my lap, crying.

There was a boy at infant school called Michael Napps. We called him Nappy-pants.

He was a small boy, with rather a large head and lots of thick, curly hair that sprang upwards in gravity-defying rolls, making his head seem even bigger. His mum made him wear white socks, like a girl, and elasticated-waist shorts that he pulled up too high, so that they came almost up to his chest. And he talked to himself; we'd seen him.

Sometimes, when we were bored, we'd look out for him. We'd spy him wandering around the playground on his own, muttering to himself and making strange noises, and we'd creep up behind him and shadow him. He seemed to imagine he was driving some kind of car, and when he realized we were following him, he'd make weird little peep-peep noises out of the corner of his mouth, shunt up an invisible gear and try to run away.

And we'd run after him, chasing him into the trees that ran along the far side of the playground.

He'd try to hide behind a tree, but we'd find him.

'Nappy-pants! Nappy-pants!' we'd taunt, rounding on him. His trying to hide worked to our advantage, for it meant that the dinner ladies couldn't see him if they looked over from the playground; they could only see us, a bunch of sweet little girls playing nicely by the trees.

He was like a scared animal when trapped. Once caught, he didn't even try to escape. He'd just stand there pinned against the tree, quivering, and staring at us with watery-bright eyes.

'Nappy-pants!' we'd hiss at him, putting our faces up close to his. 'Nappy-pants!'

If we did this for long enough – and that was the aim, of course, to do it for long enough – he'd start to fart, out of nerves, I suppose. We'd have our faces up close to his and suddenly we'd notice it, the stink, coming up.

'Urgh!' we'd shriek, wrinkling our noses in horror. 'How *disgusting*! Nappy has pooped in his pants again!'

This was just a little something we did for a change now and again, when we got tired of picking on Heddy.

What fun there is to be had when you are young, and fortunately perfect. It seemed to me back then that some people are born to be picked on, and others to do the picking.

*

Thomas, Arianne and I arrive at my parents' house just a little bit late for lunch on Tuesday, with what I hope will be enough clothes stuffed haphazardly into the back of the car. I didn't have time to pack properly; I'm sure it will be noted. My parents live all the way out past Exeter, way further from Ashton than the couple of hours or so that my mum likes to think it. I'm sure that when they moved she envisioned all our holidays and weekends spent hacking down for visits, but in fact this is only the second time I've been. Somehow that's all I can manage, however much they mind and expected it to be otherwise. They want me to go down for a full week in the summer, with the children, and I've said I will because I can hardly say no. And I want to, of course I do. As my mother tells me, it's good for the children.

The children, the children.

They are tired and fractious and hungry when we finally get there. Thomas is feeling sick and Arianne has wet herself because there was absolutely nowhere to stop for the loo for the last hour. Hardly the arrival my parents were expecting. They are standing by the road looking out for us. So are one or two of the neighbours.

'You're late,' my mother says through her china smile as we stagger out of the car. 'I've had lunch waiting for over an hour.'

And lunch has to wait even longer while I sort out the children, who don't want to eat at all, by which time my mother is almost as stressed as I am.

'I expect they had too many sweets in the car,' she says as the children pick at their food.

'They didn't have any,' I say.

'You used to get travel-sick. You'd grown out of it, mind

you, by the time you were Thomas's age. It's in the mind, mostly.'

Thomas glares at her, and then at me. 'It's a long journey,' I say, as nicely as I can.

My mother crumbles a bit of dried-up bread between her agitated fingers. 'Isn't Arianne toilet-trained by now?' she says, and poor little Arianne, who is mortified, starts to cry.

But still.

They've a whole schedule lined up for us. They've gone to a lot of trouble. There's no time to be aimless, or bored, or introspective. Walks, picnics, trips to the beach, where every move the children make, every nuance in their behaviour and every phase in their development – forwards or backwards – is observed. It's all *Do you think it's a good idea for Arianne to be sucking her thumb? Have you noticed any improvement in her coordination yet? Do the ballet lessons help?* And *You really should encourage Thomas to learn a musical instrument, Laura. It will help him to focus. He does have a bit of a temper, doesn't he, dear?*

It's exhausting, but only what I expected.

Then Arianne lets it out, about Nathan.

We're walking across the field behind the village, coming back from feeding the ducks. My mum and Arianne are up ahead, with Thomas bounding alongside, and my dad and I, somewhat quietly, bringing up the rear.

My mum and Arianne stop and turn, and wait for us to catch up, and when we do my mother says, 'Arianne tells me you've had a little boy to stay because his mother is ill.' There's something slightly accusatory about the tone of her voice, as if she's offended that I hadn't already told her such news myself. Arianne seems to notice this too and she's looking at me a little guiltily, a little confused. But it is typical of my mother to take one of the children aside in this way and quiz them for information. 'She tells me that the little boy lives in Forbury, Laura. Is the mother anyone I know?'

I wonder if she knows. She *can't* know. She can't have put two and two together that quickly.

But who else do we all know who still lives in Forbury? Lie, and I'll be digging myself a hole, I know it.

So I say, 'It's Heddy actually.'

I carry on walking, looking at the view, looking at Thomas with his stick, looking anywhere rather than at my parents, who are both staring at me now.

'Oh?' asks my mum.

I shrug. I say as little as possible. Just, 'Mrs Partridge phoned and needed help. She had to go and see Heddy in hospital, so I looked after Nathan. Heddy's son.'

I hope that will be enough, but it isn't, of course. They want to know everything, and though I tell them as little as I possibly can, it's still as if the Partridges are right there with us. Heddy and me, lumped together again like in the old days, so that once again I can be judged and found failing.

'You will do what you can for them, Laura?' my dad asks and there it is, that same old warning in his voice.

'Of course I will,' I say a little hotly. I don't *want* my father speaking to me like that. I am thirty-six years old for heaven's sake.

But he just says, 'Good,' and nods his head. 'Good.' And somehow this really, really annoys me. I feel like I am being reminded of my manners.

My mother, she says, 'I'm glad that you are being so mature about this, Laura, and putting your past differences with Heddy aside.' And this is big of her. We don't talk about awkward things in our family. And Heddy Partridge is one of the awkward things in our family. Another is what I did to my wrist when I was fifteen, of course. We don't talk about that, either.

We leave early on Friday. I say I want to beat the traffic and we're on the road before eight. I try not to look too hasty, but really it is just such a relief and those four hours stuck in the car back to Ashton are probably the most stress-free that I have had, and will have, for quite some time. Even the children don't complain.

I use the journey to do some thinking. And that evening, as soon as the children are fed, and bathed, and tucked up in their beds, I phone Mrs Partridge.

The phone rings for a long time before she eventually answers, with a very anxious-sounding hello. I suppose she must dread the phone ringing, always afraid it might be the hospital, phoning up with more tales of woe about Heddy.

'It's Laura,' I say, and then I have to wait as she clears her throat. It's a horrible sound. I can hear voices shouting in the background, the screeching of brakes, and a car blasting its horn. I realize it must be the television.

'Just a minute, dear,' she says when she's finished coughing, and there's a clunk as she rests the phone down. For a second or two I hear the TV so clearly I can make out the words, then there is a short scraping sound and the voices become muffled, but don't fade altogether. She must have the phone in the hall. I didn't notice it when I was there, but I recognize that scraping noise as the sound of the living-room door catching over the carpet as it is pushed to. I picture her in that hall, having come out stiff from watching the TV. I picture the hall itself with the bit of plastic on the floor to protect what's left of the carpet, the overloaded coat rack and the narrow stairs that disappear up into the dark. I picture it as it seemed to me as a child, every time I had to go in there to wait for Heddy, and I feel the same mixture of revulsion and dread tightening in my stomach.

If anything, this sharpens my resolve.

'Sorry, dear,' she says when she picks up the phone again and, stating the obvious, she adds, 'Got the telly on a bit loud. It's Nathan. He likes to watch the car chases.'

'How is he?' I ask, and she replies as if I was some distant stranger to him, which I don't think I am, now that I've looked after him, and held him on my lap, and comforted his tears.

'Oh, fine, fine. He's growing up fast,' she says, which strikes me as the most ridiculous thing to reply.

'And Heddy?' I ask. 'How's she?'

Mrs Partridge launches into a weary account of Heddy's troubled week. I hear about the tears and the pills and the toing and the froing and the doctors who are always too busy and the endless, endless gloom. To me it is all starting to sound more than a little monotonous. The whole miserable situation will go on forever if I don't do something to break it.

I butt in with my plan.

'I thought I might go and see her,' I say, interrupting Mrs Partridge, who is complaining that Heddy got roast beef for her dinner yesterday and that's no good at all, because you can't mash up roast beef and Heddy can't chew, not in her state of mind.

'Tomorrow,' I say, loudly, because I really don't want to hear about Heddy's inability to chew. Of course she can chew. She's got teeth. She's not helpless. I ignore the memory that is pushing up in my head of Heddy's vast body, inert in that hospital bed, obliterated way out of functioning normality by drugs, and pain. I am on a mission. I won't be diverted.

'I thought I'd go and see her tomorrow. Because it's a Saturday. And you can't.' I want this to come out right. I want her to believe that I am helping. I *am* helping. 'I thought if I went to see her, sometimes, on my own, on the days that you can't, I might be able to talk to her.' I pause for a second. There is silence, apart from the faint and distant murmur of the Partridges' TV. So I carry on. I've got to do this. I can't not, now that Heddy Partridge has been pushed into my life, overgrown and unwanted. I've got to push her back out again. 'I thought it might help,' I say. 'What do you think?'

The silence lingers for a moment, and I am willing Mrs Partridge to agree. Thank God she does. Her voice comes thin, and suddenly tired. 'That would be nice, dear. Very nice. Poor Heddy would like that very much,' she says, and I realize that this is what she wanted all along. Exactly what she wanted.

She thinks that I want to do whatever I can to get Heddy out of hospital. And she's right. I do.

I'll do whatever I can to get Heddy Partridge out of hospital, and out of my life for good.

I wish I hadn't thrown those clothes away.

I wish I hadn't thrown them away because now I'll need to find another outfit to sacrifice to hospital visiting, and this time I'll wear it and wear it and wear it, until I am absolutely sure that I will never, ever need to wear it again.

I pick out another pair of black trousers. There are so many black trousers in my wardrobe that really I don't suppose I'll miss them. And I pick out two tops, a white wrapover blouse (nice, but the collar sticks out a little further than I'd like) and a printed long-sleeved T-shirt (pretty, but very last-year). I'll alternate these tops. After all, there won't be many times that I'll be needing them, surely?

Fatalistically, I decide on the same shoes. I've never liked them, since I replaced them the first time. They remind me of Heddy too much. Every time I look at them I can practically hear them squeaking on the hospital floor.

I tell James I'm getting my hair done.

I tell him this with some irony, because he never notices when I've had my hair done. In fact he is so grateful for the hint to tell me I look nice when I get back that he doesn't even complain at being left with the children, even though Chelsea are playing on TV.

It only takes me forty minutes to get to St Anne's, taking the direct roads instead of following Mrs Partridge's out-of-the-way bus route, but parking is harder than last time. Saturday is obviously prime visiting time, and the hospital grounds are crowded with cars queuing for spaces, and with couples huddling under umbrellas and families with children weaving their way through the traffic, trying not to get themselves run over. I end up parking in a side road, a few minutes from the hospital. I think how this would please Mrs Partridge, as it means I don't have to pay.

It's raining, but I don't have a jacket as I did not want to have to sacrifice one for this cause, and mules are not the best shoes to be dodging puddles in. I make a dash for it under my umbrella, getting somewhat wet-toed in the process, but I don't care. I can afford a little discomfort. It'll be worth it, to get Heddy off my back.

I stop to buy some flowers at the stall just outside the main entrance. They're typical hospital flowers, going limp already and wrapped in damp, crumpled paper. I tip them upside down to shake off the rain. Heddy won't notice them, but they'll make me look like a better visitor.

Walking along the corridors I feel confident, and decisive, in a very glacial, one-dimensional sort of way. In fact I feel the way I always felt when I was about to tell Heddy what to do. *Go away*, I'd say, and she'd go. *Get lost*, and she'd stare at me with those hurt dumb-dog eyes, but off she'd shuffle. This is not so very different. *Pull yourself together*, I'll say, and she will, because I told her to. *Pull yourself together, and disappear*. I haven't thought up exactly what I'm going to say, but that doesn't matter. I don't need to pretty up my words for Heddy Partridge. I'll tell her what to do, and she'll do it.

The nurse who lets me into the ward is small, Irish and very young. She seems pleased that Heddy has a visitor.

'We're schoolfriends,' I tell her, giving her my most winning smile.

I follow her to Heddy's room. She has the brisk, optimistic walk of the newly qualified. I wonder what it must be like for her, dealing with people like Heddy all day. I suppose some people are just naturally kind.

The door to Heddy's room is open today and the nurse walks straight in, and over to the bed where Heddy is half-sitting and leaning to one side, face turned away from us. I stop just inside the doorway, holding the flowers in front of me like a shield and trying not to flinch at the smell of Heddy's unwashed body. She smells of milk, left out in the sun, and gone off.

'You've a friend come to see you, Helen,' the nurse says brightly, plumping up the pillows behind Heddy and gently shifting her round so that she's facing straight ahead. She's very strong for such a small woman. 'Not doing too badly today, are we, Helen?' she says. 'Not bad at all.' When she's finished straightening up Heddy, she smiles at me and puts her hand out for the flowers. 'I'll put these in a vase out in the corridor,' she says. 'That's where we keep our flowers.' Then she mouths, 'Health and safety, you see,' in case I hadn't realized, which, of course, I hadn't.

When we are alone, I put myself right in front of Heddy, so she can see me. And she can see me all right. She looks at me with dull, red-rimmed eyes.

'Hello, Heddy,' I say, and I hold her gaze. She knows who I am, I'm sure of it. It occurs to me that I can say whatever I like. There's no one else here to listen. And Heddy won't tell. She never did. It's the school loos all over again.

'Your mum wants me to help get you out of here, but I can't do that. The only person who can do that is you. You've got to help yourself. You've got to stop cutting yourself up.'

There. I've said it. It's pretty straightforward really. I break away from her gaze and look around the room, at the bleakness, at the walls painted a washed-out hospital blue, at the window, closed to fresh air and half slatted out by the metallic blind, cranked up wonky on one side. I can hear Heddy breathing, in and out, slowly, heavy in the chest. Suddenly I feel this horrendous depression, bearing down. This is my payback, but for what am I paying? For my meanness to Heddy, or for what I did to myself, all those years ago, for what I did to my arm? The walls were this colour then, I remember, at Redbridge A & E. I remember opening my eyes from my play-death and staring at the wall beside me, at paint the colour of old bras gone blue in the wash. And I remember the sound of that nurse's voice, the high, tinny pitch, the vowels dragged wide as a Saturday night.

'You're all right, love, we'll soon patch you up. But what d'you go and do that for, eh? What d'you want to go and do a silly thing like that for?'

I shudder and bring myself back, and focus again on Heddy, just lolling there in her vastness, staring at me. I want to slap her, for doing this to me.

I stare at her and she stares back with those dark, nightmare eyes. What does she see, what does she feel, and why do I even *care*? Like a wall coming down, I revert to type. 'It's not very nice here, is it?' I say and I hear myself, prissy, bitching up. Her eyes are so blank I want to hurt her all over again. 'I can't think why you'd rather be stuck in here than at home with your son. But maybe you prefer it. It's a weird choice, Heddy, but it is your choice. Every time you go cutting yourself again you're *choosing* to be here instead of with your son.'

There is a bad, bad feeling, like power, creeping up inside me. I'd be lying if I said it was a new feeling. It's an old feeling, like coming home, like knowing who I am.

Oh yes, this is me all right, bitch that I am, that ever I was. My feet slide into the shoes and I find they fit, easy as ever.

'But tell me, Heddy, what kind of a person does that make you?' I say. 'I mean, what kind of a person would *choose* to be stuck in here like you are, instead of being at home, being a decent mother to her only son?' I pause and if there's a little voice in my head telling me that I may be oversimplifying things just a little, I bat it away. From where I'm standing, things *need* to be simple.

'He sat on my lap,' I say. Heddy's eyes are black, limpet-wet. 'He sat on my lap and I held him while he cried. Your son, Heddy. The other night, when he stayed at my house because your mother was stuck here with you. He sat on my lap, Heddy, crying for you.'

Do I see a flicker in those eyes? Do I?

I talk at her, on and on. I talk like I will talk until I have rammed it home. Like I will talk week after week, for as long as it takes for her to get the message, for her to wake up and pull herself together, if not for herself, then for the child out there that needs her.

That that child's been with me, I'll use.

That that child will be with me further still, I'll use.

And I'll see Heddy screwed up with that knowledge until it has her fighting herself and out of here.

THIRTEEN

Now here we are, seated around my glass-topped dining table, the Littlewoods, Juliet and Andy Borrel, and James and me. There's a big mirror on the wall in my dining room and in it I can see us all, and I think what an advert we women are for André's with our uniformly blonde hair. I bet you couldn't tell us apart from the back. Suddenly I wonder if at André's the stylists only do one style. Probably they do. Probably among themselves they call it 'the housewife', and slap it on us if we want it or not. I mean, how would we *know* if we wanted it or not? It's just what happens. It's what we are.

'Glass is so lovely,' Juliet said as soon as we sat down. 'Oh, I'd love a glass table. But don't you find it impractical with the children? I mean, how do you keep it clean?'

'I make them eat on the floor,' I said, and Juliet laughed uncertainly, and wiped her fingers back and forth across the glass, leaving behind a nice little smear.

They gobbled up Nicola Blakely's monkfish in a citrus crust with honey-glazed vegetables.

Fiona was most impressed. 'This is wonderful, Laura,' she declared, more than a little surprised. 'You must give me the recipe.'

Even James said, 'Mmm, this really is good, Laura.' Somehow he managed not to notice the knock on the back door at seven o'clock, and the lack of chaos in the kitchen.

And now we're talking about schools. I keep trying to steer us off the subject, but as soon as I think I'm getting somewhere, Juliet has us reined in and back again. It's driving me senseless. I mean, what would we talk about if we didn't have children at the same school? Would we even be here, like this? Would we know each other? Would we even *want* to know each other?

There must be something else. But with Juliet it's all: the kids, the kids, the kids – in which category she includes her husband. Once I asked her what she was doing at the weekend and she breezed back with, 'God, we've got so much on. Two parties on Saturday and another on Sunday.' And I was thinking *Lucky you* and feeling a little miffed about all these parties going on and me not being invited – when I realized she was talking about children's parties. She was just doing the chauffeuring. That was it. That was her weekend. And the thing is, she was happy with that.

Now she's going on about the fund-raising committee for the simulated rainforest in the sensory garden at school, and that gets Fiona's husband joining in with his oh-so-slightly-superior but hey-I'm-down-with-the-mums inside knowledge on the subject. He's a governor. Well, he would be. And Fiona of course practically *is* the PTA.

They refer to the headmaster by his first name. I can't do that. It makes me cringe. But they're in the know, you see. First-name terms with the lord of it all. It's a status thing. Clocking up points. It's all about catchment areas and who's in and who's out, and who ought to be in and who ought to be out. Elbows to the fore, folks, it's all shove, shove,

shove around here. It's years until any of our children will be going to secondary, but the battle started at birth. Let's face it, the options around here are private if you can afford it, Catholic if you can't. And if you can't manage either of those, it's all-out war, charging your kid through music lessons to try to get them into Elmsmead. And if you can't even get into Elmsmead, you'll have your personal PR campaign working overtime trying to convince everyone else that you really *wanted* little Freddy to be getting down and under with the locals at Watts Lane High.

Juliet and Andy can't afford private, and they're not Catholics. Mention secondary-school options to Juliet and she gets these weird contortions in the muscles of her neck. Peter Littlewood mentions it now.

'So where will you be sending your two when the time comes?' He says it to Andy, but Juliet answers.

'We haven't even *thought* about it yet,' she lies, with a laugh.

'*Really?*' Fiona and her husband say at the same time, both of them overdoing the horror, and you know damn well that there were tutors, music lessons and school-fees plans lined up for each of their gifted little darlings the minute they were conceived.

'Well, anyway,' Juliet says, stiff-jawed as her neck tightens up, 'we're thinking of moving.' Which is of course the other option with regard to catchment areas, and gets us on to property. And how much it costs. And the right time to move. And blah, blah, blah.

I catch James looking at me with the faintest hint of a smirk on his face. He's enjoying all this. Normally I would be too, in a way. In that I've-got-to-sneak-out-to-the-kitchen-and-down-myself-a-gin-before-I-kill-myself-laughing kind of way. But tonight I can't find it funny. I mean, why do we do this? Why do we sit through such mind-numbing hell just so that we can laugh about it later?

It isn't funny. It isn't a game. This is our lives.

They start talking about the old people's home in Chestnut Drive. It's up for sale, apparently, as the old people can't afford to live there any more. There's a rumour going round that it's going to be knocked down and replaced by afford-able housing, for key-workers: teachers and nurses and other much-needed types.

'We need our key-workers, of course we do,' Fiona gushes. After all, she can hardly purport to say otherwise. 'But the thing is, how can we be sure that the people the flats are meant for won't sell on? And then who will we have living there?'

A shudder works its way around my table.

'It'll totally change the face of Ashton,' announces Peter Littlewood with finality.

'It comes down to parking in the end,' Andy says, and Juliet nods vigorously in agreement, although we all know it isn't really about parking at all. That's just a cover. It's really about the wrong sort of people, parking the wrong sort of cars. 'Sixteen flats, let's say two cars each. That's thirty-two parking spaces needed.' Andy pauses while we absorb the brilliance of his maths. 'It's hard enough already trying to park around here.'

'Tell me about it,' agrees Peter, who owns two cars himself, the BMW that he drives to work in and the little Mazda that he likes to run around in at weekends. This is, of course, in addition to the people-carrier that his wife ferries the chil-dren about in. 'Sometimes I can't even park outside my own house. The last thing we need around here is more cars.'

I drink my wine. I know I've had too much. Something pops inside my head.

'It's already been decided, hadn't you heard?' some mischief makes me say as I dole out the dessert into glass dishes. 'It's going to be used as a refuge for asylum seekers.'

The silence lasts for just seconds, but it is glorious.

Then, 'Good God,' gasps Andy Borrel, and turns an alarming shade of mauve.

'That is the final straw,' states Peter Littlewood, and flings down his napkin with a flourish.

The wives are staring at me, horrified. My husband is staring at me as if he wonders who on earth I am.

'Well, they have to put them somewhere,' I say sweetly, as I pass around the cream. 'So why not here, in Ashton?'

Fiona Littlewood, who is spooning one of Nicola's excellent profiteroles into her mouth, appears to accidentally swallow it whole and starts to choke. It soon becomes necessary for her husband to smack her on the back, which unfortunately causes her to slurp a little chocolate sauce down the front of her blouse, which even more unfortunately is made of silk chiffon. Instantly Juliet launches into a stream of advice on how to remove stains from delicates, and leans across the table to dab, dab, dab at Fiona's breast with her napkin.

All around me faces are purple, faces are white. My husband is watching me with narrowed eyes.

'Coffee, anyone?' I ask.

'What's with the asylum seekers?' James asks, later, as I am stacking the plates and bowls for collection in the morning.

'Just a little joke,' I say lightly, and I try a little laugh, but it comes out all wrong, like the brittle snapping of bones.

James is standing behind me. I can feel him watching me as I put bowls on top of small plates, small plates on top of large. I wonder if he will notice that they are not our plates and bowls. He doesn't. I wonder if he is going to ask me what's wrong, but he doesn't. What I'd like is for him to put his arms around me and hold me, but he doesn't do that, either.

He just stands there behind me as I create a perfect pyramid out of Nicola Blakely's white china. I find myself unable to turn around. I put the last bowl into place slowly, in order to prolong the task. I wish he would touch me, I wish he would laugh, say something funny – anything – to break the isolation that is wrapping itself around me like a shroud.

Finally he moves. I hear him take a glass down from the cupboard. Still with my hands and all my concentration on the balance of that last bowl, I hear him pick up the whisky bottle, unscrew the cap and pour.

There is a silence while he drinks. I wait for the tap as he puts the glass back down on the side, but it doesn't come. Instead I hear him opening the kitchen door.

'You're in a strange mood tonight,' he says, and he leaves me alone.

I stare out of the kitchen window at the blackness outside and I am flooded with many, many unwanted feelings.

I still have one finger on that last bowl, keeping it balanced in place. Both the bowl and myself are perfectly still, but there is a veritable cocktail of emotions racing through my body.

James has gone up to bed; I heard his foot on the stairs, then the landing, followed by the quiet opening and shutting of doors. Now the house is silent, and here I am, attached by one finger to my china pyramid.

I cannot think what made me stack the plates and bowls so high, and I have the sudden urge to give that top bowl a little wobble. I twitch my finger; nothing much happens. I twitch it a tiny bit harder and the bowls creak in protest. I watch, fascinated, as six bowls, six small plates, six dinner plates and three serving dishes begin a slow gyration underneath my finger, leading from the top down. I hold my breath as they sway precariously and then resettle in a dangerous imitation of their former alignment. My heart is pounding, anticipation, excitement blocking out everything else. My whole self homes in on the thrill.

There is a voice in my head saying *What if? What if?* It is a voice I remember well.

I hold my finger still. All of me is so still I can barely breathe. There is just my heart, jumping.

Dare you, the voice says.

I crook my finger, then push it out.

The bowls slide from their tower like divers, synchronized, and smash onto the floor. I count them down. One, two, three, four ... They explode into petals at my feet, hitting the tiles and dancing out to a fanfare of exhilarating sound. Each crash hits my ears like a whip.

Bowls five and six rock, hesitate, and stay where they are.

After the noise comes the silence, clean as ice. I am standing in a sea of confetti. I expect to hear my husband come charging down the stairs, but I hear nothing. He must be whiskied away, sound asleep. There is just me, and what I have done.

It's like a blood-letting.

Now I move, and the broken china crunches under my shoes. I think of Thomas and Arianne coming down here in the morning, and the guilt floods in. I think of their bare feet, pink and soft and vulnerable. I know I must clear up every last broken piece. I take the dustpan and brush from the cupboard under the sink and feel the sharp slivers catching and splintering under my feet as I move. I sweep and I sweep, cleaning away my shame. When I have finished sweeping, I go down on my knees and feel into the corners with my hands. The floor is cold under my skin as I spread my hands across the tiles, seeking out every last tiny shard. And I gather them all up, picking them up with my forefinger and my thumb.

I think I am done, when I find a small dagger of a piece, hidden under the dishwasher. I pick it up, and suddenly I wonder how it would feel, now, to cut its sharpest point across my skin. I am wearing a black lace shirt – I never go sleeveless if I can avoid it – and I bend my left elbow and tip up my hand so that the sleeve falls back. The skin on my inner arm is pale and the scars even paler, a cobweb of ghostly lines. I could trace over them, and draw them all back in. I prick a line in my skin and my fingers curl up in defence. I scratch it down and feel it sting. A tiny drop of blood creeps out and beads there; I tilt my arm and it runs, a mere trickle, over my skin. I watch it, mesmerized. My breath is in my throat, caught; needles prickle inside my chest, and flashing behind my eyes, one right after the other, are all the things, all the awful, wicked things, that I ever did to Heddy Partridge.

And stuck in my head there's this phrase: *What goes around comes around. What goes around comes around.* A stupid old cliché, going round and round, on autoplay.

Where did it come from, this need to hurt? And where does it ever end? It lies too deep, too buried.

The cut is thin and sore and mean. There is no thrill. There is no escape. Already the blood is drying. I lick my finger, smear it over the red, wetting it up again, rubbing it away. My life crowds in on me and I am filled with shame.

I throw my dagger in the bin along with the rest of the swept-up, broken china. In the morning I'll pay Nicola Blakely for the broken bowls. I'll tell her that I dropped them, clearing up.

I'll tell James the same, and that I cut my arm in the process, if he asks. But he won't. Why should he? We are pinned to our lives, blind. He cannot see. I cannot let him see.

At first I sleep the thick, black sleep of too much wine, but then I wake up suddenly, with a jolt. I thought I heard someone crying. I lie still, listening, but all I can hear is my heart, and James's heavy breathing.

My eyes feel bruised and prickly. I squeeze them tight, wishing myself asleep again, but my mind is racing, and there is a thin worm of anxiety crawling over the bumps in my spine.

I slip out of bed and cross the landing on leaden legs to my children's rooms, at the front of the house. I look in on Thomas first. He is sleeping upside down with his feet on the pillow and his head and most of his body hidden down under the duvet. It used to scare me, him sleeping like this. Several times in a night I would turn him up the right way, only to have him wriggle back round again. Now I drop a kiss onto the sole of his left foot and watch his toes twitch in response.

Then I creep into Arianne's room. She's curled up on her side, thumb just fallen away from her mouth and her beanie doll tucked up in the crook of her arm. She is an angel with her white-gold curls and her pink rosebud mouth cupped around the ghost of her thumb. The curve of her cheek is so beautiful and so perfect that it makes me ache. Gently I bend and kiss her, and breathe in her warm honey scent. Her skin is like velvet under my lips.

Sometimes my love for my children feels so huge and all-consuming that I want them back inside me, unborn. Surely every mother must feel like that? Surely even Heddy Partridge, slashing up her arms and condemning herself and her son to this prolonged and painful separation, must feel like this?

And sometimes my fears for my children are too fast and too wild, spreading out roots like trees, too far, too tangled. How much are they really mine? My Arianne, so sweet, so eager to please. Blemish-free, waiting to be soiled. Could I ever have been like that, even just a little? And Thomas with his temper, quick in fists and kicks. *You need to watch that temper*, my mother will say to me, if ever she sees him shout, or throw a toy, or stomp off in a huff. Like she should know.

I had no temper. I kept it in, until the anger slithered out of me anyway, poisonous and slow.

FOURTEEN

André is a terrible gossip.

He's like the village notice board. We all come into his salon with our little bits of information, and he gathers it all together, and passes it on. He is central to our lives and he knows it; he is hairdresser, flatterer, adviser and Ashton's own jungle telegraph. All communication passes through André.

Naturally we use this to our advantage. If there is something you want known, you tell it to André. As you can imagine, there are times when this is very useful. For instance, Tasha told André how much Rupert got for his bonus last year, so now we all know how rich they are without Tasha having had to tell us herself and risk boasting. And we know that Samantha Brook's husband bought her diamond earrings *and* a necklace for her birthday. And if someone's having a party, André will know who's going, and who isn't.

Today he is commiserating with me over the hassle of finding a decent cleaner. Penny had told him I was looking for one, and now he has a whole list of recommendations from his other ladies. He's even written down their phone numbers for me. André is far more useful than any agency – and a million times better than the one who sent me

Delores, this morning, who arrived nearly half an hour late and with one arm in a sling.

'You're very late,' I said when I let her in.

'Is okay,' she said, and shrugged.

'And how will you clean with one arm?'

'Is okay,' she said again, though it very clearly wasn't. But any cleaner is better than no cleaner, and I had my appointment at André's to get to, so I left her to it. But I have to find someone else. Someone permanent. Soon.

'Oh, you have to be so careful, don't you, though?' André sympathizes as he lifts up a section of my hair and wraps it up in tin foil. 'One of my ladies had a cleaner once who robbed them of *thousands*, went through the drawers, found the husband's bank details, and wham, cleared him out before doing a runner. And another had her house burgled by her cleaner's son. He'd had her keys copied. She kept little labels on the keys, saying which one was for which house, you know? He took everything. All her jewellery, everything. Never got any of it back.' He shakes his head at me in the mirror. 'Sitting ducks,' he says.

I listen to these horror stories with dread, and find myself a little anxious to get back and check on Delores.

'Oh, and you'll never believe this,' André says with sudden mischief. In one hand he has a length of foil, in the other he's holding up several strands of my hair, which he waggles now in excitement. I have no choice but to waggle my head along with his hand, attached as we are by my hair. 'One of my ladies came home early one day and found her husband, and her cleaning lady, *in bed*.'

I round my eyes, waiting for André to tell me who this particularly unfortunate lady is, as I'm sure he will if prompted. But he suddenly changes tack entirely.

'Oh, I know what I meant to say to you. A friend of yours was in yesterday ... who was it now? The one with the awful children.'

'Juliet?' I suggest and feel instantly ashamed. Eloise and Jemima aren't really awful. They're gifted.

'Yes, that's it,' André says as he starts painting on the bleach. 'She had some shocking news. Said they're turning the old people's home in Chestnut Drive into a refuge for asylum seekers. She brought a petition in. I've got it up behind the desk. You can sign it on your way out.'

The next day I'm meeting Tasha and Penny for lunch. I walk into Chico's at one and they're there already, sitting side by side, coffee cups on the table in front of them. They must have arranged to meet up early, to talk without me first. I try not to feel annoyed. I try not to feel pushed out, but Tasha's busy talking on her phone and doesn't even look up at me, and Penny just gestures impatiently for me to stay quiet, then turns back to Tasha and listens in on her conversation with this ridiculous proprietorial look on her face. So I sit down and listen in too.

'I know, I know,' Tasha keeps saying. 'I know ... I don't know *what* we're going to do. It's just *awful* ... '

Penny tilts her head towards me and stage-whispers, 'Tasha's had some *bad news*.'

My stomach does a little half-turn. It must be something to do with the baby. 'When I think what might happen ... ' Tasha says into her phone, and her voice wobbles and she starts blinking back tears. Penny's hand shoots out and squeezes Tasha's arm, and I wonder if I could have shot my own hand across the table any quicker and beaten her to it.

'I know, I know,' Tasha says. 'I'll try, thank you ... ' Then she puts her phone back in her bag, and sighs and dabs at her eyes.

I sit there, and prepare myself to say the right thing.

'Poor Tasha,' Penny says, still with her hand on Tasha's arm. 'You okay?'

Tasha manages a small, brave nod and looks at me at last. 'Hi, Laura,' she says sadly.

'Tasha, what *is* it?' I say.

But before Tasha can answer, Penny leans across the table at me and says, 'You won't believe this. You know the old people's home opposite Tasha and Rupert's new house? You know it was up for sale?'

I nod, and keep my face carefully blank.

'Well, it *has* been sold, and now it's going to be used as a refuge for asylum seekers!' She sits back, breathing hard. 'Isn't that just awful?'

'It's just *awful*,' Tasha echoes beside her, looking pale and frail and beautiful.

'Oh,' I say. And I'm thinking *Oh shit!* Part of me wants to laugh, but then I somehow miss the moment. They're both looking at me with matching expressions of tragedy and outrage. And they're waiting for me to say something more than just *Oh*. 'Well, is that all?' I say. 'I thought you were going to tell me something awful.'

Penny tuts and blinks her eyes dismissively, and Tasha says, 'It *is* awful. We spent a fortune on our house, and now it'll be worthless with a load of asylum seekers living opposite.'

'Yes,' Penny says. 'I mean, how would you feel if it was in your road, Laura? You'd never be able to sell your house. You'd never be able to let your children outside your front door without worrying about asylum seekers crawling around all over the place!'

I ought to tell them I made it up. I ought to laugh and say *Hey, girls, it was a joke. I only said it to wind up the Littlewoods and the Borrels. You should have seen their faces!* And then we'd laugh and laugh.

Only I don't think they would laugh. Their faces look much like those other faces all puffed up and boggle-eyed around my dining table.

'It might not be that bad,' I say, somewhat lamely.

'Of course it'll be that bad!' Penny snaps.

And Tasha says in this slow, quiet voice that's designed to really drive things home, 'Laura, do you have any *idea* how much we paid for our house?'

I can feel my face getting hot. When Tasha speaks like that it makes me want to slap her, friend or no friend. Suddenly I don't want to tell them it was a joke. I want to let them sweat it out for a whole lot longer. I force myself to smile sympathetically. 'Why don't we order some lunch?' I say, but Tasha closes her eyes in disgust.

'I couldn't eat a thing,' she says.

'Me neither,' bleats Penny.

And so I have to sit there just nursing a coffee until it's time to escape and collect Arianne. And I listen to them, and the things that they're saying, and I find myself wondering *What kind of friends do I have?*

The answer that comes back to me is cold and unwelcome. The friends that I have are the friends that I deserve.

Even James is not amused.

'I ran into Rupert Searle on the train,' he tells me over supper a couple of nights later. 'He's not a happy man.'

I raise my eyebrows over my wine glass and say nothing.

'He told me it had come to his attention that the property opposite them is to be used to house asylum seekers,' James says.

'So what did you say?'

James shrugs one shoulder. 'I said, "Oh dear, that's tough."' He pauses to spear an artichoke and stick it in his mouth. 'Apparently he's thinking of enlisting a lawyer.'

'It was only a joke,' I say, but James isn't laughing. He's studying me with this dark, remote look in his eyes, like he's trying to suss me out.

'Rupert Searle doesn't think it's a joke,' he says.

'So why didn't you tell him?'

James takes a long, slow sip of his wine, and puts down his glass. 'I think that's up to you, Laura, don't you?' he says. 'This is your little game, after all.'

When we first bought this house we made love in every room, except Thomas's of course, and Arianne wasn't born then. It took us over a week, including bathrooms. And it was the best sex ever, slamming against sinks, and walls and tiles.

When it came to the turn of the living room we lay on the sofa afterwards, surrounded by all the boxes we'd still to unpack.

'Do you think this is the sort of thing they do here in Ashton?' I asked into his chest.

'I should think most definitely not,' he replied, and I felt so close to him then, as close as I ever could.

It seems like a very long time ago.

FIFTEEN

It's my job to do the class list at school. You know, that precious A4 sheet with all the children's names on, and next to them their parents' names, their addresses and phone numbers. The idea, of course, is that it makes organizing your child's social life so much easier if you have everyone's details all ready to hand. For example, if Thomas says he wants to invite Ben home for tea and I don't happen to know Ben's mother terribly well, I can just look on the list and there she is, name and phone number. So easy.

Only there's a lot more to it than that.

Not everyone is on that list. Oh, all the children are on it, but not all the parents' names, not all the addresses, and not all the phone numbers. Some of the children have just blank spaces next to their names, and the way we see it in our little town is that there is only one reason for that, and that reason is that their families are not the right sort. If they were the right sort, they would have complied, so that everybody else could look at the list and *see* that they were the right sort.

So what you have, by being on this list, is in fact access to an exclusive club. You can see at a glance which children have the right sort of mummies and live at the right sort of addresses, and therefore are the right sort of children for your own child to invite home for tea. For example, if – and this is such an unlikely if – Thomas was to say he wanted to have Brendon Stone home to play, I could take one quick glance at my list and say *Oh, I don't think Brendon is very suitable. Why not have Milo* [oh, the joke of it!] *or Toby instead?*

And if Thomas was to ask me why Brendon Stone wasn't suitable, I could reply in a discreet and evasive tone, *Because he's not on the list.*

And heaven knows what Thomas might make of that. That kids whose parents haven't given their details live in dilapidated, haunted old houses where the parents eat other, nice children (like Thomas) for supper, perhaps. Or maybe that they live in no houses at all. Maybe that those few unfortunate children who are so discriminated against by this useful little scheme just disappear at the end of the school day, as they will eventually disappear from the lives of children like Thomas altogether one day. It's a filtering system. It starts so young.

Today I am updating the list because a new girl has joined Thomas's class, and her parents are obviously familiar with the rules. I have their names (both parents with the same surname – good), their phone numbers (home and mother's mobile – very keen, very good) and their address (also very good). No doubt little Lydia will have lots of nice new friends inviting her home very soon.

I wonder if there are class lists at Nathan's school. I expect there probably are, but I doubt if his details are on one. His name will be one of those with the glaring blank spaces beside it. I think this, and there is a horrible, tight feeling inside my chest as if my heart is being squeezed. And I wonder now what the stories are behind the few unadorned names on Thomas's class list. I mean, what is going on in their parents' lives that touting their precious little darlings to all the other parents in this dog-eat-dog convention isn't top of their to-do list?

I've never given a thought to those other lives before. Before, I've just thought of the importance of being in the right club. Because it has always seemed to me that that is the only safe place to be.

At my junior school we split into two tribes at lunchtime. Packed-lunchers – like me – just went straight into the hall and sat where they liked, but school dinners had to line up with their trays, shuffling along in a queue to get their runny mince and cabbage or whatever doled out, and then try to find somewhere to sit. No one had school dinners if they could help it, except for some of the boys, the kids from the council estate, and Heddy Partridge.

We'd sit with our neat little sandwiches in our neat little lunch boxes and watch Heddy piling up her plate, face flushed, and eager and ashamed. More mashed potato for Heddy Partridge, more custard on that sponge. Then we'd watch her, trying to squeeze her way through the rows of tables to find somewhere to sit, and wherever she sat she was never far away, never too far to hear us snorting and grunting like pigs as she tucked into her scoff. Sometimes we'd make her cry, but she'd still carry on eating, shoving it in through her wobbly lips, tears and snot mixing in with the gravy.

I tripped her up once. I stuck my foot out as she tried to get past our table, and over she went. Right over, sprawling across people's backs, sending shepherd's pie and chocolate pudding flying through the air and splattering everywhere.

There was mashed potato in Ashley's hair; hot chocolate sauce all down Zoe's back. Everyone screamed, pushing back their chairs. Zoe screamed the loudest, and then she started crying and shaking and had to be taken to the medical room to have ice put on her back.

Everyone laughed, of course, when they'd stopped screaming. Everyone except Zoe, and those of us who were friends of Zoe. Those of us who were friends of Zoe were angry and disgusted with Heddy, and remained angry and disgusted for a very long time. How would she like it, we kept asking her, if someone poured boiling hot sauce all down her back?

We had no need of class lists when I was at school. We'd got it all worked out by ourselves.

Belinda is standing in the doorway at Carole's when I drop off Arianne, with a clipboard clamped to her chest. On it, in brightly coloured letters, are the words *End-of-term celebrations*. Oh joy. At school we already have Fiona Littlewood rallying us all over prom parties, and picnics and balloon send-offs – even though it's weeks until the children break up. And now we have Belinda doing the same, here.

'I'll speak to you on your way out, Laura,' she calls after me as I sneak past, trying to ignore her. 'That's what I'm doing. I'm catching everyone on their way out.'

Sure enough, there's no escape, not for me, not for anyone. She's blocking the only exit and there's a queue of women trying to get through.

'Now what can I put you down for?' she demands when it's my turn. 'We're doing a zoo trip on the Monday, helpers needed. Hampton Court with a picnic on Tuesday, again helpers needed. Wednesday Ruby Bassett's mum is doing a cordon-bleu cookery demonstration for the children and the mums – you are coming, aren't you? Thursday we're having our sports day in the park – mums *and* dads needed for that one – and Friday we're having the end-of-term party with a magician, and I'm getting a committee together to arrange a carousel and maybe donkey rides, *though I'll have to keep a bit of an eye on the ticket prices*' – this last said in an exaggerated whisper, just in case there's anyone around who wasn't planning to spend their entire holiday budget on all this fun, fun, fun. 'And we thought we'd do what they're doing at the school and have a balloon send-off, right at the end. All the children can write their names on a little piece of paper, tie it onto the balloon string, and at the count of three they all let go.' She pauses for breath and grins at me. 'I think it's so sweet when they do that, don't you?'

'I think it's awful,' I say and the grin drops right off her face. 'I mean, where do all the balloons go? All that plastic, littering up the countryside, choking the birds. What's it going to be like if every school and nursery up and down the country starts letting balloons go at the end of every year? It'd be an environmental disaster.'

Behind me someone coughs – I'd forgotten I wasn't last in the queue, and of course I'm not the only one who just wants to get out of there.

I watch the colour rise in Belinda's face as she puffs herself up. 'It's not me you should be telling off,' she says huffily. 'That bit wasn't actually my idea. Though I happen to think it is a very good idea, and we shouldn't start bringing politics into matters concerning children.'

I laugh. I can't help myself. She carries on regardless.

'Actually it was your friend Tasha's idea.' Boy, she says it with such smug, self-righteous satisfaction. 'So maybe you should be speaking to her if you have a problem with it. Though I have to say that *Tasha* has been extremely helpful with the preparations, and I have her name down here on my list' – she glances at her clipboard – '*several* times, even though she has enough on her plate at the moment, what with being pregnant *and* having the asylum seekers to deal with—'

'There *are* no asylum seekers.' I say it just to shut her up. She tips her head to one side and looks at me for clarification.

'Excuse me,' she says, 'but I think that you'll find that there are.'

'And I think you'll find that there are not. It was a joke, Belinda. I made it up.' I speak slowly and she stares at me with her mouth hanging open. I can see the metal of her fillings, cluttering up her teeth like a scrapyard. 'There never *were* any asylum seekers, Belinda. But just look at how you all reacted.'

Suddenly the hallway leading out of Carole's house seems very quiet. Whoever it is behind me who was coughing and sighing so impatiently is now silent, clearly hanging on my every word. It seems to me as if the whole world has drawn in its breath right then, and vaguely, in some far-distant corner of my mind, I wonder what it will be like when there is no one left around here for me to offend. Belinda's mouth is still open, and she is blissfully lost for words. That in itself makes it almost worth it. Almost, but not quite.

I spot my moment to escape and take it. 'Sorry, Belinda, I'll be late for yoga. I'll get back to you about your list, okay?' And I scoot past her outraged form and out of there, resisting the temptation to turn round. It feels as if there are a thousand eyes boring into my back.

I go straight home after yoga, and sit on my own, in the quiet. Not for a minute do I underestimate what I've done.

Inside my head there is a self-destruct button, and I have both hands on it, pressing down.

I'm late collecting Arianne, and rush in and rush out, managing to avoid everyone. I arrive latish for Thomas, too; the hordes are coming out of the school gate as I dodge my way in, keeping my head down. I grab Thomas by the hand and escape. Amazingly, no one stops me. No one says a thing.

But it's only a matter of time.

This is the quiet before the storm. And there will be a storm.

The moment James comes in, and shrugs off his jacket and throws down his briefcase and makes his presence generally known, the phone rings.

It's Tasha.

'Laura,' she says in this brittle-bright, icy polite voice, 'I wonder if you might tell me exactly what it is that I have done to offend you so?'

'Nothing, Tasha,' I gush back, equally bright. 'Honestly, it was all just a joke and not aimed at you at all. The Littlewoods—'

'How can it not be aimed at me?' Tasha says and my skin prickles up, all the way into my hair. 'I mean, I am the only one who has recently bought a house right opposite the supposed asylum seekers, am I not? I am the only one whose husband has just spent an absolute fortune on that house.

Tell me, have you any idea how much time Rupert has put into finding the right lawyer to get rid of those supposed asylum seekers? Laura, Rupert is a very busy man!'

'Oh, Tasha, he hasn't. I mean surely—'

'He wanted to speak to you himself. Rupert wanted to come round to your house and knock on your door and speak to you himself, and I had to stop him, Laura. I had to stop him coming round and speaking to you himself.'

She pauses now for a response, and I'm not sure if I'm supposed to be scared at the prospect of Rupert coming round or grateful to her for stopping him. Both probably. Instead I try laughing it off, at which James, who has been loitering and apparently listening in, sighs exaggeratedly and glares at me.

'Really, Tasha, it was all just a joke.' I laugh again, and it sounds a little manic. 'And it got a bit out of hand. You know what people are like around here—'

'Rupert doesn't think it was much of a joke,' Tasha snaps. 'And nor do I. And frankly, Laura, this is not the kind of behaviour I expect from someone who likes to call themselves a friend of mine.'

She slams down the phone. She does; she tells me off like that and slams down the phone. I am left standing there, stunned, and stinging all over. I look at James, and again I try to laugh.

He doesn't laugh back. He just looks at me for a minute with his eyes narrowed, then goes into the kitchen and helps himself to the supper that I have prepared for him, and ignores me.

The phone rings again, almost straight away. I think it will be Tasha calling back, or Penny or Fiona Littlewood, or God knows who else wanting their say, so I let it go to the answer-phone.

It's Mrs Partridge.

'Laura? Is that you, Laura?' she shouts into the hall and I close my eyes. 'It's Violet Partridge calling, dear. I wondered if you'd be visiting Heddy again this Saturday. Only I was wanting to take Nathan into Fayle for a new pair of shoes. His feet have grown, see.' She pauses and I can feel her searching for words. 'I do believe your visits have made a difference to my Heddy. The nurse said so, just the other day.' I hear this and I close my eyes. 'So kind of you to go to the trouble,' Mrs Partridge says. 'So kind.'

There's a long pause before she finally hangs up the phone, as if she's thinking what else she ought to say, or waiting for a reply. In that space, I hear the crackle of the phone as she moves it about, and the faint, background murmur of the TV. I hear her breathing, tired, old, lonely. I hold my own breath lest she should hear me back. Lest she should know that I'm there.

Kind, she says. But I was never kind.

I stand alone in the playground to collect Thomas on Friday. All the other women are huddled together, in a group, as far away from me as they can be. Out of this group Fiona Littlewood extricates herself, and bravely walks over, clip-board in hand.

I smile as if I am pleased to see her, and unaware of my so obvious isolation.

She smiles back, short, tight, just a clenching of the cheek-bones and the eyes.

'I'm organizing the end-of-term celebrations,' she says, as if I didn't know, and her cheekbones tighten further, 'and gathering volunteers. But I won't be asking you, Laura. I think we all know now that you have different priorities to the rest of us.'

And then she walks away again, back to the others, and I am left standing there, grinning like I couldn't care less, which, quite frankly, I couldn't.

It is James's football night. He comes in from work, he winds up the children, and he goes out again. He barely speaks to me, just the coolest of hellos as he passes me on the stairs where I am bent picking up the discarded socks and Lego bricks and other various items scattered there by his children.

I am glad he is going out, and taking his cold shoulder with him. There is nothing I hate more than the feeling of being judged, especially by my own husband.

As soon as I have finished resettling the children, and tidying up, and picking up wet towels from the bathroom floor, I pour myself a glass of wine and slap some bread in the toaster for my supper. And my mother phones.

'How are you?' she asks.

And I lie, 'Fine.'

'And the children? How are they?'

'Fine too, thank you.'

And then we have the usual conversation in which she says too much and I say too little. News from the village, and the advice she has given to various committees on various issues; the advice she gives me now on Arianne's teeth and Thomas's boisterousness (well, he is a boy), et cetera, et cetera. My toast pops up and goes cold.

And then she asks if there is any more news on Heddy Partridge.

'Not really,' I say, somewhat woodenly. The last thing I want to talk about is Heddy Partridge.

'Will you be seeing her again, do you think?'

'I expect so.' I can hear my own voice sounding tight and a little huffy, as if I am a child again, wanting approval.

'That is good,' says my mum, and there we have it: approval given.

'I'm not so sure about that,' I say, just a little sarcastically.

'Of course it's good.' And then she gets to the bit that really matters: 'Your father will be pleased. He sends you his love. He'd come to the phone, only he's in the greenhouse repotting his tomatoes.' And before she goes she adds, 'It used to trouble him greatly, you know, your ... unfriendliness ... to Heddy in the past.'

Oh, I know that all right. I hang up the phone and there is a tightness in my chest. I think of my father too busy with his tomatoes to come and talk to me himself. It is always best for my father to be too busy with something.

There was a disco for us up at the secondary school, a sort of advance welcome. Everyone was going – and not just us, but the new intake coming up from the other two junior schools too. It was the biggest deal – and my dad went and offered Heddy a lift.

Not only that, but he didn't even tell me until we got to the end of our road and turned left, instead of right.

'Where are we going?' I so innocently asked from the back.

And my dad said, 'We're picking up Heddy.'

'We're *what*?'

'We're picking up Heddy,' he said again, calm as anything.

'We can't' – panic had me bolting forward in my seat – 'we're picking up Jane.'

'Well, we're picking Heddy up too.'

I stared at the back of his neck in disbelief. 'But *why*?'

'Because Mrs Partridge doesn't want her walking home alone in the dark.'

'We're not bringing her home too?'

'We are.' He spoke in this infuriating, fake-reasonable voice, but I knew he wasn't reasonable at all. I knew he was sneaky and mean and he'd deliberately not told me before; he'd deliberately given me no warning, no way to duck out.

'Dad, I can't go in with her,' I pleaded, starting to cry.

'Yes, you can,' he said. 'You can all go in together.'

'Dad, I can't.' I was really panicking now. We were mere moments from Heddy's house. 'Dad, I won't!' I leaned forward, grabbed hold of his arm. 'Dad, I won't go in with her!'

'Let go, Laura,' my dad said, and he tried to shake me off, but I hung on, pulling at his sleeve. 'Laura, let go!'

But I wouldn't. I pulled at him and I pushed at him, crying and pleading and begging him not to ruin my life, and my dad snapped.

He spun around so that the car started swerving across the road, and he slapped me once, twice, three times, his hand slamming down on me, on my arms, my legs, whatever bit of me he could reach. His face was scarlet and spit sprayed out of his mouth as he shouted, 'Shut up! Shut up! Shut up!' And down came that hand, down and down as I screamed and tried to coil away from it, and the car zigzagged down the road.

We stopped outside Heddy's house. My dad had both hands on the steering wheel now, and he was staring out the windscreen, breathing heavily. I was curled up on the back seat in a ball with my knees drawn up, and was shaking uncontrollably. It seemed as if we stayed like that for ages, but

Heddy Partridge must have been eagerly looking out from the house for us, because suddenly there she was, opening up the car door and plonking herself in beside me where Jane should have sat, smelling of chips and old fried eggs.

My dad unlocked his hands from the steering wheel, and started up the car. Slowly, I uncurled my legs. I couldn't stop crying; I pressed myself back into the seat and turned my face to the window, trying to sniff quietly. I could feel Heddy staring at me. No one said a word. Then we got to Jane's house, and Jane got into the front seat, and she kept turning around and staring at me too. But still no one said a word; not until we pulled up outside Forbury High School and then my dad actually had the nerve to say, 'I'll pick you up at nine-thirty. Have a nice time.'

Have a nice time, indeed. I didn't even go into the disco. I spent the evening in the toilets, crying my eyes out and watching the bruises coming up on my arms. I don't know what Heddy did all evening, and I really didn't care.

I don't remember my dad ever speaking to me properly again after that, and I certainly haven't ever spoken properly again to him.

SIXTEEN

I force myself to go and see Heddy again on Saturday, and this time I don't make up excuses about hairdresser appointments or anything else, and this time James doesn't even ask.

I try to tell myself that I am doing this so that I can get Heddy and her family back out of my life, so that things will all go back to normal. But it isn't that. Not any more. The normal that I had wrapped up and painted so perfect and so nice is fast unravelling. I don't think it ever really existed.

And I find myself thinking more and more what it must have been like for Heddy. I don't want to think about her, but she creeps into my head anyway, and the guilt is starting to swamp me. It pulls at my limbs; it drags me down.

It's the young Irish nurse on again today, and she lets me in with a smile.

'Oh, hello there,' she says, like we are old friends now. 'You'll find Helen a lot better today. A lot better.' She puts her hand on my arm; her fingers are small and very white, as though they have been scrubbed to death. 'It's a grand job you're doing there,' she tells me so sincerely. 'Your visits have made a massive difference to Helen. Massive. Doctor was

saying so just yesterday.' And then she pats my arm and she's
off again, shoes squeaking down the corridor.

A massive difference, the nurse says, but how could anyone
ever tell when Heddy says nothing, does nothing, just sits
there with her eyes so black and empty? She's propped up
on top of the bed wearing what is either a dress or a nightie,
shapeless over her own shapelessness, a ghastly purple colour
and made of the sort of material that would go up with a
crackle and a bang if you stood too close to a fire. It reminds
me of that old party dress she wore all those years ago.
Someone must think that purple suits her. And I don't know,
maybe it does, but who'd ever look properly at Heddy to
see?

She watches me as I close the door behind me, and carries
on watching me as I pull over the chair and position it
midway between the bed and the door. I sit down, and I am
close to her feet, which are naked and splayed wide on top
of the covers. Her dress comes halfway down her calves,
revealing the mottled and lumpy skin of an old lady, and on
her feet the bunions and sores. Her vulnerability disgusts me;
it is too close, too real.

'Hello, Heddy,' I say, and still she watches me with those
dark, slow eyes. How can I ever know what she sees and what
she doesn't see? What she remembers about me and what she
doesn't? 'I hear that you are much better today,' I say, and I
start on my lecture, going over and over the same stuff: how
she must make the effort, take charge of herself and her life,
and be there to be a proper mother to her son. And on and
on. I hear my own voice, sharp, preaching at her, and I hate
it. *She* must hate it.

My God, how she must hate it.

Again I wonder what I'm doing here. And I think just how desperate Mrs Partridge must have been to ask for help from me, of all people. Half an hour is all I can do – half an hour of breathing in that air that stinks of cabbages and shit, and repeating the same old stuff over and over until my throat is dry; but I would die, and I mean die, rather than drink from the same water jug as Heddy Partridge, however many spare paper cups there are piled up on the side.

Half an hour drags like a very long time. And all that time Heddy watches me. I say, 'Do you want anything? Can I get you a drink or anything?'

She doesn't answer, of course. I look around the room to avoid her gaze, but there isn't much to look at. It's a bright day outside and sunlight is forcing its way through the slats of the blinds, but once inside the room it wastes into greyness. I drift away from Heddy, and start thinking about the mess of my own life; about the school playground come Monday morning and how I must walk into it, and that I am the one nobody wants to talk to now. And I'm thinking *How can it even matter?* It cannot matter. And yet it does, it does. You have your kids and there you are, forced back into the playground whether you like it or not. And then that stupid old saying comes grating back into my head: what goes around comes around. And the irritation, and the monotony, and the whole awfulness of all of this have me snapping, 'Oh, for God's sake, Heddy, do you not think we'd both rather not be here?'

And then Heddy moves her foot. Her right foot. She turns it in an arch so that it is pointing inwards instead of outwards, and then she kicks it back out again. I glance at the foot; I glance up at her face, and panic jolts in my chest. She is staring at me with those same dark eyes, but then she squeezes them shut, screwing up her face. She shakes her head, she opens her eyes again, and they are flooded, inky with seeing.

'Why are you here?' she says, and I am so used to her silence that it throws me completely.

'To help your mum,' I reply, and my heart is starting to pound.

'Why?'

'Because she asked me.'

'But why?' she says again.

I cannot hold her gaze. 'I don't know,' I say, and stand up to leave, but I stand too fast and the blood rushes in my ears. For seconds I have to just stand there, holding on to the back of the chair until the sparks leave my eyes. Then I drag the chair back round to the other side of the room, pushing it up against the wall, and when I look back round at Heddy her eyes are shut again.

I tell myself she is asleep. I want her to be asleep.

She fancied Christopher Chapman. You could see it all over her face. You could see it in the way she followed him around with her big, dopey eyes, and the way she went bright pink if ever he looked at her.

Christopher Chapman and Heddy Partridge? What a joke! Christopher was the most popular boy in the class.

Back then, there was this weird system where we lived that meant we didn't move up to secondary school until we were twelve, coming up thirteen, and in the last year of junior school we were a bad mix of hormones and boredom. We played this game – and really, it was just a game – where we took it in turns to get off with each other, whenever we had the chance. We played it at school, that last summer. At lunchtime we'd go down to the far end of the school field and lie in a row, boys on top, girls underneath, and snog. Not everyone, of course, just the popular ones. In class we'd circulate the list, choosing who would be getting off with whom. That's how you knew if you were popular – someone would put your name on the list. One day, someone wrote Heddy Partridge next to Christopher Chapman. And the list went round and round, and everyone who saw it laughed or gagged or pulled a face like they'd just eaten shit, while poor Heddy just sat there staring at her desk with her face gone scarlet and her fat chin wobbling.

Christopher didn't laugh or gag when he saw it, though. In fact he got really annoyed and snatched the list away, then screwed it up and shoved it into his desk.

That's what gave me my idea.

I set Heddy up. I wrote her these letters, pretending they were from Christopher. I made my writing square-shaped and untidy like his; it was easy enough to do.

Take no notice of anyone else, I wrote. *You're the only one that matters*. And, *When anyone is mean to you, it really hurts me. I care for you deeply*.

Jane and I thought it hilarious. I tucked the notes under Heddy's pencil case at break time, and watched her reading them when we came back in, secretive, with her head bent down and her greasy hair falling forward like a shield. She got this ridiculous soppy-coy look on her face, like she'd got a sweet in her mouth and was trying not to suck it.

'Ah, look,' whispered Jane. 'She'd almost be pretty if she wasn't so ugly.'

Please don't reply, I wrote. *Our feelings must stay secret. I don't want anyone to laugh at us again*.

'Brilliant!' said Claire, and it was brilliant.

Heddy lapped it up. On our way out to assembly she stood

back as Christopher walked past her, and he noticed, and looked at her. And because Heddy Partridge never made eye contact with anyone if she could possibly avoid it, but here she was staring right at him with this big, hungry smile on her stupid face, he looked at her, and looked at her again.

It worked like a dream. Especially as Christopher had stopped playing the snogging game now, since we'd all laughed. She must have thought he was saving himself for her.

I want to see you alone so we can talk properly, I wrote. *Meet me in the graveyard after school. I'll be waiting by the statue of the Virgin Mary.*

'Where's the statue of the Virgin Mary?' Claire asked.

'Don't know,' I said.

'*Is* there one?'

'I don't know that, either.'

Claire clapped her hand over her mouth, eyes wide.

'She won't come,' Jane said, and I have to say, I did wonder if I'd gone too far. None of us were allowed near the grave-yard on the way home – some man had strangled his girl-friend there years ago, and the horror of it still had the whole town freaking out. But I wanted to see just what I could get Heddy Partridge doing for love, and besides, it was the only place I could be sure of us being alone.

Claire and Jane wouldn't come, though.

'No way,' Claire said. 'My mum will kill me if I don't go straight home.'

'You can't go,' Jane said. 'She'll never turn up.'

But I was on a roll now. I knew that Heddy Partridge would turn up, and I wanted to see it. Besides, if I backed out now I'd just look stupid.

Jane did come with me in the end, though she said just for five minutes. We got out of school quickly and ran on ahead. Heddy was always last out, lumbering along behind everyone else. The graveyard was opposite the church on the road out towards the river, about ten minutes from school. It was down its own little lane and you couldn't see it from the road at all. You'd never go there unless you had to – I mean, unless you were being buried or something. It was the creepiest place and went on forever, basically field after field full of dead people, and the graves near the entrance were the oldest, all slipping and sliding into the loamy earth, the tombstones crumbling and the grave beds opening up from the force of the tree roots underneath. *Here lies Eliza Wood*, I read, but it didn't look much like she lay there any more with her grave cracked wide open; you could see right inside, right into the blackness, down into the ground.

'This is scary,' Jane bleated. 'I want to go back.'

I shushed at her to be quiet. Our voices were too loud, too out of place. It was a humid, sultry day, and away from the street there was no sound apart from the birds in the trees and the whisper of overgrown grass against our legs, and the snapping of twigs, underfoot. You wouldn't believe how stuff grew in there: trees, brambles, stinging nettles and grass as tall as our thighs in places, and so much ivy, tangling itself around the gravestones, all thriving on so much human nourishment.

'What would a Virgin Mary look like?' Jane hissed.

'I don't know. Like an angel, I suppose.' We'd gone quite far in, but so far it was all crosses and slabs.

'I don't want to go any further,' Jane said.

'Just a bit,' I said, leading onwards through the bumps and dips in the ground.

'She'll never come.'

'She will.'

And then suddenly there it was, the perfect Virgin Mary. You couldn't miss it; she was standing high on square steps with her head bowed, much taller than all the other gravestones. Heddy wouldn't miss it. Just to make sure, I took off my red school jumper and draped it over the statue's head, so that Heddy would see it and think that it was Christopher's. Then Jane and I hid and we waited – and sure enough, just a few moments later, along Heddy came.

I saw her first and nudged Jane, and we ducked down, peering through the gap between the gravestones so that we could see Heddy, but Heddy couldn't see us. She was tiptoeing along at quite a speed, looking nervously from side to side. Every few steps she stopped and looked behind her, before scampering on again. It didn't take her long to spot the statue with my red jumper dangling off it. And from my hiding place I saw her looking relieved for a second, before confusion and anxiety set in. She crept all the way around that statue twice, as if expecting Christopher to jump out from the other side and say *Boo!* Then she stood turning circles on the spot, looking all around her, clutching and unclutching her hands, and then she went back around the statue the other way. Jane and I were almost bursting with the effort of not laughing. Heddy was making this strange, low murmuring sound, like a hum gone wrong.

'I can smell her fear,' I whispered to Jane.

And Jane whispered back, 'That's not her fear, it's her bum.'

Heddy heard us, or heard something; heard us snorting back the giggles most likely, and glanced our way, but couldn't see us.

'Oh. Oh,' she kept saying, and she started flapping her hands at her sides.

'She's trying to fly,' I whispered and Jane screeched and fell backwards, giving us away.

Heddy watched us as we struggled to stand up, clutching at each other, half-collapsing again with laughter. She had a look on her face of absolute jaw-dropped horror.

'What's the matter, Heddy?' I said. 'Have you seen a ghost?'

'There are lots of ghosts out here,' Jane said. 'Lots and lots.'

'Yes, look!' I gasped and pointed. 'There's one right there. And there, look!'

Heddy turned to look, and so did Jane. Just then a bird or a squirrel caused a rustling in the bushes right beside us, and all three of us jumped. Jane screamed, and Heddy began to make a low groaning noise in her throat.

'Where's Christopher?' she asked, as if she actually thought he might be there.

'I don't know, Heddy,' I said, all quiet and mysterious. 'Is he here somewhere? Is he?' I put my finger to my chin in concentration and looked slowly around, peering through the trees and gravestones, and Heddy peered with me. Then I took a sharp breath and pointed to my red jumper, hanging off the statue. 'His jumper is here,' I whispered. 'And so he must be, too. But where can he be? What do you think, Heddy? Where can Christopher be?'

Heddy shook her head, and kept on looking around with her frightened, pleading eyes. She was clutching her skirt at the sides with both hands, bunching it up, pulling it shorter across her thighs.

'Do you think – do you think something could have happened to him? Something *awful*?'

'Let's go now!' Jane said. 'You're scaring me, too!'

I was scaring myself, but I couldn't stop.

'Do you, Heddy? Do you think something really terrible has happened to Christopher?'

Heddy screwed her skirt up even tighter; her thighs were practically wobbling with fear. And still she was making that groaning sound. I began to creep from side to side in front of her, slowly moving in on her.

'What if he's been murdered? What if he came to meet you and, while he was waiting, he was murdered? That would be your fault then, Heddy, wouldn't it? It would be your fault if he was murdered because of you.'

She was snivelling now. Snot was running out of her nose; she curled her tongue up over her top lip to meet it. She filled me with revulsion: her fat thighs, her snotty nose, her *stupidity* in thinking someone like Christopher would ever be interested in her. And every time I moved, she moved. It was like my birthday party all over again, but Heddy was well and truly trapped this time. She could run off into the depths of the scary graveyard, but she couldn't run past me.

'Do you think that's what's happened, Heddy? Do you think he's been murdered?' I shivered as I said it, and at the same time a bird came batting its way noisily from the leaves of a tree above us.

'Come on, I'm going,' Jane said and started heading for the exit, but I was too wired up now, driven on by all the anger, all the resentment I had ever felt towards Heddy Partridge.

'What were you going to do with him anyway, Heddy? Were you going to snog him? Were you planning on meeting Christopher Chapman and *snogging* him?' I tipped my head back and laughed; the sound of it crackled out, witch-like in the heavy air. 'Did you really think that Christopher would actually want to snog *you*, Heddy Partridge?'

Heddy was panicking now, looking round for an escape, but there was none. She moved to the left, I moved to the left. She moved to the right, I moved to the right. Then suddenly she turned and just *ran*, going I don't know where. And straight away she tripped over an old tree root or something, and fell so hard that when her top half hit the ground, her lower half bounced up again, like in a cartoon, and her skirt flew right up, showing off her big white knickers. And I was laughing so much I was going to wet myself if I wasn't careful.

'Come on!' Jane called from the gate and I called back that I was coming, but not before I saw that the wrist Heddy had landed on was broken, the bone sticking right out, the hand discolouring already.

She tried to pick herself up from the ground, but got no further than her knees. She wasn't even crying, just breathing in short, hard gasps. And then she retched, and threw up all down herself.

And I turned and ran after Jane, and I left Heddy there.

Heddy wasn't in school for the last days of term. Out of sight was out of mind as far as Jane and Claire were concerned; they seemed to forget about the whole thing instantly. They didn't know about Heddy's wrist, of course. No one did. No one would be interested in why Heddy was off school. No one would even notice.

But I expected there to be some kind of comeback.

It wasn't my fault that Heddy had broken her wrist. It wasn't my fault that she ran and tripped. It wasn't my fault that she wanted to go sneaking into the graveyard to meet a boy after school. She should have known better.

None of it was my fault. I went over and over this reasoning in my head and absolved myself from blame.

And then one evening over dinner my mum said, 'I saw Mrs Partridge in the chemist's this afternoon – she was in there getting something for poor Heddy. She told me something shocking. Heddy's been in an accident. Apparently she was chased by some older boys on her way home from school and she tripped over. She's got a broken wrist and a huge gash on her forehead, according to Mrs Partridge. Isn't that awful?' And then she said to me, 'Do you know anything about this, Laura? Did they say anything at school?'

The gash on the head was news to me. I shook my head, unable to speak.

'That's terrible,' my dad said. 'Did they call the police?'

'I asked her that, but she said not. They ought to have done, but you know ... ' My mum shrugged a shoulder, raised an eyebrow, saying so much about the Partridges with so few words.

'I'll go and see them,' my dad said, and I waited in fear to be found out.

And I waited and waited.

Either Heddy lied to her mum because she'd be in trouble for being in the graveyard in the first place, or because she was scared of what I'd do to her if she told the truth. Either way, my dad came back with the same story.

We'd all quit Guides by then and now she stopped going to ballet too – after all, she'd look pretty stupid prancing around with her arm in plaster. And we moved up to secondary school, and that was it: Heddy Partridge was finally out of my life.

And it seemed that I'd got away with it.

And yet, and yet.

I picture myself lying prone and bleeding on her mother's worn old sofa, offering myself up like some badly bodged sacrifice. And I think how she always seemed to be there in the distance, watching as I chiselled out the shape of this not-so-perfect life of mine, and I think of what she saw.

She saw what I really was. She saw what I had done to her all those years, and what that had done to me.

I can't face going straight home, so I drive round and round, catching myself in the endless loop of the one-way system, then I veer off following the signs to the multi-storey car park, and park up, and find my way down to the shopping precinct. And there I wander from shop to shop in search of anonymity; I blend myself in with everyone else, just like any other woman, on any Saturday. But it brings no respite. I cannot lose myself because my self comes with me; we are anchored, chained together, inseparable. Myself and my ghosts. All that I did, all that I am.

So I go back to my car, and again I just drive, slotting myself into the stream of crawling traffic, and I end up taking the route back that I took with Mrs Partridge that first day, following the bus route back to Forbury, through concrete street after concrete street. We are near the airport out here, and today the planes are frequent and low, roaring in and out of my consciousness. The air is sour with kerosene, and I close my window and switch on the air filter, closing myself into my bubble.

I don't know why I am doing this. This is no pleasant trip down memory lane. I drive through the council estate that leads into Barton Village. Living in Ashton, you could almost forget that places like this exist, and yet this is the world just forty-five minutes away. This is life. These are the people I was at school with, and it could be me, too, but for chance and determination.

At least there's the odd field out here, and the hills along-side the reservoir. Forbury seems almost rural, the houses small, the cars even smaller. I drive past the turning of Fairview Lane and turn down the road where we used to live, my mum and dad and me. I drive past our old house; there's a huge builder's skip in the driveway and a half-built exten-sion on the side. All those years I lived here and now it belongs to someone else – it isn't even familiar. My family are scrubbed out, just as we are from the shop in the High Street where my father and my grandfather sold carpets for so many years. I drive up past here and I would never, ever recognize the place. The pizza delivery bikes parked up outside, the skinny, spotty boys clustered around smoking their cig-arettes, talking on their phones. It is so strange, how things can be one thing for so long, and then so suddenly and so quickly they are entirely gone.

Yet the damage lives on and on.

Finally, I drive round past our old junior school, and from there to the little lane going up to the graveyard. Outside the school there are crossing places now, traffic lights and speed bumps, all new. The road bends and narrows into the old part of the village, to where the church is, and opposite that the lane down to the graveyard. I haven't been down here for years, not years and years. My mother wanted me to get married in this church. She thought it appropriate. 'This is where you grew up, after all,' she insisted.

Exactly, I thought. And I picked a registry office as far away from here as possible.

The road is too narrow really for me to stop, but I pull up opposite the lane to the graveyard for just a moment anyway, and park half up on the pavement, with my hazard lights flashing. There's a sign up at the entrance to the alley now, telling you where it leads to, the opening hours of the graveyard, and that no dogs may crap on this land. But other than that it is as creepy as it ever was, going nowhere other than to death.

I sit in the false safety of my car and I just look. Wild horses wouldn't drag me down there, now.

It's late when I get home, and James is in a sulk and the children are whingeing, all because I wasn't there to get tea.

I stand in the doorway of the kitchen and watch James as he slams cupboard doors open and closed, as if hunting for clues, and I feel strangely detached and misplaced. James huffs and he puffs, and he pulls out a packet of spaghetti, and a tin of baked beans, and bangs them down on the counter. Yum, yum, I think, but I resist the urge to take over. Instead I turn to Arianne, who has come grizzling into the kitchen to wrap herself round my legs.

'Thomas is being horrible,' she wines.

'Thomas, don't be horrible,' I say automatically.

Thomas comes into the kitchen too, shoving past me. 'I don't want baked beans,' he says.

'Well, you're getting baked beans,' snaps James. 'As there doesn't appear to be anything else.'

I almost laugh, but Arianne starts to cry, and so does Thomas. I say, 'They are your children too, you know, James.'

'I don't need you to tell me that,' James replies, clattering all the cutlery in the drawer as he searches for the can opener, which he doesn't need because there's a ring pull on the tin.

'There's a ring pull on the tin,' I say, and James turns and glares at me.

'Thank you, Laura,' he says. 'I think you've made your little point.'

'I wasn't aware that I was making a point.'

A thin stain of red rises under the ridges of James's cheek-bones. 'You could have phoned,' he says.

And childishly I say, 'You could have phoned me.'

James stands there with the tin of baked beans in his hand, and he is staring at me as if he really doesn't know me at all. Which, I realize, he doesn't. And he never really will, not if we stay together for another forty years.

When you are born blonde and clever and pretty like me, you have it all. You are Mary at Christmas, year in, year out. Then you're the May Queen in summer. Because you're good at sports as well, you always come at least second in all your chosen races at sports day, and when you start secondary school there's no question that you'll be captain in netball. You've got to be good *and* popular to be captain. And so you have the power of picking the team. And you pick the team like you pick your friends: from the prettiest down. The same way you pick your boyfriends when you're older, the same way that I picked James.

I can picture him now: the first time I met him in the student-union bar, with all his friends fawning around him. Good-looking, popular, clever. It was like looking in a mirror. It was like seeing who I am: the top of the box, no need to dig any deeper.

SEVENTEEN

On Monday, the stripes are back on Milo Littlewood's face.

Arianne and I walk into the playground at half-past three just as the children are spilling out of the double doors, and see that Mrs Hills is holding Thomas back. I mean literally, holding him back. It is taking both her arms and a lot of effort to restrain him. He is furious.

'No, I won't say I'm sorry! I'm not sorry!' he shouts for everyone to hear as he struggles against her, and my heart sinks. I grip Arianne's hand and walk steadily towards them, trying to appear calm.

Fiona Littlewood – who *always* arrives early for pick-up – is standing to the left of the doors, clutching Milo dramatically to her side. Milo is sobbing loudly with his mouth wide open, his cheeks all pink and freshly scratched. Fiona glares at me as I approach, her face tightened up with anger, and my heart starts to thump. As soon as I'm near enough she takes two steps towards me and says, 'Really, Laura, this is *too* much,' in a voice that whips out sharp across the playground. And then she flounces off, still with the wounded Milo clamped to her side.

Thomas starts crying too, now that he's seen me, and the sight of his desperate little face makes my own eyes smart.

'What's the matter with Thomas?' Arianne pipes up beside me, and I hush her, quickly, with a tug of the hand. Mrs Hills loosens her hold on Thomas and straightens herself up. She is hot, and flushed, and clearly not amused.

'Mrs Hamley, I am sorry to have to tell you that there has been *another* incident,' she says, and again I have to listen to her complaining about my son's unacceptable behaviour with regard to name-calling and cheek-scratching and Milo Precious Littlewood.

I do what I have to do. I look shocked. I say, 'Thomas, what on *earth* is this about?' in the most appalled voice I can manage, so that Mrs Hills, and anyone else listening, knows that we certainly don't approve of violence in the Hamley household.

'It's your fault,' Thomas cries and lunges at me, pushing me in the stomach.

'Thomas, for heaven's sake!' I grab hold of him and he falls against me then, and clings on.

'He said you're a twisted fuck-head,' he cries into my skirt. 'And he kept saying it. He said his dad said it, so it must be true.'

I'm looking at Mrs Hills over the top of Milo's head as he says it, and I see the colour drain out of her face. We stare at each other, stunned to hear these words come out of my son's mouth. I stare at her the longer, stunned that they came out of Peter Littlewood's mouth. Part of me wants to laugh at the very idea of Peter Littlewood calling someone a twisted fuck-head, but I can't laugh because that someone is me. I stare at Mrs Hills and I'm blinking and blinking my eyes, but I can't think what to say.

She speaks first. 'Would you like to sit down, Mrs Hamley?' she says in a gentler voice than I've ever heard her use before,

and I guess I must have gone even whiter than she did. I shake my head. I just want to get out of there.

'I think we'd better go home,' I manage to say, to which she agrees, and nods her head a little too keenly. I feel her watching as we make our way out of the playground, we three, with me in the middle trying to hold on to my dignity.

I haven't been called a name like that ever before in my whole life. Not ever.

I'm still reeling, hours later. I'll be reeling for days. When we get home we sit on the sofa together, Thomas, Arianne and I, watching *Scooby-Doo*. I give them fish fingers and ice cream for tea, and see Thomas looking at me wondering why he's getting such treats when he was expecting a telling-off. But I can't find it in me to tell him off. I mean, who am I to criticize his behaviour when it stems from me? The best I can do is say, 'There is no excuse for violence, Thomas.'

And when Thomas complains that he hates Milo Stupid Littlewood, I say, 'I know you do. But can't you just try to be nice?'

Oh, irony of ironies.

All that I am and all that I have done: the past lives on within me like a measured ghost.

'Mummy,' Arianne says, like she's been mulling it over, 'what does fuck mean?'

And when I don't answer she asks Thomas. 'What does fuck mean, Thomas? Thomas, what does fuck mean?'

And Thomas, in his six-year-old wisdom, says, 'It means bum.'

I'm crying when James gets in. He dumps his briefcase in the hall, walks into the kitchen, sees me sitting there at the table and stops. Horribly, I am reminded of those days after Thomas was born, when he'd come home and find me crying. He has that same look on his face, the look that says he wants to turn around again and walk straight back out.

'Now what is it?' he asks with trepidation, as if he really doesn't want to know. And he stands there, and I know damn well that all he wants is his dinner, and to be left alone.

Slowly I say, 'Peter Littlewood has been calling me a twisted fuck-head. I know this because his son told our son at school today. And so I'm feeling a little upset.'

I see him wrestling with himself. I see the fact that he thinks maybe Peter Littlewood has a point cross his face, followed swiftly by outrage, the pumped-up, don't-insult-my-wife-or-you-insult-me obligatory outrage of the husband. And let's face it, I am in James's eyes not so much an extension of himself as an *attachment*, you know, like I'm an ambassador when things are going well, and a parasite when they're not.

What we have is a marriage, after all.

'Well, what do you want me to do?' he asks, throwing it back at me.

I shrug.

'Do you want me to go round there and thump him?'

And he would; he'd go round there and thump him. He would, my fine, handsome husband. He'd go round there and thump Peter, and say *Leave off my wife*, and then come back here and blame me for making a thug out of him.

We have a marriage, but it's a thin and fragile thing.

I look at him and he swims in a sea of tears. 'I don't know what I want,' I cry. 'But I don't want this.'

He almost rolls his eyes. 'What do you mean by *this*, Laura? Do you mean this little mess you've got yourself into,

or do you mean more than that? Do you mean me, *us*? Our children, our home, our *lives*? *What*? I mean, if you don't want *this*, then what is it that you do want, Laura?'

The question hangs in the air. James's voice is too loud; I see it cross his mind just as it crosses mine: *Don't wake the children.*

'I don't *know* ... ' I stare at him and he stares right back, his blue eyes stone-hard. I blink and blink again, breaking the focus. 'It's just living here, the way we live, the way everything that should matter doesn't matter and everything that shouldn't does ... Don't you ever wonder why we do it, James? Don't you ever wonder why we live here like this?'

'Then where would you have us live?' James asks, and he kind of laughs, dismissively, *coldly*, like he hasn't got a clue what I'm on about. 'Would you like me to give up my job and go and become a postman in rural Scotland or something? Would that make you happy?' Again he laughs, shaking his head as if he thinks I am *mad*, and I hate him for it. 'This is life, Laura,' he says. 'This is what I *thought* you wanted. And anyway, what makes you think it would be different anywhere else?'

Once, I nearly told him, about the cuts on my arm.

He asked me about them, and I got this sudden confessional urge – something I'd never had before and I've never had since – something to do with being in love maybe, softening my head, letting my defences down. We'd not been together long, and you know what it's like when you're on that high. You get carried away. You want to find trust.

It was a Sunday afternoon, late, just as the daylight was dipping and fading out. We'd been to the cinema, then gone back to his place, and back to bed. And we were lying there, half-dozing, half-dreaming, cocooned in shadows. He asked me out of the blue, asked me like he'd been wanting to ask me for some time.

'What happened to your arm?' he said, trailing his fingers over my scars. And just for a second I nearly told him. But then this warning voice came bolting through my head: what if he already knows or thinks he knows, and what if he really wants me to tell him otherwise?

So I did. 'I cut it falling through a glass door, years ago,' I said, and it was the right thing to say, because he accepted it, just like that.

I knew I'd never tell him then, but no matter. It was from a different life, gone.

Fuck-head means nutter, everyone knows that.

I lie in the dark, curled away from my husband's sleeping body, and I want to be gone, far, far away.

EIGHTEEN

Round here, I've no choice but to brave it out.

I deliver and collect my children from their daily obliga-
tions as usual, and I shop, and I run, and I go to yoga, with
a smile etched upon my face. And I watch as the little groups
of women in this place huddle and split and re-form again.
Tasha and Fiona are suddenly best friends, though they never
spoke to each other before – they've got something in common
now: me. And so Penny's put out and has to jockey for position, which she does by shoving Liz out, and so Juliet spots
an opportunity and homes in on Liz, and round and round
it goes.

And James comes home with a pissed-off look on his face
and tells me nothing of his day. And he goes off to his football, but when he comes back he creeps in beside me in the
dark, and although I'm awake he no longer shares with me
the pub talk, the secrets of the men in this little town.

I am outside now. I am on the outside of my own life, and
observing from the sidelines as it so easily comes apart.

And then, late on Wednesday morning, just as I am bracing
myself to collect Arianne, Ian Partridge phones.

'Laura,' he barks, 'Ian here,' in that over-familiar way that makes my skin crawl. 'Got something I need to talk to you about. About Mum. I was thinking I could meet you for a drink or something. Hang on a minute . . . ' There's a radio playing in the background, for a moment it blares out even louder, and then a door bangs and the music fades out. He's in a corridor; I can hear his footsteps echoing off the floor, and the crackle of his phone as he carries it, stomping along. In those few seconds I am ready with a definite No.

But then he's back saying, 'Got good news about Heddy. Doctors reckon she'll be coming out soon. And me and Linda, we've been wanting to get Mum moved up here with us, and Heddy and Nathan, but it's not been possible, you know, with Heddy in the hospital. Listen, I'm coming down at the weekend. Thought maybe you and me could meet up then, have a bit of a chat.'

And I am so desperate to find an end to all this that I agree to meeting Ian Partridge in the Red Lion in Forbury High Street, on Friday night.

I have to get a babysitter in, as James is out on Friday too, but I think that is probably just as well. I don't really want him to know where I'm going, and it saves lying.

I wear my jeans, and a plain black top. I'd wear my sunglasses too if I could, and a wig. I haven't been to the Red Lion in Forbury High Street since I was seventeen. I imagine it, still full of the people from school, the girls all mums now with tired faces, the boys all starting to bald. God forbid that I should recognize anyone, or have anyone recognize me, out on a Friday-night date with Ian Partridge.

We arranged to meet at eight, so I arrive at five past and go in the back entrance from the car park.

huddled outside. It's not just the Red Lion I haven't been in for years; I haven't been in *any* pub. The odd bar maybe, but not a *pub*. I walk across the dirty dark-red carpet to the bar, and feel as if everyone is staring at me.

I'd have got my own drink, but there he is, Ian Partridge, propping up the bar with his pint and waiting for me.

'Laura,' he says, loudly, so if there were anyone there from school they'd hear, and maybe look, and maybe put two and two together. 'Good to see you again. What you drinking?'

And I have to stand there like his date while he kisses me on the cheek again, and orders me a Diet Coke. And then we both walk across that dreadful carpet to a little round table next to the fruit machine. Ian sits on the built-in seat that runs along the wall and I have to either sit next to him or perch on the stool opposite. I take the stool, obviously, but have you ever had to sit on one of those stools? It's impossible not to cross your legs and lean forward, showing too much thigh and cleavage. Thank God I'm wearing jeans, so there's one less distraction at least.

Ian takes a big gulp from his beer and licks the foam off his lip. And then he belches, keeping his mouth shut to hold it in, so that his face kind of jerks back into his double chin for a second and his cheeks puff out. When he speaks I get the faint whiff of sulphur off his breath. 'Yeah, Mum says the doctors are pleased with Heddy. She's making good progress.'

'That's excellent news,' I say, though I can't help feeling uneasy. But Heddy's kept my secrets all these years; surely she's not going to go letting them out now? Or maybe she will – maybe that's part of the therapy, the letting go. Shame eats at my conscience, but it's the shame of being found out.

'Yeah,' says Ian. 'And Mum says it's part down to you. She's very grateful to you, Laura.'

'Really, I've done nothing,' I say and the shame bites a little deeper.

'But the thing is, it's too much for Mum, looking after Nathan and Heddy. Me and Linda, we've been trying to get her to move up near us for ages. Mate of mine's got a house just up the road. He bought it for his mum, but she don't need it now; she's gone into a home, poor dear. He don't want much rent and it's just sitting there, waiting for her. Got a lovely little garden, it has, just right for Nathan. Course they couldn't move while Heddy's stuck in the hospital.'

How selfish of Heddy – the thought rises out of old habit and flashes through my mind. And it's followed by another thought, probably equally unreasonable: how come I didn't know about this house before?

'I worry about Mum,' Ian says. 'It would be much easier if we were nearby.' He picks up his glass again and looks at me a little shiftily over the top of it. 'Thing is, Mum gets a bit funny about moving. She's lived in that house for years, ever since she first married my dad. She's got all her memories and that.'

It takes me a moment to realize what he's getting at. I'm too busy thinking that there can't be that many good memories. I mean, watching your husband becoming ill and then dying, and being left to bring your kids up on your own and having one of them wind up the way Heddy has, and basically just scrimping and scraping and struggling all your life. Would that give you memories to cling on to? Probably it would, if you were Mrs Partridge. Probably you'd treasure whatever you had. Your life is your life, after all.

'It would be nice for her to be so close to you and her grandchildren,' I say, and I just feel so incredibly sad suddenly. Sad that anyone should have a life like Mrs Partridge's.

says. 'I don't know what me and Mum and Heddy would do without you.'

For an awful, guilt-hewn moment I think things are going to get embarrassing again, but then he's back talking about how he'll give the house a lick of paint to brighten it up for his mum, and about his kids and how they're looking forward to seeing their nanna every day . . . And I sit there and I listen and I am overwhelmed by just how much Ian Partridge loves his family. His wife and his kids and his mum and his sister and his nephew . . .

I see how much they all love each other, the Partridges.

I see a lot of things now, that I couldn't see before.

And so we go to collect Nathan the next day, Thomas, Arianne and me. The children are just delighted to see that old car again, and wait out the front admiring it; Nathan comes out of the house to join them. And I stand in the doorway of the Partridges' house and force myself to embrace Mrs Partridge's small, tired bones in a quick, fast hug.

'Mrs Partridge, it's fantastic news about Heddy,' I say, and I can't understand why she doesn't seem even just a little bit thrilled. She flutters in my arms like a bewildered bird and I think maybe I've pre-empted things. Maybe Heddy isn't definitely coming out after all.

But then there's Ian, striding up the hallway behind her. 'Thanks, Laura,' he says. 'Going to take Nathan with us when we visit tomorrow, all being well. Looking forward to that, aren't you, Nathan?' he calls out, his voice loud, booming against the narrow walls. 'Going to see Mum tomorrow.'

Nathan, who is crouched down with my children beside that car, looks back at the house, bashful, shy. But Mrs

Partridge says nothing other than, 'Yes, dear, I think so, dear,' and, of course, 'Thank you, dear.'

I whisk Nathan away and bring him back to my house. We have lunch and then go to the park. All is going well enough until the Littlewood children turn up at the park too, complete with their dad, with his put-upon face and his arsed-up attitude, and his phone stuck permanently to his ear.

I hear him coming before I see him. He drones into his phone with his loud, bored voice so that everyone has to hear him. Goosebumps prickle over my shoulders and I want to hide, but where can I hide, here in our bright, sunny park? So instead I act like I am as happy as can be on this most carefree of days, laughing at everything the children say, pushing swings, throwing balls, and absolutely 100 per cent delighting in all that they do.

He has no choice but to acknowledge me. 'Laura,' he says gruffly and stands, uncomfortably, an arm's length away.

And I don't even look at him. I can't bring myself to. 'Peter,' I say, equally curtly, and he has to stand there suffering while his children play with mine. Even I can't stand it for long, though. I round up Thomas, Arianne and Nathan and head for the exit, smiling as I go. And I'm thinking *You'll think twice before you go calling me a fuck-head again.*

James has been out playing golf, but he comes back earlier than I expected. We're just back from the park ourselves, and the children are having drinks and biscuits at the kitchen table when I hear his key in the door.

James has never met Nathan before and knows nothing about him. This should be no big deal – kids come back here to play all the time without James knowing anything about it, and I'm sure he wouldn't even know what half his children's friends look like. But this is different. Nathan is different. He *looks* different, sitting there at the table with my two with their blond hair and their bright eyes.

James strides into the kitchen just as Nathan is stuffing another biscuit into his mouth.

'Daddy!' Arianne cries and then both she and Thomas launch into their tales of our trip to the park and, more unfortunately, our trip preceding this to the house where the funny car is, with its rusted old wheels and the doors hanging off, to pick up Nathan.

James listens, but he's looking at Nathan, curiously. And I can see that James is thinking that Nathan is different. I can see him taking in the paleness and the puffiness of Nathan's face and the sore patches round his mouth as he munches on his biscuit, and the dirt ground into the skin around his nails, even though I had them all wash their hands when they came in. And it annoys me that he should see all this, and judge as he cannot help but judge.

James looks at me, and he raises one eyebrow, just slightly.

And later, when I have returned from taking Nathan home, and the children have been fed and finally settled into bed, James and I face each other over the chasm that is growing between us.

Out of habit, we sit opposite each other and eat the pasta. Out of habit, we drink the wine.

And James takes a big sip from his glass and says, 'Well then?'

Not so long ago that would have been the prompting for a story, and not so long ago I would have obliged. Tonight I say, 'Well, what?'

'Who's the boy?'

Carefully, I say, 'He's my friend's son.'

'Your friend's son?'

'The girl I told you about. The one who's had the break-down. If you remember.'

'I remember,' says James. 'But I didn't realize that she was your *friend*.'

I feel like I am being cross-examined, and I force myself to eat, feeling as if I could choke on it. 'I just want to help her out,' I say.

And James says, 'Oh, I'm well aware of that, Laura. I just hope your guilty conscience isn't clouding your judgement.'

I look at him sharply, half-expecting him to laugh. But I see that he is perfectly serious.

'I have a right to know who our children are hanging around with,' he says. 'And I don't like them playing on wrecked old cars.'

'Oh, for God's sake, they weren't playing on it.'

But James appears to have had enough of sitting and talking with me. He picks up his plate and his glass and decamps to the living room, where he turns on the TV. And so I have the choice of either staying where I am, alone, or joining him on the sofa, still more or less alone. Either way he has made his point. There is no room for my past in our marriage. Of that I am very clear.

NINETEEN

I am nervous as hell when I pick Mrs Partridge up on Tuesday to take her to the hospital. I've booked Arianne in to Carole's for extra hours, just in case. Mrs Partridge's appointment with the doctor, Ian told me, is at half-past eleven, but doctors, of course, can often run late.

Mrs Partridge is ready, as usual, and is grateful, as usual. She sits beside me in the car, buttoned up to the chin in her coat, even though it is a hot, humid day, and clutches her bag upon her lap. I expected her to be happy, and I can't understand why she isn't. She isn't even speaking, much. It's like she's locked into herself, filled with her own fears.

'It's good, isn't it? About Heddy?' I say.

And Mrs Partridge, who is lost in her own thoughts, says, 'What, dear? Oh, yes, dear, very good.'

'When will she be home? Do you know?'

'Soon, dear, the doctor said soon.'

'Well, that's fantastic, isn't it?'

Mrs Partridge sighs. I glance sideways at her. She's staring out of the windscreen in front of her with a deep frown on her face, and chewing on her lip. 'My Heddy,' she says at last, 'she's up and down. Up and down.'

And I see her wanting Heddy home, and not wanting it, as she sinks under the weight of her own life.

'This house,' I say. 'You didn't mention it.' I try not to sound accusatory. After all, what business is it of mine?

Mrs Partridge says nothing, and stupidly I can't help feeling a little hurt. But I carry on, 'It'll be so much better for you, won't it, to be living near Ian? Better for all of you. Easier, for you especially.'

And Mrs Partridge says, 'Of course it will, dear. It would be lovely to see the children growing up.' She says it in the same tone that I imagine she might say she'd like to win the lottery one day, or travel the world. Like it's in the never-never, the dreams that are not for her. And I realize that this is just one more thing for Mrs Partridge to deal with. However good the outcome, she can't see beyond the getting there, beyond the *one more thing*. The future is a luxury Mrs Partridge has never dared to think of; she's too crippled by the struggle of now.

'Mrs Partridge, I'll do whatever I can to help you,' I say and my eyes are suddenly burning with tears.

We've time to see Heddy first, before we see the doctor.

More than anything, I don't want to see Heddy again.

I don't want to see her eyes, looking into mine, and remembering again what I did to her. I don't want her mother to see it.

And yet I walk along that corridor beside Mrs Partridge with my heart pounding out my dread, and I know that this is my punishment. This is the circle, turned all the way and closing up again. I've no choice but to see it to the end.

She's sitting up on the bed, against newly plumped pillows. She looks at us as we come into her room, her mother and me, and what can that be like for her? I force myself to say, 'Hello, Heddy. I hear that you are feeling much better.' And I load my voice with kindness, with brightness, as if I could make her think that I am nice now. As if I could make her forget.

'Say hello to Laura,' Mrs Partridge chides, bustling around Heddy, adjusting her pillows, smoothing her sheets. She shifts Heddy over a little; Heddy's dress is caught up underneath her and I get a glimpse of the fat underside of her leg, white, naked. Like a firework exploding in my head I see her falling head first, the plump flesh of her twelve-year-old thighs exposed and quivering, her pants, tired and old, sticking to the crack of her bum. I see it and I see it.

And I hear myself laughing, gorged up with hysteria, *ha-ha-ha-ha-ha*.

Heddy's hands are on her lap, clasped tight. I can hear her breathing, the heavy, whispering puff. I feel her looking at me, but I cannot meet her eyes.

Mrs Partridge fusses over Heddy. She says, 'Laura brought me in the car today. So kind of her, so much quicker than the bus. We're to see the doctor, in a little while. About your coming home, Heddy. What about that then, eh? What you got to say about that then, Heddy?'

Heddy says nothing, so Mrs Partridge carries on, 'Ever so grateful to Laura, aren't we, Heddy?' She perches herself on the edge of the bed. 'Cat got Heddy's tongue again today, Laura. Funny that. She was quite chatty, at the weekend. I think perhaps she's a bit shy around you, Laura.'

And, coward that I am, I say, 'Listen, I'll go and wait for the doctor. Give you some time on your own.' I force myself to look at Heddy and I see her face, down there in all the grass and the weeds, deadly white, stripped raw with pain, twisted round and staring up at me, terrified.

And in the shadows at the edges of my eyes I see the powder-white chunk of her bone, fresh as a new tooth, forcing its way out through the skin of her arm.

I blink. I swallow. I feel a thin bead of sweat trickle its way down between my shoulder blades, inside my shirt.

'All right, dear,' Mrs Partridge says. And, 'Don't you go minding Heddy now. She'll talk to you when she's ready.' She reaches out and puts her own thin hand on top of Heddy's, and squeezes Heddy's sausage fingers, and then pats them. 'She's much better now, aren't you, Heddy? Much better.'

I make myself speak. I say, 'I'm glad. Really I am. I'm so glad.'

Mrs Partridge doesn't really need me with her to see the doctor. It's a short meeting, a mere tying up of ends so that Heddy may be dispatched upon her way.

We see Dr Millar himself this time; he's older than the other doctor, and relaxed and to the point. In his hands he has a large file with Heddy's name on it. I wonder what is written inside. More to the point, I wonder if I am in there somewhere, and I feel the colour rising in my face.

Dr Millar looks at Mrs Partridge and at me, and he smiles. He bends that file between his two hands like a card pack, about to be dealt. 'We've a final assessment scheduled for Thursday,' he says. 'And social services will have their own report. But I see no problem. Helen has made remarkable progress.'

'Is she ready to come home, though?' I ask, on behalf of Mrs Partridge, who in the presence of authority has once again shrunk into herself.

'Of course she is.' His smile deepens. 'We can't keep Helen here forever. There are other people waiting, who need to be here much more than she does.' I sense Mrs Partridge brist-ling a little at this, but then he says, 'The best place for Helen now is at home, with her family, leading a normal life.'

Normal, he says, but however do you define normal?

'I've plans for Heddy and myself and little Nathan to move up to Birmingham, to be nearer to my son and his family,' Mrs Partridge says suddenly, and the way in which she says it leaves me in no doubt that this plan really has been there for a long time. And that she just chose not to mention it to me.

'I think that's an excellent plan,' Dr Millar says.

We make the journey home in near-silence, Mrs Partridge busy no doubt with her thoughts, and me tortured by mine. I've a splitting headache and the sun is too bright, too intense, driving into my eyes.

When we pull up outside her house I say, 'Do you plan to move soon then, do you think?'

And Mrs Partridge says, 'Oh, I think so, dear. There is no reason for my Heddy to be wanting to stay down here.'

She looks at me and she's going to say something else, but stops before she's begun and instead says, 'You're ever so pale, dear. Are you well?'

'I've got a headache,' I say. 'That's all.'

And Mrs Partridge reaches her bony hand across the gear stick and pats me on the arm. 'Dear, dear, and all this rushing around on our behalf. Come inside and have a cup of tea before you go, dear. Do.'

Her kindness is my undoing. I am so wretched with my own guilt that I follow her into her house, into the dark, creeping stillness, redolent with cigarette smoke and the rancid memory of chip fat. She unbuttons her coat and hangs it on the rack. Already I'm regretting coming in with her, but there is something I have to know. I stand in the doorway of the kitchen, the soles of my shoes sticking tackily to the lino, as she unplugs the kettle and fills it at the sink. The water hisses in the pipes and spurts out from the tap in angry bursts. The morning's breakfast things are stacked on the rack, washed and waiting to be put away, and hanging over the edge of the sink is an old dishcloth the colour of slate.

'Mrs Partridge, I haven't got time for tea,' I say. 'I've got to get back for the children. I'd love a glass of water, though, if you don't mind.'

She hands me a tumbler; on it are engraved the words 'Happy Christmas' and the faint remains of a snowman. 'Sit yourself down, dear. Make yourself comfortable.'

The kitchen table is tiny, and pressed up against the wall. To sit at it, I have to pull a chair out half into the hallway. On the table, next to the ashtray and the salt pot and a pair of folded-up socks, is a pile of papers and letters, some of which are from estate agents. I don't want to pry, but there they are, right in front of me.

Mrs Partridge catches me looking. 'Ian picked those up for me. At the weekend. I'm to read through them all,' she says, 'and choose.'

'I can help if you want,' I say. 'You know what estate agents are like.' Though, of course, she doesn't.

She makes her tea, squeezing out the teabag with her bare fingers and dropping it into the sink. The fridge, when she opens it, smells of old milk, and starts up a rumble. The pain in my head is throbbing harder now, in time with my heartbeat.

Mrs Partridge sits herself down on the other chair, wedged in between the table and the sink. We are very close, crowded in there. Too close. She pats her pockets and finds her cigarettes, and sticks one in her mouth. It hangs there, bobbing from her lip as she fishes again for her matches. She strikes one, lights up and exhales upon a sigh. And I am engulfed in smoke.

'Mrs Partridge,' I blurt out and my head is really pounding now. 'That time Heddy hurt her wrist, when we were still at junior school ... ' A wave of nausea rushes up inside me and I have to swallow it back. 'Do you remember?'

Of course she remembers. She sucks on her cigarette and her face is tense, shadowed with remembering. 'Yes, dear,' she says. 'A terrible business.'

I swallow again and force myself to carry on.

'We'd gone to the graveyard. There was this boy—'

She talks right over me. Loudly she says, 'A gang of boys. My Heddy was chased by a gang of boys. On her way home from school.'

'No, Mrs Partridge, it was—'

'Yes, yes, dear. She was chased and she tripped. On her way home.'

'Mrs Partridge, I—'

'She was chased and she tripped,' she insists. 'That's what happened, isn't it, dear? That's what I told your parents.' She grinds out her cigarette and her face is tight, pinched. 'Always so kind, your parents.' I'm about to speak again, and again she talks over me. 'Did you have to get back for your children, dear?' she says. 'Don't want to rush you, but goodness it's getting late.' And she stands, leaving her tea untouched. 'And my Nathan will be home soon. I need to be thinking about dinner.'

But I cannot leave it like that. 'Mrs Partridge,' I say desperately on my way out of the door. 'I wasn't kind to Heddy.'

'No, dear. Maybe not always, dear,' Mrs Partridge says. 'But your parents were.' And there is something in her voice, something more than just gratitude and denial.

She knows.

She knows what I did to Heddy, and I think she's always known. But who is she trying to protect by denying it? Not me, surely?

Herself, maybe. Maybe she just doesn't want to face it.

Or is she trying to protect my parents? Is she covering up for me to spare them the pain of what I have done? But why would she bother to do that? And why, oh why would she want to have anything to do with me now?

If anyone ever hurt one of my children the way that I hurt Heddy Partridge, I would want to tear that person apart, ripping at their limbs and clawing out their eyes. I wouldn't sit there drinking tea with them. I wouldn't be giving them second chances.

And yet she knows, I'm sure of it.

The shame blossoms inside of me. Every part of me is stained.

TWENTY

Meanwhile, back in my own little world, it comes to my attention that Tasha has sent out the invitations to her house-warming party. I can't help but notice this because, as well as the usual flurry around the forthcoming end-of-term extravaganzas at school and at nursery, there is additional excitement, a *buzz*, if you like, centred on Tasha. Every time I *see* Tasha these days she's got Fiona Littlewood fawning all over her, and giving her the benefit of her advice on everything from canapés to glass hire to godforsaken patio heaters. And Tasha just laps it up. Everywhere I go there are women twittering away like birds, and it's *Tasha this* and *Tasha that*, like they have a little competition going on to see who can say her name the most.

Tasha, our own little celebrity, with her big house and her rich husband, famous around here just for being Tasha. Everyone wants to be Tasha's friend. So, of course, did I.

Even Belinda has an invitation. She tries to collar me at nursery with her schedules and her lists, and there it is, pinned to the front of her clipboard. Like a badge, for all to see. How proud she must be.

Two weeks ago it would have pissed me off no end that

Belinda has an invitation and I don't, but now do I care? Do I?

Of course I do, just a little.

Then Arianne tells me that Phoebe doesn't want to be best friends any more.

'But I don't mind,' she says, her little face all serious. 'I can be best friends with Sophie now instead. She's got red shoes *and* a pet rabbit.'

Arianne, so innocent, so unaware of the ways of our world. I think how I steered her as I steered myself, keeping us up there where I thought it mattered.

'Well, it's good to make new friends,' I say to Arianne now, and I talk to her about choosing them wisely, and for the right reasons. Advice I could have done with myself.

But Thomas is not so easily consoled, and cries at night because he's got no one to play with at lunchtime. 'I want to play football,' he sobs. 'But Milo won't let me.'

'Why is it up to Milo?' I ask.

'He says it's his game.'

'Well, can't you play with some other boys?'

But Thomas says, 'All the boys play football. Except for me.'

And I cannot have that.

So I do what I should have done already. I speak to Mrs Hills.

I say, 'I don't like to make a fuss, but this has been upsetting me for quite some time. This really isn't the sort of school where language like [I mouth it] *fuck-head* is acceptable. I do not expect my child to hear, and repeat, words like that at school. I'm sorry, Mrs Hills, but I really do feel you need to speak to the mother. And really, I think this is a matter for the headmaster, don't you? After all, Mr

Littlewood is a governor and, really, do you think that is the kind of example we expect from a governor of this school?'

Poor Mrs Hills has no choice but to agree, and it fills me with cold satisfaction to arrive early to collect Thomas on the Friday of that week and see Fiona Littlewood summoned in for a word. I would love, so dearly love, to hang around and see her face when she comes out again, but that would be too crass. I have to content myself with imagining it, and imagine it I do.

I write a letter to the headmaster too, explaining my distress at my child being bullied so by the son of a governor, and also that a governor should abuse his position in such a way rather than remaining professional, and impartial, always.

It works like a dream.

Peter Littlewood is no longer a governor. I know this, because a note comes around asking for nominees for a new one.

Soon afterwards, a note comes round looking for a new head of the PTA. Fiona Littlewood has resigned, in defence of her husband. The end-of-term celebrations are in chaos. I see Fiona standing, arms folded, in the playground at pick-up time, with a look on her face like a pinched squirrel. It is not a look that Tasha would enjoy seeing over lunch.

Am I a little over-the-top here, in doing this? Maybe.

Does it make me feel any better? Yes, it does, a little, for a while.

Now everyone wants to know why Fiona Littlewood has resigned from the PTA, and of course she isn't going to tell them. So I carefully let it out that I know. It's amazing, then, how many people suddenly want to talk to me again.

I don't tell them, though. I let them sweat. And I watch as they rush about the playground like hens, fevered up with speculation, busy jostling for position.

Always jostling, jostling.

And then I run into Tasha; she's coming out of nursery with Phoebe, just as I'm going in. And in the second before she hides it, I see something like panic crossing her face. Like what does she do now? Ignore me, drag up the whole asylum-seekers thing again, or try to act like nothing's happened?

She makes a poor attempt at the last.

'Laura, *hi*,' she says, just *so* much friendlier than she's been for a long time. 'Haven't seen you for *ages*.'

'Well, no,' I say, *equally* friendly back. 'I've been very busy actually.'

'Really?' Tasha says. 'What have you been doing?' And it is so obvious that she thinks I can't have been doing *anything* if I haven't been having lunch and coffee with her.

'I've been helping that family, you know, the one with the girl I was at school with. The one who had the mental break-down. You remember, I told you about her?' I say this straight, as if I expect her to remember, though it's quite clear to me that she doesn't. I mean, why should she remember some-thing as unimportant to her own little world as that?

'Oh,' she lies. 'Yes, of course.' And then she starts searching in her handbag, and out comes my invitation to her party, at last. 'I've been meaning to give you this,' she says, presenting it to me like a prize. 'Only I wasn't sure if you'd want to come.'

'Oh, right,' I say. 'Thanks.' And I stick it in my bag and forget all about it.

TWENTY-ONE

They leave in dribs and drabs.

Most of their stuff is for the bin: old sheets and bits of curtain kept just in case, endless odd mixing bowls and baking trays with literally decades of blackened fat crusted into the corner, school books and worn-out shoes and, would you believe it, Heddy's old Brownie dress. There's even an ancient suitcase full of Mr Partridge's old trousers stuffed under Ian's bed and forgotten about. I'm there when Mrs Partridge opens the suitcase up and finds them all; I hear her sharp, indrawn breath and the clatter of her teeth as her chin starts to wobble. And I see her face, raw with shock. She takes those trousers out, and she folds them again, smoothing them down with her brittle hands. And I think if it wasn't for my being there as a misplaced witness, she'd be gathering them up in her arms and burying her face into their smell and crying.

As I am crying, just having to watch.

I try not to let her see, but all of this is *heartbreaking*. Seeing the way Mrs Partridge so carefully sifts through the hoarded-up scraps of her life, I realize that every frayed little bit is precious to her. *Everything* is a memory to Mrs Partridge. All this junk, all this rubbish ... it's her *world*.

I want to help her, but what help am I, coming over with my Sainsbury's boxes and saying you can keep only this much?

Downstairs Heddy sits on the sofa in that hideous blue sack of a dress that is the only thing that fits her, with her hair looking as though it hasn't been washed once in the whole week since she came home, and she watches TV. And when the TV is gone, she watches the space where it was.

And Nathan, when he comes in from school, sits on the floor near his mother and watches her as if he doesn't know quite what to make of her, now he's got her back.

Every now and again Mrs Partridge finds something upstairs that she wants to show Heddy. 'Oh, look at this!' she cries. 'Heddy, it's that old Christmas tree we had before we got the white one, do you remember?' Or 'Look, Heddy, here's that hot-water bottle cover I knitted you because your feet got cold. Oh, look, Heddy, it's still got the hot-water bottle in it, and it's still filled . . . '

Up and down the stairs Mrs Partridge scurries, bringing Heddy this thing to see, and that thing, and leaving stuff on her lap until Heddy is piled up like a jumble-sale table.

And Heddy just sits there, and does nothing to help, and says not a word.

We stack the boxes against the wall in Mrs Partridge's bedroom, until there is barely room for her to get into her bed. She doesn't want them in Heddy's room in case it upsets her, though I don't see why it would, and Nathan sleeps in the boxroom; no room in there for anything anyway, apart from his bed and the few clothes and toys upon the floor.

Mrs Partridge's room is Heddy's old room – they've swapped around. They've swapped beds too, so that Mrs

Partridge lies alone at night in a single bed squashed up against the wall, while Heddy gets the double in the bigger room, the better to take her weight.

I wonder how Heddy feels, having to sleep in her parents' old bed, the bed in which her father lay and coughed and slowly died. And it is the same bed, I'm sure. It has to be. It's so old that with the covers pulled straight, as they are now, I can see how the mattress sags in the middle. And I see how Mrs Partridge sits herself down on the edge of the bed now, hands absently, lovingly smoothing over the blanket at her sides, as she looks around the near-bare room. How many memories can there be for her here in this one room? She sits with her thin shoulders hunched up slightly, and her head tilted to one side. Her eyes are glassy bright, and I look away and concentrate on stuffing Heddy's old clothes into bin bags. Clothes that should be going to the recycling, but Mrs Partridge won't hear of it. Mrs Partridge won't go throwing away perfectly good clothes, no matter that they don't fit anyone any more.

'My Heddy was born in this room,' she says suddenly and her voice wobbles over the words. 'We would have gone to the hospital, but Mr Partridge was out working and we didn't have a phone back then, and by the time I'd gone next door to use theirs, and by the time we'd tracked Mr Partridge down and called the ambulance – well, my Heddy was on her way by then.' She laughs a fragile laugh as she speaks, but she's sniffing too, and digging around inside her sleeve for a bit of tissue, which she rubs across her eyes with a trembling hand. 'Dear, dear,' she says, 'look at me being all silly.' And she stands up, shoving that tissue back up her sleeve and patting her hands briskly against her thighs before getting back to the sorting, the folding, the stuffing into boxes of all this musty, dust-covered *stuff*.

I shouldn't *be* here.

We find Heddy's old school reports. I can't bring myself to look at them for even a second, and stick them in a box before Mrs Partridge sees them. And a photo, of all of us, in our last year of junior school. I know that photo. My parents have a copy of it. I'm there in the front row near the centre, my blonde hair cut shoulder-length and tucked back behind one ear. Is Heddy in it? I guess she must be, somewhere.

My throat is so tight I can barely speak. 'Mrs Partridge, I really am so sorry … '

'Sorry, dear?' Her hands work fast, shaking out and folding, pulling off stray bits of fluff.

'I'm sorry for all the times that I wasn't nice to Heddy.' What feeble words I use. 'When we were children.'

'Your parents have always been very kind to us, Laura, and for that I am very grateful.'

'Yes, but I wasn't kind. They kept forcing Heddy and me together and I was *horrible*.' My heart is pounding. 'Mrs Partridge, why did you never tell them what I did?'

Mrs Partridge's face is very pale, but there are two dark-red dots rising on her cheeks. 'I'm sure your parents only wanted the best for you, Laura,' she says. In her hands she holds a single blue woollen glove, from which she carefully unpicks a loose thread, and snaps it off, fast, between her fingers. 'Just as I wanted the best for my Heddy.'

And did wanting the best for Heddy mean accepting the kindness of my parents, in the hope that it was real? Kindness is never kindness if it comes at such a price.

Why could we not just have kept well away?

For a week, Ian chugs back and forth along the motorway in his van to take away the wardrobe, the boxes, the TV and the various carpets all rolled up like sausages, until the last day, when he makes several trips one after another, until there is nothing left but the sofa with Heddy sitting on it and the kettle and two cups. It is a Thursday; the schools have broken up now, and I am here with my children, to say goodbye. They're out the front, playing on a mattress that's been left for the council. And Ian and Mrs Partridge are outside too, trying to work out if they can squeeze the sofa into the van now or if Ian will have to come back for it, and there's just me and Heddy left inside.

The house smells strange now that there is so little in it. I mean stranger than usual, like it's been flossed out like a set of dirty teeth. And the stains behind the furniture are so stark now they're revealed, like yellow nakedness. Fluff clings along the skirting boards and it seems that you can hear the noise from right down the end of the street, now that the carpets have gone.

Heddy sits there, and I wish I knew what she was thinking.

I sit down beside her on the brown Dralon sofa and I say something stupid like *Isn't it nice to hear the children having fun?* I feel so thin and insignificant next to the bulk that is Heddy, and I feel that anything I have to say will be thin and insignificant too. But I have to say *something*.

'Heddy, I hope you'll be happy now,' I say, but even that has the edge of a threat in it. So I try again. 'I really do wish you and your mum and Nathan every happiness. I really hope it works out well for you all.' I sound so wooden. How can I ever find the words to say what I really mean?

Heddy sits there, looking at her hands in her lap. Her lower lip is sticking out slightly, and there is just the faintest rise of colour in her cheek. I know that Heddy hates being looked at, and here I am, sitting gawping at her, searching for absolution. And of course I've seen her at her worst. I've come along like a voyeur at a freak show and seen her felled by drugs and misery, lolling in the prison of her own body, unable even to wipe the dribble off her own chin.

My God, how she must hate me being here.

Outside a car has pulled up. I hear the metal clunk of the door as it is closed, followed by Mrs Partridge's high-pitched *Oh, hello*, and then a new voice, a man's. The estate agent has arrived and they'll all be coming inside in a moment to talk to me, because it's me that will be dealing with things when the Partridges have gone.

Suddenly, Heddy speaks. 'I always hated living here,' she says. 'It just makes me think of my dad all the time.' Her voice is low, quiet. She's still staring at her hands and I can only just hear her. 'And now you're here, and that makes me think of your dad. Your dad loved you whatever you did. My dad went and died.'

I don't know what to say. Of all the things I thought she might home in on, it certainly wasn't this.

She turns her head to face me, but she can't quite look me in the eye; instead she looks just past me, and it's to the corner of the room, where old Mr Partridge used to sit in his chair. 'However horrible you were, your dad still loved you. That time you fainted in the street and your wrist was bleeding ... your dad picked you up and he carried you in here in his arms. I wished I had a dad to carry me.'

As she speaks I see a thin tear slide its way down the side of her nose. I see this and I feel as if my heart is going to burst in my chest.

'Oh, Heddy ... ' Without even thinking I reach out to

touch her arm, but she almost flinches, and looks down again, at her hands. And another tear plops onto her dress and streaks its way down her chest. 'Heddy, I'm so *sorry* ... '

I can hear the boys laughing out the front, and Arianne shrieking *My turn, my turn!* and Ian Partridge slamming the van doors shut, and Mrs Partridge saying *Are we done, then?* And then they're making their way up the path, Mrs Partridge, the estate agent and Ian.

'For everything, Heddy. I am just so sorry.'

My heart is hammering. I feel like the inside of my face is burning, I am trying so hard not to cry. I put my hand on her arm again and this time she lets me. But then the front door opens and swings back against the wall with a bang, now that there's no carpet for it to stick on, and Mrs Partridge says *Ooh, steady there*, and the estate agent laughs his estate agent's laugh, and the moment is gone.

Mrs Partridge boils the kettle and makes tea in the two remaining cups, and gives one to me and one to the estate agent, like we are guests of honour. And she has bought Mr Kipling cakes, two packets, which she opens and puts on the arm of the sofa, and which the children somehow sniff out and come running in from the garden to scoff.

Despite the fact that we have everything written down, she is starting to panic and fuss now, and she uses the plastic cake packet as an ashtray and stubs her cigarette out right through it, into the arm of the sofa.

'Oh dear, oh dear,' she clucks, and starts licking her thumb and pressing it on the burn.

'Mrs Partridge,' I say, 'please don't worry. Everything will be fine. I'll come in twice a week for the mail and to check the boiler, and if there's any problem Mr Jarvis can call me.'

'I'm sure there won't be any problems,' Mr Jarvis says and he drinks his tea as fast as he politely can, and leaves. He already has a buyer lined up. Some young couple, with not much money, but plenty of enthusiasm – and boy, will they need a lot of that!

And then it is time for me to go, too.

I thank God for the children, then, for their noise and their chaos and their general distraction, because it feels so weird now that this moment has finally come. Any second now I'll be crying. I tell myself it's just the relief that they'll be gone and out of my life at last, but it isn't that, it isn't that at all.

I think it's quite the opposite.

'Goodbye, Heddy,' I say, but she doesn't look up again and really, what did I expect? Forgiveness? How could Heddy Partridge ever forgive me?

Then Mrs Partridge is bustling me out of the door with her endless thank-yous and last-minute instructions for the boiler and the postman, with Ian crowding out the hallway behind us. Outside, the sunlight spears into my eyes and I am blinded for a second. Mrs Partridge grabs me suddenly with her bony fingers digging into my arms, and pulls me against her tiny body in a hug, and it's all I can do not to cry like a child.

'Mrs Partridge, I am so sorry,' I whisper again, into the nicotine and sweat-scented nylon of her housecoat.

And she replies, 'I believe you are, Laura. I believe you are.'

And then Ian snatches me away from her and he hugs me, too. Eventually I stumble into my car, blinking back tears, and in the back the children wind down the windows and they're yelling *Bye, Nathan*, and Nathan and Mrs Partridge and Ian are calling *Bye* back and standing there and waving at us, as I start up the engine and drive away.

'I liked that car best,' Thomas chants in the back.

'I liked those pink cakes,' chants Arianne.

'I liked the yellow cakes,' chants Thomas.

'I liked that mattress,' chants Arianne. 'Mummy, mummy, can we put a mattress in the garden to play on?'

And Thomas says, 'Mummy, when can we go and visit Nathan again?'

We're not even out of Forbury and I have to pull over. I feel as if I can't breathe properly. I tell myself it's just the relief that it's all over. I stop the car at the bus stop before Forbury High Street and try to steady my head.

'Why are we stopping, Mummy?' Arianne asks. And, 'Mummy, why are you crying?'

I just sit there for a second with my eyes shut, trying to get a grip.

'Are you sad because Nathan's moving?' Arianne asks.

And Thomas says, 'Don't worry, Mummy, we can go and see him in his new house.'

As if we ever would.

I feel Thomas's little hand tugging at the back of my hair as he reaches forward to stroke me, and my head is just a boiling mass of tears, but then a bus comes up behind me blasting its horn and I have to pull myself together and move on.

TWENTY-TWO

All the next day I wander about my house, aimlessly, moving from room to room. The place is a mess because I've spent so much time at the Partridges' lately; there's dirty washing spilling out of the basket on the landing, and no food at all in the fridge. And yet I cannot get on with anything.

I feed my children honey sandwiches and sit by as they run in and out of the house still in their pyjamas, trailing mud across the floor and dragging all the pillows and duvets off their beds and into the garden to make a camp. Our duvet ends up out there too, and the new cushions off the sofa, which cost ninety pounds each from Osbourne's.

I feel so disoriented. I tell myself it's just a reaction, to all that has happened. I tell myself this, but my self is not convinced.

I just can't get it out of my head, what Heddy said about her dad, and about *my* dad. I can't stop thinking about *that day*, when my dad did as Heddy said and carried me into her house in his arms and laid me on her sofa. And how she stood there looking at me, and how she was feeling what I now know she was feeling.

And what of my dad, who loved me whatever I did? When I lay on that sofa with my eyes squeezed shut and heard him tell Mrs Partridge and Heddy and Ian that I was okay, *I* thought he sounded disappointed.

Disappointed with *me*, yet again.

And what about me? The only feeling I could register in myself at the time was embarrassment, that I hadn't put on a better performance and made the cut a bit deeper.

Suddenly I remember my first concert at Forbury High, and I remember how nervous I was because I'd got a big part dancing, not just in a group, but on my own too for some of it. My mum helped with the catering because that's what my mum always did; while I was dancing she was organizing cakes onto plates and overseeing the cup quota. She missed the performance entirely, though she took the complements happily enough in the interval. *Oh yes, Laura's very good at her dancing, very good*, she agreed, pouring out the teas.

My dad, though, he was there in the audience, right near the front. I saw him sitting there, and gazing off into the space beside the stage with a frown on his face for the whole time I danced. And so he missed it all, too.

Though you wouldn't know it to hear him afterwards. 'Excellent show,' he agreed with my mother, with the other parents, with anyone else who was listening. 'Laura did very well.'

That's Laura for you, folks – all-singing, all-dancing, always putting on a good show. And there are my parents, doing the same.

When I took my little wrist-slitting show to the Partridges' front room I got my dad's attention then all right. But what good did it do?

I've a hollow inside me, an ache, like an old, old hurt. Like there's a cry inside me, cut off, mid-shout. Hurting myself could never make up for what I did to Heddy Partridge. Each wicked thing that I did sits upon the track of my life like so many twisted knots. They can never be undone.

When James comes home the children are still up, their faces and their pyjamas all sticky with honey and mud. They run in from the garden to greet him, leaving yet more dirty footprints on the living-room floor, and start clamouring for his attention. They haven't spoken to him for days, as all week he's been in too late to see them, and they've lots to tell him, about playing at Nathan's house and all the cakes that they ate and the mattress that was as good as a trampoline. James stands there, braced against the onslaught, trying to keep their grubby hands off his suit. And every now and again he looks at me over the top of their heads with a slightly raised eyebrow and a pained expression, especially when he realizes that the mattress was outside the house, and when he hears about the camp I've let them make in our garden with our own crisp and pristine bedding.

'Well, I think it's time you put your duvets back on your beds now, don't you?' he says.

'There's a snail on Thomas's pillow,' says Arianne.

And, 'Mummy said we could sleep out there,' says Thomas.

James looks at me again, in disbelief.

'Well, I didn't say that they couldn't,' I say. I am curled up on the end of the sofa. I try to raise myself up from my lethargy, and find that I can't.

James carries on looking at me, and his eyes narrow. 'Would our new cushions happen to be out there too?' he asks.

I don't bother to answer. The children are starting to whine now, deflated by James's lack of enthusiasm. 'Right,' he snaps,

'I think it's time for bed.' And with Thomas and Arianne hanging off his sleeves, he marches out to the back garden and marches in again, dragging duvets and pillows and wailing children; and out again, and in again, until all are deposited where they should be, dirt and all. And then he comes back down the stairs, leaving the children crying in their rooms.

Still I cannot stir myself.

James stands before me, with his hands on his hips. He looks hot, and he looks angry, and there is a large yellowish splodge on the front of his lapel. 'Are you doing this just to wind me up?' he asks.

'Why would I do that?' I reply, but he just huffs and rolls his eyes in exasperation.

'I don't suppose there's any supper?' he says and, when I look at him blankly, 'You know I have just come in from a long day at work.'

'I thought we could get a takeaway,' I say, a little lamely.

James is looking at me intently, *critically*, as if trying to suss me out, and I curl my legs up a little closer. Then he says, 'You know, I've some interesting news of my own.'

'Oh, really?'

'Yes, really.' He takes his hands off his hips and folds his arms now, in front of him, barrier up. 'Guess who I bumped into on the train tonight?'

I look up at him. I wait.

'Rupert Searle.'

'Oh.'

'Yes, and guess what he said to me? He said: are we going to their party tomorrow night, as we've not yet replied?'

'Oh,' I say again.

He tilts his head to one side and laughs this bemused *what's-going-on-here?* laugh, which isn't really a laugh at all.

'Laura, do you *realize* how embarrassed I felt? I didn't even know they were having a party.'

'No,' I say. 'I'd forgotten about that.'

He laughs again, in disbelief. 'Since when did you ever forget about a party?'

'Yes, well, I don't want to go.' The TV guide is on the floor next to the sofa; I bend and pick it up. Anything to avoid looking at James. Upstairs both of the children are still crying; one of us will have to go up in a minute.

'Why don't you want to go?' James asks, standing there with his arms crossed, and I shrug.

'I'm just not in the mood to go spending an evening with those people.'

'*Those people* are our friends,' he says, and I snort; I can't help myself.

'I'm not so sure about that.'

James reaches down and snatches the TV guide right out of my hand. When I look up, he starts nodding his head, slowly, as if realization has finally dawned. 'This is about that thing over the asylum seekers,' he says.

'Well, look how they reacted! I mean honestly, James, some people around here don't care about anything except the price of their houses!'

'Laura,' James says, 'do you not think people have a right to be pissed off when you start spreading around rumours like that? Do you not think you'd be pissed off, if one of your friends did that to you? And if Tasha and Rupert have the good grace to invite us to their party after all that, do you not think we ought to have the good grace to accept?'

'Look, I just don't want to go.'

'Well, maybe *I* do. *I* want us to go, and I want us to be nice to these people.' Then, 'Oh, for God's sake! Now what?'

Arianne has come out of her room and down the stairs, and is now standing in the doorway, howling.

'It's okay, Arianne,' I say to her, getting up at last from the sofa. Because people like us, we don't fight in front of the children. That's what we like to think. We simmer and we snipe and we circle each other in resentful isolation, but we don't fight. Oh no.

And so I can't stop myself from saying, 'You know, James, the children were perfectly happy until you came home,' before I take Arianne back upstairs and comfort her, as I have comforted her so often. And then I settle both the children, as I have settled them both so often.

When I come back downstairs James has gone out. He comes back a while later with a takeaway in a polystyrene box that he sits and eats in front of the TV, jabbing angrily at noodles with a plastic fork. He doesn't speak to me again all evening, until later, when he sees me struggling to change our duvet cover, which is covered in dirt and grass stains from the garden.

'Not such a good idea after all, was it?' he says then, ambiguously, and takes himself off to the spare room, leaving me to sleep alone.

And thus I am punished.

Still, I do go with James to the party. Damage limitation, James calls it, but for me it is just a swansong.

We walk there, in strained silence, through the pleasant, leafy streets. And all the while James is just fractionally ahead of me, so that I have to walk too fast in my heels to keep up. It doesn't bode well. When we arrive there are already loads of cars parked up outside. Only Tasha could get away with having a party in July; people will have booked their holidays around this. Just as we get to the door, James turns to me and says, 'Please, just don't do anything else to embarrass me.'

But before I can reply – and believe me, reply I would – the door is opened and in we go.

Brittle smiles greet me as we walk the length of the hall to the kitchen. Warmer smiles greet James. It's all *James, hi, good to see you*, followed by *Laura, and how are you?*

Again and again and again.

I have the weird feeling of not belonging to my life any more. Surprisingly, I don't really care. I feel strangely free, like a ghost walking through, just watching. James cares, though, I can tell. Not out of any loyalty to me, you understand, but as a reflection upon himself. There is a marked difference. I see it clearly.

Poor James. He couldn't come on his own, but he doesn't want me there, not really.

And then we are set upon by Tasha. She too greets James first, draping her delicate arms around him, kissing him fondly on the cheek.

'So glad you could make it,' she gushes, and to me, stoically, 'I hope that tonight we can all be friends.'

I know why she says this. Just beyond her, at the far side of the kitchen, I can see Fiona Littlewood poking things on sticks into a giant watermelon. She glances my way and catches me looking, and turns away again, and in no time at all is huddled up with a group of what we always referred to as the mums from school, all of them with their backs to me.

'Drinks are in the garden,' Tasha says. 'Do help yourselves.'

And so we wander through. Outside, they've a table laden with champagne glasses and some sort of fountain-thing going on, and a couple of girls I recognize as ex-babysitters loading up trays to circulate with.

'Let me get you a drink,' James says a little tersely, and leaves me standing on the patio, from where I can look out at the good and the great, and the not-so-good and the not-so-great, scattered across the perfectly striped lawn. There are fairy lights strung from the trees, and plenty of patio heaters, pumping out their fumes. Not that they are needed; it's a fine, warm night. Everywhere people are gathered in little groups, chatting in that fast, urgent way that people chatter at parties – you know, making out that everything they have to say is just so funny and so amazing. Oh no, nothing can ever be dull, or just plain ordinary, or *serious* in any way. The laughter trills out, carrying for miles.

'Here,' James says, returning briefly to hand me a glass. And then I watch him as he so casually wanders over to a group of the men of this town: Rupert, Peter Littlewood and the like, and so smoothly moves in on them, slapping backs, telling jokes. And I see how they respond, just as he wants them to. Clearly he is not to be blamed for the failings of his wife.

The thing is, it is unthinkable for James to be anything other than popular. It was unthinkable for me, too, until recently.

'Hello, Laura.' It's Liz.

'Hi,' I say, and I slap on my party smile.

'I'm glad you came,' she says. 'Haven't seen you for ages.'

'Well, you know ... I've been kind of busy.'

'So I heard,' she says, and she sips her drink. She's had quite a lot to drink; I can tell this because she sways, just ever so slightly, like a flower in her pink strappy dress. 'They'll get over it, you know.'

'What?'

She points with her glass to the far side of the garden by the arbour, where Tasha is holding court now among a crowd of followers. She's showing off her dress, in which she looks gorgeous, even though she's five months pregnant. 'Them,' Liz says, and she leans a little closer to me and whispers conspiratorially, 'you showed them up for what they are and they didn't like it. I think it's hilarious.'

And then off she totters again, back across the lawn to the others.

I don't want to stay. I am not a part of this any more.

To interrupt James and tell him I'm leaving would be to induce a scene, of one type or another. So I just go. Quietly, I slip back through the house, and out of the front door. And the sense of freedom I feel as I start walking down that street, on my own, in the soft balmy air, is heaven. It's still not completely dark and I can see the shapes of the clouds in the sky above the trees, purple on purple. There are just big houses in this street, set back from the road behind hedges. No one is about. Not a single car passes me by. It would seem that the whole world is at Tasha's house and I am completely alone. My heels hit the ground too noisily, and the sound hammers back with an echo, so I take my shoes off, and I feel the pavement gritty under my feet. Now there is silence. Now I can truly disappear.

Emma from across the road is babysitting. She jumps up from the TV when I walk in, surprised to see me back so early, but I pay her for the night anyway and send her on her way. And I wonder what I am going to do now.

I look in on my children, and see them sleeping the sweet sleep of oblivion. I straighten their covers and close their doors again, and creep about my house in the half-dark as if I don't belong here. I feel I should wait up for James and give him some sort of explanation. I think of texting him, but remember he doesn't have his phone; we took mine tonight, for the babysitter. So I pour myself a glass of wine and sit in the living room, in the silence and semi-darkness.

I feel so detached from my life. On the wall beside the mantelpiece is a photo taken of us all last year: a studio shot in which we are tumbling together against a background of white, bare-footed and laughing. You know the sort of thing; you'll have seen similar photos of similar families in similar houses to ours. It shows us in our uniform, our disguise. See how good-looking we all are, with our perfect teeth and our shiny hair. It's a PR shot. It shows us as we want to be seen, not as we really are.

And I remember all those photos clustered around in Mrs Partridge's front room, of her children and her grandchildren, the people she loves and who love her. The snapshots and school photos of gap-toothed, bed-haired kids, of Heddy in her wedding dress. No air-blown perfection there, no need for artifice. Just the real thing. So lovingly Mrs Partridge packed them all away into old cardboard boxes, carefully wrapping each one in newspaper. I think of their lives. Always, for evermore, I will think of their lives and feel the hole that has opened up in mine.

I wait for James and I wait. I feel so strangely calm, weightless, as if I have already let go. But he comes in late, very late, and by then I have given up and gone to bed. I hear his key in the door; I hear him banging doors. He will be drunk, then, as well as angry. I hear him go into the kitchen and pour first one glass of water, then another. I lie in our bed, completely still, hidden in the dark, and listen.

After a while he comes upstairs, but he doesn't come into

our room. He goes straight into the spare room. And this is where he will always sleep from now on, for the remainder of our marriage.

It is a hot night and against my skin the sheets feel cool. I lie so still I could almost be floating. I close my eyes and I picture my life as a box, held together with string; undo the string and one by one the sides fall open, and inside there is just me.

I feel the layers of myself, peeling away.

TWENTY-THREE

I am up early in the morning, long before James. I find some cereal for the children and put the washing on. Strangely, I feel the urge to be a good wife now that I feel I will not be one for much longer. I load up the dishwasher and clean out the fridge, which is more or less empty apart from some suspect milk and a bag of old apples. I am sitting at the table with a cup of coffee, and writing a list for Sainsbury's, when James comes down.

He comes into the kitchen and he stands there in his bathrobe and says, 'Why did you do it?' in this quiet, pained voice. He is looking tired and a little haggard; he runs his hand back through his sleep-messed hair, tilting his head to the side. Does he mean to be patronizing? Sometimes I find it hard to tell. 'Will you please just explain to me why you find it necessary to humiliate me like that?' He pulls out a chair and sits himself down opposite me, and then waits, as if he actually expects me to answer.

'I don't find it necessary. I don't mean to humiliate you.'

'Then what else is it, Laura? Why else would you come to a party with me, and then just leave without even *telling* me?' His voice is rising now. The children are in the living room watching TV – they'll hear. 'I didn't even know you'd gone,' he says. 'Till near the end and I'm looking for you and I can't find you, and I say to Tasha, "Have you seen Laura?" And she says, "Oh, James, didn't you know? She left ages ago. I do hope nothing's wrong."'

'You didn't miss me then.'

'Do you know how stupid I felt? Do you know how ashamed? Everyone else knows my wife's just walked out, without even saying goodbye to anyone, and I don't.'

So I didn't escape unseen, then. I picture them all, gossiping. How they must have loved it.

'If I'd told you I wanted to leave, you'd have tried to stop me.'

'Well, of course I would have. You don't just walk out of someone's party. Don't you think that's just a little rude? You could at least have made an excuse or something. I mean, God, Laura – there I am trying to smooth things over after the last thing you did, and you just go and show us up all over again. Why, for God's sake?'

'I just didn't want to be there.'

'You just didn't want to be there,' he repeats back at me, incredulously. And we sit there, and we stare at each other. From down the hall in the living room comes the hyper-jolly laughter of kids' TV.

'James,' I say tentatively, 'you may not have noticed, but I've had a lot on my mind just lately.'

And straight back James says, 'Oh, I've noticed all right. How could I not have noticed? You're hardly ever here and when you are, *God*—' He breaks off, he shakes his head, and he laughs that short, humourless laugh. Anger, hot and fast, shoots its way up my spine.

'James, do you really think it so strange that I should want to put right some wrong that I did in the past? That I should want to help someone I was unkind to?'

'I really wouldn't know, Laura,' James says, 'but I don't want it affecting us like this. Maybe you could do us both a favour and remember that we'll still have to live in this town, long after your little project with the headcase has finished.'

I move before I think. I *don't* think. I pick up my coffee cup and I *hurl* it at James. It hits him somewhere between his face and his chest and he reels back, scraping his chair across the tiles and yelling, '*Jesus!*' The cup smashes on the floor, and there's coffee everywhere, all down James's chin and his front and the wall behind him. He's got his arms raised up like he's expecting something else to come flying at him, and he's looking down at himself and kind of gasping – I don't hang around to see what he'll do; in seconds I'm up from that table and I've snatched up my bag and my car keys and I am out of there. I hear him shouting, 'Laura!' and the children calling, 'Mummy!' as I slam the front door behind me, but I don't stop. I throw myself and my bag into the car and I am gone.

Though God knows where I am going.

I drive too fast, almost in *panic*. I can't believe what I have just done. I've got my fingers gripping on to the steering wheel tight and my teeth digging into my lip, and I can hardly breathe I am so angry. He referred to me as if I belonged to him, and I don't. He spoke as if I'd want to still carry on living as we do, but I don't. I really don't. But what kind of a hypocrite am I, telling him that I *wanted* to help someone I was unkind to? I didn't *want* to help Heddy. I was coerced into it. All I really wanted to do was get her and her family out of my life again. And what James said, about my *project with the headcase* – well, that's nothing worse than what I might have said myself just a month or so ago. What kind of people are we, James and I? What kind of lives do we lead? And what will hold us together now that the glue's come unstuck?

There are two main roads out of Ashton – the one into London and the one out, westwards. I take the latter because it's faster and I just want to get as far away as I can. I don't even think where I'm going, and I've got nothing with me except my handbag. I can't go far, but I can't go back, either. I need a destination. In my bag I've got the keys to the Partridges' house: I head there.

My anger's fizzled out into a kind of low gloom by the time I get to Forbury, and I pull up outside Mrs Partridge's and just stare at the place for a minute. Without curtains, and in the bright light of the day, the windows are black and empty. That mattress is still outside, and there are rubbish bags stacked up around the bin. One of them has been ripped open by the foxes and there are eggshells and teabags scattered across the path, and the For Sale sign has slipped over and is leaning to one side.

I sit there in the false comfort of my car and my heart slides. I mean, how bleak can one house look?

Mrs Day comes out from next door with a milk bottle and stops and gawps at me, so I feel I have to get on with things. I get out of the car and do my best to look composed and businesslike as I walk up the path. I pick up those eggshells with unwilling fingers and poke them back in the sack, knowing full well they'll be dragged out again later. The teabags I leave; they've split as they've dried out, and their contents are smeared into the concrete like black tar. It is so weird opening that front door. No safety locks here;

one turn of the key and the door flings open onto silence.

They've only been gone a couple of days, so there's not much mail, just pizza leaflets and other junk. I pick it up, closing the door behind me, and there's that smell again, that Partridge smell, left behind like their ghosts, here forever. I'm supposed to check the boiler, which clings to the wall in the kitchen, and the pipes in the airing cupboard upstairs, which are prone to leak. The boiler seems fine, if a little hissy. But I can't help thinking maybe someone should have attacked this place with some bleach or something before they left; *everything* is coated in grease. Still, the new people will probably strip it all out anyway.

My shoes are loud on the hall floorboards, but Mrs Partridge left the carpet on the stairs because it was too old and worn to lift, and the sudden quiet underfoot is eerie in contrast; I find myself creeping up into the dark, afraid to make any sound. Every creak of the floorboards has my heartbeat picking up. It's just so dark and so gloomy. What must it have been like for Heddy having to come up these stairs night after night, especially as a child? Especially after her dad had died, with the fear and misery of death lurking in the shadows. It is just too, too depressing. I remember how it used to freak me out, just looking up the stairs when I came round here. And I remember the first time I actually had to climb up them to the bathroom, when I was here for Heddy's birthday, and how I was so desperate to get out of this horrible house and go home.

Heddy had no such option. For poor Heddy, this *was* home.

I check the airing cupboard and I'm about to go back downstairs – it feels so wrong, snooping around up here in the stale, fetid air. But a sudden noise stops me, a creak, coming from the main bedroom, where Heddy slept. And there it is again. I think that maybe a cat has somehow got in, or a mouse even, though the child in me is half-frightened into believing it's old Mr Partridge's ghost come back, looking for his family. It's stupid to creep, but creep I do, and my heart is racing away like a jackhammer as I tentatively push back the door to Heddy's bedroom.

They left that big old bed there, stripped of its covers. The mattress is stained and sunken from the weight of so much use; I try not to look. The huge wardrobe is still there too, emptied out now and with one door hanging open. This is where the noise came from; as I watch the door creaks and moves just slightly, feeble under its own weight. The carpet has gone from in here and I put my foot down on a wood-louse and feel it crunch underneath my shoe. I look down and see another scuttling away. The air is sour and oppressive with dust and sleep-sweat and other people's memories. I can barely breathe. I picture Mrs Partridge, sitting on that bed, thin, worn hands clutching at the bedspread as she tells me about Heddy's untimely birth. I see her eyes, over-bright, glistening with a lifetime of love and sadness as we sort through Heddy's things and pile them up into boxes and bags, and again I feel myself so wrong, so useless, so shamed.

Your parents have always been very kind to us, Laura, and for that I am very grateful. I hear Mrs Partridge's voice, the wooden politeness of unwilling need.

And I hear my own pathetic entreaty; I hear myself whining like a child. *Why did you never tell them what I did?*

Like I thought I'd got off the hook.

I close my eyes and I hate myself. I can never make amends for what I have done. Yet there is something else, something tugging at the edge of my mind.

I walk over to the window and look out and down. I see

the mattress, the bin bags and the squashed teabags, spilling their insides on the cracked and broken concrete. But in my head I see myself, at seven years old, nine years old, eleven years old, over and over, so reluctantly, so resentfully, forced up that path.

And I remember my dad once, when I objected, when I sat there in the car outside this house pleading, 'Dad, I don't want to call for her.' I remember him leaning over towards me in the car and jabbing his pointed finger right in front of my face.

'You, young lady,' he spat at me, 'do not have a choice.'

And I remember the unfairness; the anger, rising up inside, a simmering potent rage.

Your parents wanted the best for you, Mrs Partridge said. *As I wanted the best for my Heddy.*

Is that all?

Mrs Partridge must have known how much I hated being here. Just as she knew how cruel I was to Heddy. Did she really think that was the price to pay for their kindness?

Years ago I asked my mother why it mattered so much that I should be nice to Heddy Partridge all the time, and she gave me some strange, half-explained reason about Mr Partridge having worked for my dad, once upon a time. But what kind of reason was that for foisting such a damaging kindness upon the Partridges? And for forcing me, so obviously unwilling, upon Heddy?

Why did my parents do it? Could they really not see what was happening?

I go back downstairs and lock up the house behind me. In the car I check my phone, even though I know I'd have heard it if James had rung. That he hasn't leaves me with a deep, slow dread. Though, of course, I should phone him. After all, I threw the cup. And I walked out. These things, I fear, are final. But what can I say? Somewhere at the sides of my mind I'm starting to think *What will I do? Where will I live? And what about the children?* Always, always, the children. But I cannot let these thoughts in. I cannot. Not just yet.

I don't phone James, not even to tell him where I'm going. And I don't phone my parents either, to warn them I'm coming. I just drive, picking up the M3 and then the A303, and joining the holiday crawl down towards Devon. I don't know what I'm going to say to my parents when I get there. But I don't think they were quite as kind as Mrs Partridge would like to believe, and I think there must have been something else binding Heddy Partridge and me.

TWENTY-FOUR

It's a three-hour drive down to Devon at the best of times and this is a Sunday, in peak season. The A303 just crawls along, and I've plenty of time to change my mind.

But I don't.

And as I drive I feel my marriage seeping further and further away from me. Across my shoulders, I feel the lightening of constraint. No more will I be an embarrassment to James. I can't even think how angry he must be. First, all the social humiliation, and now this. And that I should walk out and leave him like that, dripping hot coffee and unable to have the last word – he won't forgive that. Oh no. And he won't clean it up, either. The coffee will be left where it hit, drying into the walls and staining them indelibly, a constant reminder of my faults.

When I eventually reach the village where my parents live, I almost do change my mind. I have to slow right down to drive through narrow lanes crowded with hedgerows and twee, flower-decked cottages, and I can feel my heart thumping hard in my chest, and the echo of that thump pulsing out behind my eyes. I almost feel sick. Tiredness, no doubt, from the drive and the stress, and I haven't eaten anything since toast this morning. But it's more than that. I actually feel nervous, at the prospect of turning up at my parents' house unannounced and without the shield of my children to hide behind. And what am I going to say to them? I'm supposed to be coming here again in two weeks' time with Thomas and Arianne – though of course that may change now.

Everything, I guess, will change now.

I can see their house, at the end of the lane, and I slow all the way down to a crawl. I think what an idyllic life they have for themselves out here. And I think how it must run in the blood, this need for perfection. How we carve it out for ourselves, how we build our own walls.

My dad is in the garden with his watering can, making the most of the late-afternoon sun. He glances my way as I pull up, but he doesn't register the car as being mine, and he carries on again, tending to his plants. And so he is totally shocked when he looks up again minutes later to see me walking towards him up the path. I *see* that shock, and how it blanches out his face.

And I see him in my mind as I saw him the day I cut my wrist, the moment he looked up from his newspaper to find me standing in front of him with blood running down my arm. We never talked about that day; never mentioned it again, any of that stuff. We glossed over it, shoved it under the carpet, thinking there it would stay.

He puts down his watering can. 'Laura?' he says. 'What's the matter? Is it the children . . . ? What is it?'

I shake my head. 'Nothing,' I lie. 'I just wanted to come and see you.' But I can feel my face beginning to dissolve.

'Rita! Rita!' my dad calls without taking his eyes off me. But he stands where he is, like he's afraid to move.

My mum comes hurrying from around the back. 'Oh, my goodness!' she cries. 'Laura! Whatever's happened?'

'Nothing's happened,' I manage to say. 'I just thought I'd come and see you.'

I see my mum glance at my dad, very quickly, then she's taking off her gardening gloves and telling my dad to put the kettle on and ushering me around the back. She was going to take me inside, but it's just so lovely out there with the view and the sunlight sliding so mellow. So we sit at the garden table, my mother and I, while my dad goes inside to make tea, then brings it out to us, and then loiters nearby, in the manner of dads.

'Does James know you're here?' my mum asks and I shake my head, and see her lips thin as she draws her conclusions. 'Ah,' she says, with meaning.

'I've been spending a lot of time with Mrs Partridge, and with Heddy. Heddy's out of hospital and they've moved now, to be nearer Ian. Just last week. I'm looking after the house till it's sold. I did what I could to help them.' I want her to pick up on what I am saying. I want her to read between the lines. And I'm watching my dad; he's prodding about at some mini-tree he's got in a pot there, and he's listening. Anger is creeping in small beads through my veins, like ants on the crawl. I want their approval. All those years of being told to be nice to poor Heddy Partridge – well, I have been nice to her now. I want their approval, but I want to throw it back at them too. 'Though I don't suppose it could ever be enough.'

But my mum just says, 'That's good. Mrs Partridge has had a hard life and I'm sure it'll be easier for her if she's near her son.' I see her glance at my dad. I see him deliberately avoid her eye.

Then my dad says, a little too bluffly, 'Are they all right for money, the Partridges?'

And quick as anything my mum says, 'I'm sure they're fine.' Then, as if she realizes she spoke too sharply, she adds, 'We can't go helping everyone who's short of money. We'd have nothing left for ourselves.'

'We're not talking about *anyone*,' my dad snaps back. 'We're talking about the Partridges.' And he goes back to his little tree, snapping off the unwanted leaves with a hard, quick flick of his wrist. My mum glares at him, chewing on her lip.

The anger in my blood picks up a gear. 'The Partridges, the Partridges,' I say sarcastically. 'Here they are back in our lives once again.'

My parents are not amused. My dad abandons his precious tree and stomps off around the side of the house, where there are, no doubt, more needy plants awaiting his attention.

My mum, in a voice that could crack glass, says, 'Don't you think that it's time you phoned James?' And what she means is: don't come here causing trouble.

'I don't want to speak to him at the moment,' I say evasively, and my mum purses her lips in disapproval.

'Marriage isn't always easy, Laura,' she preaches. 'Believe me, I should know. You have to work at it, constantly. But James has a right to know where you are.'

And how could she ever understand that my marriage is part of the box that I'd wrapped myself into, lacing myself up to keep the demons away? Painting myself perfect, lest the truth might show through.

And that life is all undone now.

My mother finds some quiche and salad for me to eat for supper, which I do, with little conversation. And later, when she has given me a clean towel and a spare toothbrush and settled me into the spare room at the ridiculously early hour of nine o'clock, and my dad has stayed pottering around on the sidelines and so avoided having to speak to me again himself, she comes into me with the house phone and says, 'I've James on the line.'

At least she has the grace to leave me again.

'So now you get your mother to phone me,' James states down the line, and this is it, then. I hear the coldness in his voice; the ties that bind us stretch and thin and tear.

'I didn't get her to phone you. She took it upon herself.'

'And what the hell are you doing there anyway?' he shouts in my ear. 'I've got a meeting tomorrow morning. What am I supposed to do with the children?'

Oh, the things that really matter. I feel him drifting away. 'I'm not coming back tonight, James,' I say.

'For God's sake, Laura, what kind of a mother walks out on her children?'

'That's a cheap shot, James. I didn't walk out on my children. I left them with you.'

And so he turns. 'In the eyes of the law, you walked out, Laura.'

I almost laugh. 'Are you threatening me?' And when he doesn't answer, but just leaves me hanging on with his loaded silence spelling out all kinds of doom down the phone, I say, as calmly as I can, 'I'll be back sometime tomorrow, I expect. For our children. I'm sure you can look after them until then.'

Still that silence. And then, sorrowfully, and as if it should really hurt me that he could think this, he says, 'You've changed, Laura. You're not the woman that I married.'

And I say, 'Thank goodness for that.'

*

I wake up early and put on yesterday's clothes. My parents are in the kitchen and they greet me a little stiltedly. Surprises don't fit well in a carefully planned existence, and what a surprise I am, turning up unannounced like this. Allowing them no time for preparation, no opportunity for performance, for cushions to be plumped and cakes to be baked, for the choreography of outstretched arms and cries of delight.

I'll get all that when I come back next time, with the children. But this time, I just get the bones.

'Well, I'll leave you to it,' my dad says more or less straight away as if I *want* to be left to it, and off he goes, into the garden. And so I am left with my mum again, and that oh-so-tangible air of disapproval. I remember just before I got married, a month or so beforehand, when the whole ordeal of flowers and napkins and place-settings just got too much, and it felt as if the most important thing about my wedding was whether we were going for violet or blue. And I remember saying as much to my mother, during yet another over-stressed conversation.

'Of course it's important,' she snapped back. Followed with, 'Don't you dare go changing your mind now, or I will never forgive you.'

And I wondered if she was talking about the colour scheme, or the wedding itself.

'And how are you feeling this morning?' she asks me now, a little coolly.

And I say, 'Fine. Thank you', because I realize there isn't much point in saying anything else. To my mother, this is all about a silly argument with James. 'I'll be heading back in a while.' She nods in approval, and I see her visibly relax. 'But I'll just go and have a quick chat with Dad first.'

*

I find him poking about down the end of the garden, as far away from any possible histrionics as he can get. He starts telling me about his plans to grow vegetables, and then we just stand there, side by side, staring out across the fields to the sea, picture-book blue in the distance. I think he can sense that there's something I want to say; there's something between us, some charge. My heart is beating slow and hard. I think of Heddy saying *Your dad loved you whatever you did*. I think of that time in the car when we had to give Heddy a lift to the Forbury High disco; I think of him hitting me again and again and again.

And I blurt out, 'Heddy Partridge was in hospital because she kept cutting up her arms.' I wonder if he already knows this – if he does, he doesn't let on. His face is controlled, impassive. 'I went to see her ... lots of times. I saw her scars, just like mine.' My voice is stark and clumsy in the soft, honeyed air.

My dad lays down his garden trowel and slowly wipes his hands on the front of his thighs. I can hear the steady rise and fall of his breathing.

I carry on before I lose my nerve. 'And before they moved she said something about her dad dying ... and about you, about that day, when you took me in there, when I—' I stop. I just cannot bring myself to say it.

The silence is blistering.

And then he says, 'Is that what this is all about? Bring back bad memories, did it?'

I shake my head. 'No. It's not just that. Dad, I was so cruel to her when we were kids.' I see his face cloud with disappointment, just like it always did, shutting me out. But I won't stop now. I can't. 'But you forced us together, all the time. I couldn't understand why.' My voice is getting shrill;

I can't help it. 'I felt like you shoved me at her constantly, and constantly I let you down.'

'Was it really so hard for you to understand the concept of being nice to someone less fortunate than yourself?' he starts in that weary voice that he has used on me so often – *so* often – but I'm not having it. Not this time.

'But why did I have to be so nice to her? Why did I even have to know her? Why couldn't we just have been the strangers that we wanted to be?'

'Laura? What's going on?' I can hear my mother, coming striding across the lawn. 'Laura!' she calls, her voice sharp with suspicion.

'Heddy's father worked for me a long time ago. I felt a degree of responsibility towards them,' my dad says quickly and turns away from me, as if that is an end to it.

'Do you know how judged I felt by you all the time? And it seemed to me that she was the cause. I was caught in a vicious circle. The more *disappointed* you were with me, the more I hated her; and the more I hated her, the more disappointed you got.'

'Laura! I don't think we want to be talking about this now!' my mum barks, joining us now, her face flushed from her march down the garden.

But I carry on. 'I was so cruel to her. The things I did—' My voice cracks now. 'That time Heddy broke her wrist. It was my fault. I persuaded her to come to the graveyard after school to meet some boy, and she got frightened and she ran and fell over. It was my fault, and I just left her there.'

There, I have said it. My words fall like rocks in the morning air. My parents stare at me in shock, and the flush on my mother's face drains clear away.

She recovers first, though. And she starts off on an outrage.

'Well, you must tell them. You must apologize to Heddy and to her mother straight away. I don't care how long ago this happened—'

'I did,' I say. 'But Mrs Partridge knew already. She always knew.'

Suddenly my dad sits down, right there on the grass, and puts his head in his hands. 'My God,' he mutters, 'what have we done?'

'We've done nothing,' my mum snaps, 'except do our best for that family. Laura, you bring shame on us.'

'Do you think I don't know that? Don't you think I've *hated* myself for the things that I've done? I hated Heddy, but I hated myself too. Surely you could see that?' My voice catches and I'm breathing too fast. I feel like I am five years old again, excluded from understanding. My mother glares at me, her thin mouth working silently, dragging up the words with which to condemn me again.

But my dad speaks before her. 'Heddy lost her father,' he says, 'and I felt responsible.'

I see him sitting down there, looking so old suddenly, and so pale.

'But why would you feel responsible for that?' I ask.

And my mum says, 'David!' warningly, and to me, 'Laura!' – like who is she trying to stop? She looks from one to the other of us, arms folded across her chest, fingers digging into her skin.

Slowly my dad stands up. His hands hang by his sides, helpless, dragging his shoulders down in a slope. 'Mr Partridge worked for the firm,' he says and his voice is strained and tired. 'As a carpet fitter. He'd worked there for years, long before I took over. When his Heddy was born same year as you ... well, he was so proud. He brought photos of her into the shop, showed them to everyone.' He sighs, then comes back to the point. 'We got a big job in, at an office block in Fayle,' he says, 'replacing all the flooring.'

'It was still your father's business then, David,' my mum butts in quickly. 'Don't you forget that.'

'Yes, but I was in charge of the office.' My dad's face is grey and pinched. 'It was me that gave the instructions. It was my decision. Go on in, I said, rip it all up.' He gestures with his hand, swiping at the air. *Rip it all up.*

I wait for him to continue. Suddenly, I am afraid to breathe.

'And there was asbestos,' he says simply. 'In the old floor.'

I gasp. I can't help myself.

'But didn't you check?' I say. 'Before he started?' You always check for asbestos, *always*. Even I know that, carpet-shop owner's daughter that I am. It's the procedure. You check. You *assume*, until you know otherwise.

'I took a chance,' he says shiftily. 'We were in a hurry.'

Now maybe I am being really slow here, but I don't quite follow this. 'But you must have known . . .'

My dad hunches his shoulders. He avoids my eye. 'We needed to get the job done quickly. The business was struggling. There were bills to be paid.'

'You mean you covered it up?' I stare at him in disbelief.

'Your father did what he had to do,' my mother says curtly. 'For the sake of the business.'

'So you didn't tell them, the Partridges? They didn't know about it?'

'Of course not,' my mum says. 'What good could possibly come of that? Your father would have lost the business!'

I can't believe she says this. I think of Mr Partridge, confined to his chair, and coughing himself slowly to death. 'So you watched him die?' I say, and my father flinches. 'You sacrificed Mr Partridge for the sake of a few pounds, and then you watched him die?' My mouth is filled with saliva and I think I'm going to be sick. I swallow and swallow, but my stomach is knotting into cramp.

'Laura!' snaps my mum, and then she looks round, sharply, as if realizing she has spoken too loudly. She drops her voice to an angry whisper. 'What would you have us do, then? Ruin *both* of our families? And the man smoked forty cigarettes a day, don't forget. For all we know, it might have been them that killed him!'

I am too stunned to reply. I turn to my father for some kind of explanation and he looks back at me reproachfully with hurt, hangdog eyes, as if somehow he is the victim in this.

'I tried to make it up to them over the years,' he says and his voice is short with indignation. 'I did what I could for them. Helped them out when I could. And all I asked of you, young lady, was that you be kind to their daughter.'

And thus he absolves himself. He speaks to me in that accusatory tone, shifting, twisting the blame. He asked me to be nice and I wasn't. I let him down.

My mother – so visibly, quietly angry with me – says, 'And now there is absolutely nothing more to be said.' And then she links her arm through my father's and starts steering him back towards the house.

And so they pull away from me, as ever they did. As always, a united front. I see my mother, glancing round anxiously now lest anybody might have overheard. I see my father, small and fallible and weak.

My parents, such pillars of the community.

And I think of Mr Partridge, grey-faced and wasting on his slow slide to death; I think of that bed in their house with its stained and sunken mattress and Mrs Partridge sitting on it, clutching at its history with her thin and desperate hands.

I stand there in the bright sunshine as my parents walk away from me and I am filled with a lifetime's anger and guilt.

But who am I to judge? We're all culpable.

I sit down on the grass and have to spit, several times, to clear my mouth. I am breathing too fast and too hard and my heart is pounding. I try to calm myself. I draw up my knees and link my hands around them so that I am hugged into a ball. The sunshine is warm upon my back and there is silence now, except for the birds in the trees and in the distance the faint hum of a lawnmower. I breathe deeply and smell the grass, the flowers, the soft morning air, and I feel that I will choke.

On the day of Mr Partridge's funeral I came home from school to find my parents in the kitchen. I remember the weirdness of bounding in to see my dad sitting at the table in his black suit and tie, with his shoulders all hunched over and his head resting in his hands. My mum was there too, standing by the sink. She'd been saying something, but she shut up as soon as she saw me, and so I walked into this sudden, strange silence.

I stood there, and I wanted to say something, but I couldn't think *what* to say. The first thing I came out with was, 'Mrs Cookson kept us all in at break because some of the boys were mucking around, but *I* wasn't, so it wasn't fair.' And still there was this silence, with me in the middle of it. My dad didn't even look up. So I started saying it again. 'Mrs Cookson kept us in and it wasn't fair . . .'

It was nerves making me talk. Nerves making me say whatever came into my head. Anyone could have seen that. I was too freaked out by the sight of my dad sitting there with his face in his hands. But behind me my mum snapped, 'Laura!' to shut me up, and my eyes smarted with tears.

'*Dad* ... ' I wailed and he looked up then, at last. And he looked terrible, all pale-faced and his eyes were bloodshot with dark smudges underneath them, like bruises. I didn't want to see my dad looking like that. I didn't want to see him looking at me like that. 'What's the matter?' I said. 'It was only Mr Partridge ... '

And what I meant was that Mr Partridge was just someone we knew a bit. He wasn't family. He wasn't even a friend. I couldn't understand why my dad would be so sad.

But my dad closed his eyes, as if he couldn't bear to look at me any more, and my mum snapped 'Laura!' again, followed by, 'Go upstairs! Now!'

'Don't worry!' I shouted back, stung by the unfairness. 'I'm going!' And off I flounced, slamming the door behind me.

But in the hall I stopped, and I listened. And I heard my mother saying to my dad, 'For heaven's sake, David, you had no choice.'

To which my dad replied, 'Oh, but I did, Rita. I did have a choice.' Followed by the even scarier, 'What kind of a man am I?'

What kind of a man indeed?

I press my face into my knees, and so I sit, and I cry like a child.

Here it begins, and here it ends.

Nothing will ever justify what I did to Heddy. Nothing will excuse the taunts and the jeers and the goading. But I see my father, always turning away from me, haunted by a greater guilt. I see shame and secrecy, poisoning its way down the line.

And hurt engenders hurt.

They are in the kitchen. My father is sitting at the table looking woefully defensive. His hands are clasped on the table in front of him, like in a prayer. My mother is standing to the left of him, midway to putting the kettle on for tea. They were talking, and now they stop, and so I walk in to a hostile, loaded silence.

I am reminded of the day of that funeral. And of the secrets kept from me, the damage done. And now that those secrets are out, we are stripped bare, all of us. We are parasites, feeding off the weak.

'People like the Partridges don't matter,' I say. 'They can be manipulated, disposed of at will.'

'Laura, you are being ridiculous,' my mother says, and she turns away from me, the colour rising in her face. She holds the kettle under the tap, which she then flicks on hard so that it blasts noisily, water against metal.

'But people like us, we mustn't lose face.'

My mother plugs in the kettle and takes two mugs from the cupboard and slams them down on the counter. Two, not three.

My father grips his hands and ignores me. I look at him, and I see so much deceit that I can't think what is real and what isn't, in anything he has ever said to me. I think of that day when he carried me bleeding into the Partridges' house, and laid me down upon their sofa. I think of Heddy wishing that she had a father like mine, and of him saying to Mrs Partridge *How are you? How are you managing?*

I swallow, but the lump in my throat is a solid, hard mass.

'How can you bear it?' I say. 'Knowing what you did.'

He doesn't answer. I didn't expect him to. He closes his eyes, the better to shut me out. But what does he see there inside his head? What peace does he find?

Over by the counter my mother has gone very, very still.

'You used me,' I say. My father's eyelids flicker, but he keeps them shut. 'You expected me to somehow make up for what you had done.'

'It wasn't like that,' my father whispers.

And my mother says, 'Laura, please.'

'But how could anyone make up for what you had done? I made it worse. I hated Heddy Partridge and I hated myself, too. And the reason that I hated Heddy and hated myself was because of the guilt that you dumped on me.' I speak fast. My throat is burning. 'Your guilt.'

I leave them in the kitchen. For half an hour I sit on the single bed in their little spare room, too numb to do anything. There is no going back from this. There's a line through my history, striking it out.

The house is silent. I gather up my things.

'I'm going now.'

They are in the kitchen still, both of them sitting at the table now, the empty mugs in front of them. My mother gets up when I walk in, and starts fussing; she takes the mugs to the sink, then picks up a tea towel and starts folding it in her hands.

'You don't want to leave James any longer,' she says, to

which I say nothing. She shakes out that tea towel, and folds it again. 'And I expect you'll want to avoid the traffic.' She's relieved to see me go. They both are. It's hardly surprising.

I look at my father. His face is tensed and closed.

'We ought to tell them,' I say. 'The Partridges. We ought to tell them what happened. They have a right to know.'

For seconds no one speaks. No one moves. Then my mother puts the tea towel down and slowly wipes her hands on the front of her skirt. It's a similar gesture to the one Mrs Partridge was always making; I can't help but notice.

She says, 'For heaven's sake, Laura, what good would it do now?'

My father looks up now, and I see the anguish in his eyes. 'You do not know,' he says, 'how desperate I was. I was going to lose the business. If I lost the business, we'd lose the house.' He stretches his hands out in front of him as he speaks and clutches at the air and lets it go again, repeatedly, clutching, clutching, letting go. 'You do not know,' he says, 'because you were a child. Wanting your ballet lessons, and your parties, and your pretty clothes.' These last words he spits out, and I stare at him, stunned. I think of my childhood with its best of everything, and all of it spun from deceit. 'I had a family to feed,' he says. 'Bills to pay. I was desperate.'

'But what about Mr Partridge?' I say. 'He had a family too.'

'Do you not think I know that? Do you not think I regret what I did, every single day of my life?' He pushes his hands into his hair now, and stays like that, with his head bowed, elbows resting on the table. And I stand there and I look at him, and feel my heart stripped raw.

We won't tell the Partridges, of course. We all know that. My mother is right: what good would it do now? It wouldn't bring absolution. Just hurt, on top of hurt.

To break the silence my mother says, 'Let's hope that your next visit will be more pleasant, Laura.' But then she turns quickly away, as if realizing the improbability of her words.

They come out to see me off, though. Both of them. And I can't help but be amazed at how they slip their social faces back into place. There are one or two neighbours out and about enjoying the sunshine now – my mother waves, my father calls out *Morning!* No one would notice the slight croak to his voice. I see them looking at me, these neighbours, and I find myself holding my back up straight and keeping my face pleasantly blank. How we perform, how we always perform.

I get into the car. My mother taps on the window so that I have to wind it down. She leans in and says, 'You go home now and make things up with James,' and thus she attempts to sweep all other matters back under the carpet, where she can deal with them best. 'I'm sure everything will be fine.'

Things won't be fine, though. Of that I'm sure. Nothing will ever be fine again.

And then my father comes shuffling up, and my mother steps aside. He bends down so that his face is close to mine, and when he sighs I feel it against my skin. For a long while he doesn't speak, and I just sit there and watch him struggling for words. This is my father. There are tears in his eyes. I see his jaw tensing, fighting for control.

'I did a terrible thing,' he says. 'And I've had to live with it ever since.' He leans his hand on the car door, just below the window, and I see that he is shaking. 'Believe me, Laura, I am sorry. Truly, truly sorry. For what I did to them . . . and to you, too.'

'I'm sorry too,' I say. 'But it will never be enough, will it? It will never make things right.'

And in my father's eyes I see the damage that we have done, both of us. I see the limits of what we are.

THIS PERFECT WORLD

Discussion points for reading groups

1. Laura is a very flawed character. Did this make it difficult for you to empathize with her? Why do you suppose the author chose to narrate the story from Laura's point of view?

2. Laura is caught up in the competitive world of the middle-class mother. She sees that such things as French classes for toddlers and costumes for book week are ridiculous, yet she still goes along with them. Why do you think she does this?

3. Bullying is a central theme in the novel. Are there parallels between the cruelty that Laura inflicted upon Heddy as a child, and the way in which her own friends treat her now as an adult?

4. Is it possible to move on from the damage done in childhood? Or will it always manifest itself in one way or another?

5. The dinner-party scene is pivotal to the book. Do you think this sort of 'not in my backyard' mentality is particularly prevalent in the circles in which Laura moves or does it go on everywhere?

6. Do you think Laura acted purely out of malice in her cruelty towards Heddy? Are children ever fully aware of the consequences of their actions?

7. How much of the blame for Heddy's situation lies with Laura's parents? Was their behaviour better, or worse, than Laura's?

8. Although Laura's and Heddy's actual circumstances are very different, do you think there are emotional similarities in their experiences of new motherhood? Do you think these feelings are experienced by all mothers to some extent?

9. What did you think about Laura's observations regarding the 'class list'? Do you think Laura is right in describing it as a 'filtering system'?

10. Self-harm is another theme of the novel, and something that Laura and Heddy have in common. Did you find these scenes disturbing to read? There has been a lot of coverage in the media about self-harm lately. Do you think it is a side-effect of a modern society, or is it something that has always been there?

THE CHILD INSIDE

Read an extract from Suzanne Bugler's
next novel *The Child Inside*, published
by Pan Books.

ONE

I walked out of that hospital into the hazy sunlight, and I forced myself to smile. Other people were smiling, so I did, too. And I walked tall, even though it hurt. Andrew walked beside me, with Jonathan bounding along beside him. I did not look at them. I did not want to see them, or hear them, though see them and hear them I would, for evermore.

The car was in the long-stay car park, around the side of the building. I let myself into the passenger seat and waited, while Andrew put Jonathan and my overnight bag into the back. And then he got in, and he took a long, deep breath.

'You okay?' he said.

And I said, 'I'm fine.'

The house is in one of those tree-lined avenues between Kew Gardens and the station. I find it easily enough. I got the address from the class list and looked it up in the *A–Z*, and when I spoke to Oliver's mother on the phone to confirm she said, 'Oh, you can't miss us, we're the one on the corner with the huge skip outside.'

So I find it easily enough, but because of the skip there's nowhere to park. There's no space on the road, never mind the fact that it's all permit holders only around here, and that the drive outside the house, where we would have pulled in, has got the skip on it. So I end up driving all the way to the end of the road and across and around again, with Jonathan whining in the back, 'Can't you just park?' and 'We're *miles* away now.'

I find a meter eventually, in the next street. And as I dig around in my bag for change, Jonathan says, 'Why couldn't you just drop me outside? I don't want you coming in.'

I look up and see his face in the mirror, pink-cheeked and scowling.

'I have to come in,' I say. 'I'm not just going to drive off and leave you there.'

'Well, don't stay then,' he says anxiously. 'And don't start talking.'

'Jono, I have to be polite,' I say gently.

And he says, 'And don't call me Jono.'

He does not mean to hurt me. He does not mean to be rude. I tell myself this, and yet my heart slides into a lost place deep inside me, a place where once there was warmth and need.

We let ourselves out of the car and I lock it behind me; the bolts click loudly in the quiet street. My son cannot bear to look at me. Instead he stands there, staring at his feet and wrestling with his demons, as I feed coins into the meter, and on the five-minute walk back towards Oliver's house he keeps a constant two steps ahead of me. But when we get to the house he hesitates; he doesn't want me with him, yet he cannot bring himself to walk up the pathway without me and stops, reluctantly, to let me go first.

'Well, go on then,' I say, stopping too.

It's a big house, as are all the houses in this street: Victorian and double-fronted with a wide front porch. But it isn't the house that's making him nervous; lots of his new friends at his new school live in big houses. He's getting used to that, I think, and so am I. After all, if you scrimp and save and push to get your child into a private school, he's bound to make friends with kids who live in bigger houses than his, have better holidays and flasher cars. No, it isn't the house that's the problem; it's me. That I exist. That he even needs to have a mother at all.

He rings the doorbell and his neck is stiff with shame.

They have one of those intercom things. A woman's voice crackles through it and I have to lean over Jonathan's head to say, 'Hi, it's us. It's Jonathan.'

And then the intercom buzzes and Jonathan shoves me back with his elbows, hissing, '*Shush!*', his pink cheeks turning scarlet, and the door clicks and swings open.

Oliver is standing there, and behind him his mother. We haven't met before. She is tall and thin with fine blonde hair, and she sticks out a confident hand. 'Hi,' she says, 'I'm Amy.'

And I say, 'Rachel. It's nice to meet you.' Her hand is cool and smooth in mine; I grasp it and let it go. She folds her arms then, languidly, across her stomach, and leans slightly to one side. I find myself mirroring her movements, though I am not so thin, or so at ease.

'Sorry about the skip,' she says. 'Did you find somewhere to park? It's a nightmare around here.'

'Just up the road,' I lie. And to Jonathan, who is disappearing up the stairs with Oliver, I call, 'Bye, Jono', followed needlessly by 'I'll come back for you later.'

How desperate I sound. And how I could kick myself for calling him Jono in public. He doesn't reply. He runs up the stairs away from me. I can sense his anger from right down here.

Amy gives me a thin and, I suspect, slightly condescending smile.

'He'll be fine,' she says, as if I thought he wouldn't be.

And I should go now. I should smile back and say, 'I'll pick him up at six, shall I?' and make to dash off, as if there's something I must do, somewhere I must be. But I don't. Instead I do what Jono hates me doing – I linger as if I daren't let him go. And I try to chat.

'You've got a lovely house,' I say.

And Amy shrugs and looks about her, a little startled, as if she really hadn't noticed, and says, 'Thanks.'

Still I don't go.

'It needs a lot of work, though,' she says.

The hallway is wide, with rooms off to both sides and stairs up the middle. Further down I spot the evidence of decorators: a stepladder and paint pots along the side, and on the wall three large different-coloured swatches splashed out to view. I spot this and I latch on.

'You're choosing colours!' I gasp, on a catch of breath, and clasp together my hands. My enthusiasm has her turning, looking where I am looking.

'Yes,' she says and takes a few steps backwards down the hall, and I follow her, deeper into her house. 'Can't make up my mind between these two.' She points at the wall with a manicured finger and we stand there, side by side, contemplating the three shades of cream. She's taller than me, and out of the corner of my eye I can see the steady rise and fall of her chest inside her close-fitting sweater. She smells of lemons.

'I just adore decorating,' I say. 'We've just finished doing our house.'

'Really?' She's not as interested as I'd hoped. So I try harder.

'It is difficult, though. Choosing the right colour. You wouldn't think one shade would make a difference, but it does.'

'Mmm,' she says. 'It bores me stupid. Clive's the fussy one. He thinks all these colours are wrong.'

'Is Clive your husband?' I ask, and this is my cue for her to say, *Yes, and you know he'd love to meet you. You must come round sometime, you and your husband. You must come round for dinner.* And through my head runs a whole host of fantasies, of her family and ours, sharing summer barbecues and lazy afternoons drinking wine and laughing while the children play; of trips to the beach, where the men and boys horse around catching balls, and she and I laze and gossip on stripy towels, in charge of the picnic. We could be like those people in restaurants on Sundays: those families who always know people and come out in their crowds, to spread themselves noisily around the long, central tables and throw order after smiling order at the red-faced, overworked waiter – *Would you mind . . . ?; Could you just . . . ?* – while families like mine are squeezed onto the tiny tables in the corner, to quietly watch and wait, and envy.

She doesn't say anything of the sort, of course. She doesn't even offer me a coffee. And why should she? She'll have her friends. She'll have her busy, busy life.

Upstairs a door opens and I hear the children's footsteps running across the landing. Jonathan will be furious if he catches me still here.

I see Amy look at her watch, and quickly I say, 'Goodness, is that the time?' And, as I should have said five minutes ago, 'I really must be going. I'll come back at six, shall I?'

'No hurry,' Amy says, and she leads me back to the door. Her smile is pleasant, but distant. 'Clive and I aren't going out until eight. You can make it six-thirty.'

It's not much after three, but whatever light there was is rapidly fading. It's a dull, cold day, and everything is clouded with greyness. I walk briskly away from their house, but as soon as I am out of sight I slow right down, dragging out the distance back to my car. I've got nearly three and a half hours until I can collect Jonathan again, but what am I going to do in that time? It would take me half an hour to get home, and more than that to come back again later, because by then it will be busier on the roads. And what would I do at home anyway? Empty the dishwasher. Sort out the washing. Kill time till it is time to return.

Andrew is at home, but he will be sweeping up the last of the leaves and after that, maybe, fixing the shed door. Out there in the cold and the dark, straining his eyes under the outside light. Without Jono there we are middle-aged too soon, each of us silent in our isolation, him outside the house, me within it.

I could drive into Richmond and go shopping, but it is the first Saturday in December; the place will be packed and bustling with the heave of Christmas, and I am not in the mood. And so I just walk, wandering through these elegant streets crammed with gorgeous, elegant houses, and imagining what it must be like to live here. The roads all loop around and link together, and the second time I pass my car I stop, and feed the meter till six, after which parking is free. It's getting really dark now and the street lights are on; and the lights inside people's houses, too, giving me a good view. I see blonde-haired teenagers watching football on enormous

TVs; polished tables on which there might be a large glass bowl or a vase of flowers – roses or white lilies, cut and arranged, bought from a proper florist; thin women in twos and threes, talking to each other, and to small children, who are dressed in soft, thick cotton and candy-striped wool. I see husbands, walking through their living rooms, cracking open a beer and talking on the phone.

I see. As always, I see.

I pass a good hour in this way. Then I wander over towards the station where the shops are, and such lovely shops. Specialist food shops and gift shops, and a quaint old-fashioned bookshop. I while away another hour, thinking how nice it must be for the lucky people who live here to have all this on their doorstep. While I am browsing, some of those lucky people saunter in and greet the shopkeepers by their names, and so they are greeted back.

Good to see you, Mike.

Miserable result, Don. Chelsea relegated in the second half. Got any of those sage-and-rosemary sausages left?

In the grocer's a man wanders in with a child on his shoulders, both of them wearing neither coat nor shoes, to pick up a couple of artichokes. I watch as they leave again; I watch the way he ambles across the road in his cashmere socks, wrapped in a shroud of insouciance. In a gift shop I admire soft leather bags with frightening price tags, and hand-made jewellery of the sort I would never dare wear. The woman sitting at the desk smiles at me and says hello, but I can see in her eyes that she's clocked me, that she knows I don't belong around here.

It's gone five now. The shops are starting to close. There's a coffee shop with a delicatessen at the back; I go in there and order a cappuccino just as they are starting to wipe down. The only other customers are a young woman and a child, spread messily around a circular table right in the middle. The woman is saying, 'No, Polly, don't do that. There's a good girl. No, Polly, no', while the child picks up lumps of cake and throws them on the floor. The child reaches out a chocolatey hand to me as I walk past, and grins a chocolatey grin; I dodge around them, pick up an old copy of the *Daily Mail* and sit myself by the window.

The paper is just for cover; I don't read it. I'm listening to that mother and the way she talks to her child; listening and remembering what it was like to be so blanketed. I can almost hear my own voice superimposed over hers, saying, *There, now, Jono. Good boy, Jono. That's right, that's a clever boy*. And I feel the sweet-sad prickle of loss.

But soon they leave, packing themselves up, with a zipping up of coats and the scraping back of chairs, and leaving behind them a cold blast of air and a sudden quiet. I watch as one of the girls comes out resignedly from behind the counter with a J-cloth in one hand and cleaning spray in the other to tackle the mess left on that table. I listen to the hiss-hiss-hiss of the spray and the clatter of the plates and cups as she piles them up, and I'm thinking that I will have to be leaving soon, too.

But just then the automatic doors slide open again and somebody else walks in, and this, I feel, gives me licence to stay a moment longer. It's an old woman, wrapped against the cold in a marbled brown fur coat and hat – real fur, by the look of it, which surprises me, even for around here. Though I have to say it looks like she's had the coat forever; the fur has that mangy, slightly matted look that comes from having been alive once, and then dead for so long. Anyone dressed like that would get your attention, and I watch her march up to the counter and start ordering various items from the display cabinets, taking her time to point and deliberate and eventually make her choices in a voice that is clipped and precise, but with an underlying scratch, catching on the vowels. She wants some ham to be sliced, and so the machine that had been cleaned and covered in a red checked cloth and put away for the night has to be unwrapped again and brought back out. The girl behind the counter sets about doing this with an audible sigh, and I see her look at the other girl and roll her eyes. And this makes me feel sorry for the old woman, fur coat or not.

I watch, as she is so begrudgingly served, and I find myself intrigued by her. She is quite tall, and her legs – where I can see them sticking out from under that coat – are painfully thin, and clad in tights so laddered as to be almost shredded. Her shoes, which are suede with a buttoned strap across the top, would have been gorgeous once upon a time, but are badly worn down now at the heel, so that the material is ruched and torn. And yet I notice that the finger with which she points, as she makes her requests, sports a diamond ring so enormous that it almost covers her knuckle.

And when she leaves, carrying her purchases inside a woven canvas bag that she loops over her wrist, she glances at me briefly and I catch the glacial blue of her eyes. Startlingly blue, in the naked paleness of her face. Then she passes me by with her worn heels clacking on the tiled floor, and the doors swoosh open for her and she's gone, out into the dark street. I sit and watch through the window as she looks twice and then steps out into the road.

And suddenly the girl at the till exclaims, 'Oh no!'

'What?' says the other girl, and I turn away from the window and back to them.

'She's left her card, again. Mrs Reiber. She's gone without her card.' She holds the credit card up in annoyance, and the other girl sighs and throws down her cleaning cloth.

'I'll go,' she says, like she's said it a hundred times before, and she grabs the card and straight away she's round from behind the counter and out of the shop with it, running after the woman.

And I'm thinking, *Reiber, Reiber*, and my heart is fluttering as if there's a butterfly trapped inside my chest. I shove back my chair and stick my arms into my coat, and scramble my purse out of my bag with trembling, clumsy hands.

'Keep the change,' I say to the girl at the till because I don't want to wait. And I rush out the door, just as the other girl comes back in, her face flushed from the cold and from running.

I cross the road where the woman crossed; from there the road curves round onto the main street and then you can go either left or right. I think I might have lost her, but just then I see her: she's crossed over again and she's just turning into one of the side roads, going the same way that I will have to go when I head back to collect Jonathan. I walk fast, to catch her up. And still I'm thinking, *Reiber, Reiber*. How many people have that name? The only Reibers I ever knew lived in Oakley, in Surrey, and that, of course, was a long time ago.

I want to see her face again. I want to see her eyes.

I cross over the road and follow where she turned. She's just ahead of me now and I slow down a little. I walk just a few paces behind her, and I study the shape of her, and the way she walks. I look for clues. I walk softly in my quiet, flat boots, but even so I feel that she must sense me being there behind her, scrutinizing her like this, and I think that she will turn. *Then* I will see her eyes.

But how could I possibly recognize her? How could I know if it really is *her*? And what could I say? *Are you Mrs Reiber? Are you Vanessa's mother?*

extracts reading groups
competitions books new
discounts extracts extracts extracts discounts
competitions extracts reading groups
books new
events books
extracts new titles reading groups
interviews
events extracts
discounts
new books events
events new
discounts extracts discounts

www.panmacmillan.com

extracts events reading groups
competitions books extracts new